I Know Who Holds Tomorrow

Volume 1 of The Katrina Legacy

To Chris,
For your support
and to all your
tomorrows!
Catherine Ritch Guess
April 7, 2009

BOOKS BY
CATHERINE RITCH GUESS

EAGLES WINGS TRILOGY

Love Lifted Me
Higher Ground

SHOOTING STAR SERIES

In the Bleak Midwinter
A Song in the Air

SANDMAN SERIES

Old Rugged Cross
Let Us Break Bread Together
Victory in Jesus

THE WINSOME WAYS OF MIZ EUDORA RUMPH

In the Sweet By and By
Precious Memories

- - - - -

In the Garden
Church in the Wildwood
For the Beauty of the Earth
Tis So Sweet
Be Still, My Soul
The Friendly Beasts
In the Sweet By and By

CHILDREN'S BOOKS

Kipper Finds a Home
Rudy the Red Pig (Rudy el Puerco Rojo)
Rudy and the Magic Sleigh

MUSICAL CDS

Musical Sculptures
This Is My Song

I Know Who Holds Tomorrow

Volume 1 of The Katrina Legacy

CATHERINE RITCH GUESS

CRM BOOKS
Publishing Hope for Today's Society
Inspirational Books~CDs~Children's Books

CRM BOOKS, PO Box 2124, Hendersonville, NC 28793

Visit our Web site at www.ciridmus.com

Printed in the United States of America
ISBN (10 digit): 1-933341-31-9
ISBN (13 digit): 9781933341316
LCCN: 2009923769

TO

Jeanne Brooks,
a school librarian who has
given more for the students of her school
than anyone I've ever known

AND

to the beautiful Katrina children,
many of whom are nameless,
who inspire me and
through whose faces God radiates

LASTLY,

to James, forever and always,
wherever you are...
Your North Carolina friends love you!

IN LOVING MEMORY

To

Cheryl Karst

You shall forever be missed by everyone at the Riverside Park sand sculptures

Acknowledgments

To St. Andrews UMC, Findlay, Ohio, whose members have so graciously welcomed me and allowed me to feel a part of their church family; to Organist/Minister of Music, Bev Roby and Secretary, Deb Guthrie who are always willing to answer questions with the benefit of their "birds-eye" view

To Court Street UMC, Hattiesburg, Mississippi and the Reverend Bruce Case and to members Mike and Diann Wolf. You have a most accepting and loving congregation who truly does exemplify how ministry should be for Duke's intern students

To Doug and Debbie Snyder who continually allow me the use of the conservatory for the perfect writing room

To the Hope House, Findlay, Ohio and to Jim Baker, Chairman of the Board and Sammie Rhoades, Executive Director

To Roger Powell, my "Sandman"

To all of you Findlayites who have become like family to me, and to the many businesses who've supported my work. I love all of you!

To the residents of Hancock County, Mississippi, especially the children, of Pearlington, Waveland and Bay St. Louis whose resilience were the inspiration for this story

To Jeremiah Ritchie, and his beautiful daughter Alexis, whose story and artwork brought me closer to understanding the impact of Hurricane Katrina than anything else I witnessed

To the many Katrina children, throughout the entire affected Gulf, who allowed me the privilege of experiencing a bit of the horror of the greatest natural disaster our country has ever known as over and over I heard their stories, enhanced by the emotions written, not only in the expressions on their faces, but on their very souls. Yours is a story which needs to be heard!

To Mary whose clay rainbow showed me the breadth of the Katrina children's deep-seeded faith

To Hunter, a bright spot in the life of all who know him, and his family who fed us when we were hungry and gave us drink when we were thirsty

And most especially to the students, teachers and staff of South Hancock Elementary School, Bay St. Louis, Mississippi and to the School Board of Hancock County for allowing me to share a small part of life with your students. May you continue to grow, enduring life's hardships with pride and the same example of resilience you've shown the rest of the world!

To St. John's Lutheran Church
Concord, NC

I would be greatly remissed if I didn't dedicate a page of this book to a group of my real heroes, all the youth and volunteers of St. John's Lutheran Church whose selfless love and support unknowingly served as the instruments that turned the wheels in my brain during the writing of this first book in "The Katrina Legacy."

Never did I dream when I sat on the organ bench the first day at St. John's Lutheran Church in Concord, NC, exactly two years to the day prior to the writing of this novel, the great gift God was granting me. I was sure my days as an Organist/Minister of Music were through, after 35 years of service in that capacity, but you proved that wrong... or maybe you didn't. You see, I don't consider my work there solely with the choir members, but as a larger picture of being with God's chosen who are always willing to meet any demand, any need, any crisis as you face them nobly and generously, assured of Who is holding your hand along the way.

Having said that, the following page is left blank as a sign of silent gratitude - one of the few times you will see me silent - as I extend my utmost and sincere thanks and appreciation to all of you who have contributed in some way or shared the gift of yourself with Katrina's precious children in Hancock County, Mississippi.

May God continue to bless you and use you to bless me - CR?

Note from the Author

I Know Who Holds Tomorrow - what a perfect title for this book, for the first words of that gospel hymn by the same name are "I don't know about tomorrow." Not only did I not know about tomorrow when I started this novel of reality fiction, I didn't know the final title or setting of this book. Out of 20 books, this is the first one where God took the pages from my hand, wadded them and threw them in the trashcan, and handed me a new piece of paper.

When I was "given" the idea for ***Old Rugged Cross,*** I asked Roger Powell, my real-life "Sandman," the name of his favorite hymn. Thus, the first book of the Sandman Trilogy. About five minutes before the notes and research for that book were finished in Findlay, Ohio, Larry Whiteleather (Wayne Willoughby in The Sandman Series) sparked the second book, which immediately spun into a third book of the first trilogy.

As I completed ***Victory in Jesus,*** the finale of the first trilogy, I knew the story of Mary Magdalena Matelli had grown into a trilogy of trilogies. I was certain I knew the location for the second trilogy and had already begun research and preliminary writings for that segment of books. However, on Friday, March 14, 2008, at approximately 2:45am (EST), I was deeply engrossed in conversation with Mississippi school librarian Jeanne Brooks about our upcoming PROJECT SPLASH – a program of the non-profit organization for children's literacy through my Rudy the Red Pig children's series. She made a statement, which I don't remember, but which led to the rewriting of this first volume in the second trilogy involving the Sandman.

As I listened to her and we discussed a summer cultural arts camp and a carnival for the South Hancock Elementary School that was to open in the fall of 2008, she shared many tales of the school, the area and their losses during Katrina. Having lost everything myself once during a long battle with a deadly autoimmune illness, my heart ached for the teachers battling to provide an education for those affected students of the worstly-devastasted area of Mississippi – Hancock County.

Sensing where God was taking me, I stopped her in mid sentence and ventured to ask, "What is the one song that stuck out in your mind during Hurricane Katrina?" I knew her answer would be a hymn.

"You probably don't know it," she began, "because I grew up in a small Baptist church as a child. It's one they sang a lot." I didn't bother to explain to her that I, too, had grown up in a rural Baptist church in the South. "It's ***I Don't Know About Tomorrow,"*** she said.

"I do know that hymn," I responded, and then shared our similar religious backgrounds. "I've played it a million times." As I was telling her this, my mind was racing over the words and thinking how appropriate they were for the basis of the story already running through my mind as a result of our conversation.

I didn't tell Jeanne the reason or the impact of the question at first, but waited until the next day to unload on her that I had begun a new book and she was the inspiration. She was thrilled.

There were many things about "tomorrow" I found I didn't know as the writing of this book took shape. Thus, it was most fitting that while I sat in the conservatory of my dear friends Doug and Debbie Snyder of Findlay, Ohio, to begin penning this novel, the inspired story evolved, taking me from Hancock County, Ohio, to Hancock County, Mississippi – both victims of different circumstances, but both reeling from natural disasters. Suddenly a full rainbow appeared in the sky right in front of me. I ran to get Doug and Debbie and the three of us scurried to the front porch of their beautiful Main Street home to see the beauty that appeared out of nowhere from an eerie, ominous sky.

The rainbow proved to be my sign – as I again sat at my computer in the conservatory and watched the day turn into night – that God's promises all still hold true. It showed me God was giving me another beautiful story to share with the world about His beautiful creatures – the people of Hancock County – Mississippi ***and*** Ohio. The rainbow was followed by multiple tornado warnings, causing a well-known sign of the hurricane-ridden Gulf, "Katrina was big, but God was bigger," to come to mind. It was a sign etched on my brain from the time of my very first visit to the Gulf following the storm. As long as there was a world, there would be storms of life and signs of beauty, but no matter what, God would always be bigger, and He would always be holding out His hand for whomever would take it.

Again, four weeks before the book was to hit the press, I awoke one Monday morning and knew God had told me to trash my story and write His. Skeptical of ever meeting my approaching deadline, I sensed Him demanding that I rewrite the story, this time through the eyes of the Katrina children. I hopped out of bed and literally said, “Okay, God, if You say we can do it, we can do it. You be the voice and I’ll be the hands.” Within four weeks, this entire novel experienced a new birth as it flew from my fingers. My research was the many mission trips I’ve led to the Gulf to work with the children, during which I always knew Who held my hand.

The wish which rang loud and clear in my mind as I wrote the final words of this book for a third time, and spoke about the heroes who made this story possible, is for each of you readers to see and understand it takes so little, yet reaps such overwhelming rewards, to reach out and share the gift of yourself with others.

May you experience God’s promises for your own life as you see and feel Hurricane Katrina through the eyes of the Gulf’s children who can say firsthand...

I Know Who Holds Tomorrow!

Blessings,

CR?

Photo Credits

I wish to thank the following agencies and individuals for use of the Hurricane Katrina photos on the cover of "I Know Who Holds Tomorrow"

The inside wall of the eye of the hurricane, taken by a NOAA hurricane hunter aircraft during one of ten flights into and around the eye of Hurricane Katrina, is the background of the cover is used by permission from the National Oceanic and Atmospheric Administration, US Department of Commerce.

FRONT COVER PHOTOS:
The photograph of the water tower is the property of the US Environmental Protection Agency.

The aerial view of houses under water is property of Jocelyn Augustino/FEMA and is used by permission from IllinoisPhoto. com.

The photograph of the Katrina sign is used by permission from Margaret Kinney.

PART ONE

1

For the rest of the town of Findlay, this year's annual Holy Week sand sculpture was history. During the past ten days, which had begun with Good Friday, all the other residents of northwest Ohio's Hancock County had taken scores of photos, shared beautiful heart-warming stories, and felt the bond of a community – which had come to be called "Common Ground" – all because of one man, Joshua Redford, who had several years earlier listened to the voice of God at three o'clock one morning.

For Mary Magdalena Redford, however, who happened to live across the street from the site of this event that had come to receive worldwide attention – and who happened to be married to the sculptor's son Nick – this was her first glimpse of this year's creation in the sand. Returning home from a ten-day trip to Mississippi, she didn't even take time to pull in her driveway, but drove past it to the entrance of the Riverside Park. As she made the turn onto Center Street, she caught sight of the first man she had encountered on her initial visit to Findlay. A tiny little man – a toy soldier, actually – painted on a short fire hydrant at the street's corner that served to welcome visitors to the park. He stood at attention, ready to guard against anything happening on his beat. She brought her car to a halt next to the posts used to keep vehicles from getting on the grass which led to the volleyball courts. Volleyball courts except for this time of year, when they became the home of the Holy Week sculpture.

Vehicles, that is, she reminded herself, ***except the parade of sand trucks which line up, one after another, and have come to be a royal procession each Monday following Palm Sunday for nine years. Those same sand trucks***, her mind continued to wander as a slight smile formed on her lips, ***which drew me to Findlay the first time***.

The slight smile grew to cover Mary Magdalena's face as she recollected the first time she'd witnessed those trucks. There had been no smile on her face then, but rather a desire to curse them as she sat stalled in traffic, having to follow them through town, as she was trying her best to hurry from the University of Michigan to Fort Lauderdale on her spring break to find her "perfect man."

Spring break, she began to muse again, noting the parallel between that spring break and this year's. There was no doubt her "perfect man" had played a role in both of them. The spring break, when she first discovered the annual sand sculpture six years prior, was the exact same reason she missed the sand sculpture this year. Having experienced her own life-changing experience of a meaningful spring break back then, she had volunteered as a chaperone of ASB (Alternative Spring Break) to give students of her Alma Mater, the University of Michigan, that same opportunity during their spring break this year. Unlike her mission to find a "perfect man" to rescue her from the lifestyle she'd found herself in as an exotic dancer at a place called Northern Exposure, theirs had been to repair homes in Gulfport, Mississippi, which would explain the paint and sawdust that covered the clothes in her duffle bag.

It would also explain why she was dressed in much the same manner she had been on that first visit to Riverside Park, her dark hair, streaked by hints of rich, deep auburn from the past week's exposure in the sun, pulled into a ponytail through the back of a ball cap with wiry unruly wisps peeking out around her face. Her olive skin glowed, having also been kissed by the Gulf's sun, and her sleek Patrician silhouette was still recognizable underneath loose-fitting jeans and an oversized dark-blue sweatshirt bearing the maize-colored letters of a much-beloved alma mater. Her charismatic mystique, which came from a father's dark Italian features combined with a mother's fair skin and blue eyes, still drew people's eyes. Only now she used that natural magnetic trait to attract the children and youth with whom she worked rather than to earn dollars to pay for a college degree.

As Mary Magdalena ventured slowly and tentatively – exactly as she had six years prior – across the short path to the volleyball court which was covered in two large and several small mounds of sand, all she could make out were footprints where children had trampled, like oversized ants, across the top of the sand. Walking around the perimeter of what had been the huge sculpture, she stopped in front of an area she felt sure had been the depiction of Christ on the cross. She recognized the space where the arms and the legs would have been extended, and where a hint of red was still evident on the ground. ***A drop of blood. A drop of love.***

Suddenly her spirit brightened, as strikingly as if the sun had just burst through the clouds of gray. Which, in her mind, was exactly what happened as she was overcome by a moment of realization, a moment of truth. For here in Findlay, here in Ohio, here in the entire country, she thought of people who were walking blindly. People who owned every gadget money could buy. People who owned the finest houses, the finest cars, the finest boats. People who, in their selfish desires, had lost sight of needs. ***Or, at least, real needs***.

And then, in Mississippi, she thought of people who had lost everything. ***Everything except self, hope and faith,*** she reminded herself. People who had put up a huge sign, made from the only piece of wood left within sight, which read "KATRINA WAS BIG, BUT GOD IS BIGGER."

Mary Magdalena felt her breathing pattern change as she took in all that she could from the air of this place, which had become a holy shrine of reverence and remembrance for countless thousands during Holy Week each year. She sensed her thoughts reaching into the far, deep crevices of her memory as she envisioned her missionary grandparents, who had given up everything to serve others. It was then she realized the longing within herself. It was not a longing for "things." It was a longing to reach out, to help others who were struggling.

She remembered words her grandfather had once shared with her. "Everyone is struggling, Maggie, in his or her own way. The biggest problem is most of them don't even know it. They don't even know about the morrow, yet they think they're in control of their lives."

Her body flinched and became rigid as the last sentence, in her grandfather's voice, bolted through her mind like a flash of lightning. ***Words so similar to those used by the woman on the plane home***, she recollected.

Mary Magdalena replayed the conversation she'd had with a woman, Jeanne, on the ride home from the Gulfport/Biloxi airport. Jeanne was a librarian from Mississippi on her way to Maine to speak to a librarian's conference, among which one of the distinguished guests was Laura Bush. "My family was all scattered in different directions," she had shared when asked about her Katrina experience. "My husband headed toward Houston, my twenty-year-old son managed to get to Baton Rouge, but my mother and I were forced to go to Florida. The police wouldn't let us go to either Houston or Baton Rouge. The traffic was so backed up going both of those directions, they informed us there was only one way we were allowed to go to escape the hurricane's path. The nightmare began way before the storm hit the coast."

"How horrible it must have been for you," Mary Magdalena had replied. "What was going through your mind during the storm?"

"It's weird, I know," Jeanne had responded, "but these twelve words kept going through my mind, over and over. They were words to a hymn I hadn't heard since I was a child, but words that must have spoken comfort to me, for I heard them over and over, through shutting down the house, through securing the library, through the evacuation, and even through the trials of coming home to the clean-up, at least what little was left to clean up."

Mary Magdalena's memory stopped there, at a loss for the librarian's exact words. ***Why didn't I take down her name and why didn't I write down those twelve words?*** She felt scorned by her hindsight as her longing became more and more concerted, her heart acting as a bass drum, pounding louder and louder with each beat.

She thought one last time about her grandfather's words. "Everyone is struggling...they don't even know it...don't know about the morrow." ***Were those words running through my grandparents' minds when they accepted the call to be missionaries***? she questioned, wondering what sort of longing they had experienced to make them want to give their lives to a service of mission.

Her attention turned from what was left of the sand to her grandparents as she went home to view the large Italian painting of Saint Francis which hung in her stairway. The same painting whose hidden story had allowed her grandparents the opportunity to become missionaries.

2

"How was it?"

There was no question in Mary Magdalena's mind of exactly what "it" Evan Brightmore meant. She had developed an appreciation for not only his expertise shortly after she acquired her job at the Hope House, but for his leadership and service in so many areas, both professionally and civically. He served as an example to everyone around him, especially in his capacity as Director of Missions for his denomination's district offices. She had no idea how long Evan had been on the Board of Directors for the Hope House; all she did know was he was a valued friend and leader.

"'It' was without a doubt the most rewarding experience of my life," she answered, not at all surprised to see Evan pop in her office on her first morning back from Spring Break. "You said the trip would humble me in a way even working here couldn't. I found that hard to believe, but you were exactly right. If I had to choose one word to describe 'it,' I would have to say it was transforming." A troubling expression replaced her warm smile. "But I keep feeling there's something I didn't do. Like the transformation got cut off in midstream, like a cell phone going dead in the middle of the conversation or something."

Evan knew that symptom. He'd heard it from many who returned from mission trips. He'd experienced it himself. "You have to learn to recognize every success you make, no matter how large or small it may be. It's exactly like your work here at the Hope House. They started out nearly nineteen years ago, with only housing for ten families at a time. Look at them now. They provide services to over 1600 men, women and children annually. They're reaching their goal by not only taking the baskets of babies out of the water, but going upstream to figure out how the babies are getting in the water."

His words made perfect sense to Mary Magdalena. She'd read the same theory in their recent Hope House newsletter. ***Maybe I need to read it again***, she noted, hoping it might prove useful in helping her discover what was still gnawing at her.

"I'd already learned from working here that it's wrong to stereotype people," she said, thinking of another valuable lesson she'd gleaned from her job at the Hope House. "If that was ever true, it was so with the Katrina victims. We were near a small community called d'Iberville, near Biloxi, where we stayed at the Heritage United Methodist Church in a facility built by volunteers from Indiana. Contributions from Indiana's Methodist Conference had paid for the dorm-type facility which, as dorms go, was like the Taj Mahal. It can house several teams at one time, and has a huge kitchen and dining area, which also subs for the room to watch TV and settle in the evenings. Not only did staying there help me to learn more about myself, but about others and about the work we were all doing. 'It' was incredible!"

Mary Magdalena swirled a pencil from her desk around her fingers. "You know, I'm sure every volunteer there had God in their hearts when they went, but the people of Mississippi, the ones who had lost everything, kept telling us, 'When we forget God, we get in trouble.' They had nothing, yet were totally dependent on God and never lost faith in Him, even after the devastation and losses they suffered. I kept thinking how many people, who had been believers, would have turned their backs and declared, 'There *is* no God!'"

She shook her head. "I can't tell you how many times I heard people say they felt their lives were in God's hands during the hurricane. They didn't seem to be afraid." Her words triggered her memory as she sought for Jeanne's words again, knowing they held some similarity to the testimonial she'd just made.

"Fear keeps people away from God," remarked Evan. "When Roosevelt made the statement, 'We have nothing to fear but fear itself,' he hit the nail right on the head, no pun intended. Most of those who survived Katrina know that well, for they lived it. They are all about helping each other, and giving back to the volunteers who come to help them."

"You've got that right. I kept hearing the words from Matthew 25:35 the entire time I was there." Her comment received an acknowledging nod. "Because I was hungry, and you gave me something to eat. I was thirsty, and you gave me something to drink. I was a stranger, and you welcomed me." We went there to live that verse for others, yet we were the ones continually being fed and offered drink, both physically and spiritually. And talk about welcoming the stranger, I've never felt more accepted in my whole life."

"That's what pulled me into the world of mission," Evan admitted. "I was dyslexic. As a child, I was a slow reader and a slow learner. Back in the fifties, no one knew anything about that, so I suffered a lot because of it. People laughed at me, they picked girls before me on the teams at recess. I learned at an early age what it was like to be rejected, to be on the bottom."

Mary Magdalena stared at the gentleman in front of her. A man whose very presence showed assertiveness, self-assuredness and total control, yet whose face expressed love and humility. It was hard for her to comprehend he'd ever been anything other than a leader.

"I never forgot what that feeling was like to be an outsider. Jesus Christ loved the losers. That's why I felt, and still feel, so connected to the church. The greatest thing I had as a child was love. I was loved by my parents, by my grandparents, by my neighbors. That love overcame the disability that I had. When I became a teenager, I took care of the parsonage and even painted it once. I mowed the lawn. Whatever was needed, I did it. I'm sure that love of my grandparents and neighbors left me with the lesson that you always helped the elderly. Their love spilled over into everything I've done as I've always tried to build relationships everywhere I've been."

Evan's smile, Mary Magdalena was sure as she watched him, had opened the door to lots of relationships with people, both young and old. "I guess all that is what made me such an activist. My roommate in college was Catholic, and became the president of our class. His ideals influenced me a lot as I continually watched his example of working for peace and helping the poor, speaking for those who didn't have a voice." His smile grew larger as he concluded, "And thanks to him, here I still am."

The young woman sat silent as she digested his words. He had obviously felt some of what she was feeling now, the seeking, the anxiety of not knowing exactly which direction to go to move forward. Yet Evan had answered one part of the question for her. She needed to stay within the circle of God's encompassing love as she searched for her destiny, and through it, she would find her way.

"I think the thing I loved most was watching the Methodists install insulation, the Baptists paint and the Mennonites put the roof on the particular house we were working on," she finally said, noting how it didn't matter about the denomination, only the way of the heart. "Our group from the university went in there having no clue what they were supposed to do, but it took care of itself. In less than five minutes, they were all on a task with a paintbrush, a hammer or screwdriver. And they were having fun doing it! Everyone got along like they'd known each other forever, yet there were seventeen states represented through just the volunteers on that one house."

"I remember my first trip down there," stated Evan. "There was a crew of us working on the house of a man who worked at the banana factory. He and his wife, who was dying with cancer, lived in a FEMA trailer. We were determined to finish that house in one week for his wife. He came out and helped us every day. On one of the afternoons, we took a survey and discovered persons from twenty-five states were in his front yard."

"That's amazing! It's hard to believe such a large number of people didn't get in each other's way."

"You're right, but it's like you said, you jump in with both feet, and if God is at the heart of it, He takes care of it. You can accomplish much when you're centered spiritually. We had his house finished by Saturday evening before the last of the crews left."

"Isn't it strange how some of the volunteers I encountered in Mississippi had come here when we had the flood in 2007?" Mary Magdalena asked.

"I wouldn't call it strange. I think of it as 'what goes around, comes around.' What we did in Mississippi prepared us for graciously accepting the help of others when we needed it. During the week before the flood hit here in Findlay, some buddies and I were in the center of the river, cleaning it out and pulling tires out as we stood knee-deep in mud. The very next week, we were doing all we could to help the elderly. We helped with 96 houses, as others began to pour in, by de-mudding and then later, the demolition. It's all about the networking. Some of the ones who came here are persons from Iowa who we then went to help after their flood. We're all in this world together and we learn to give help where it's needed, and sometimes that includes home. Our congregation had as many as twelve different flood teams staying in our new facility at one point after our flood. We were equipped for them, showers and all."

The story he told reminded Mary Magdalena of the story she'd heard in Mississippi about Biloxi's Bethel Lutheran Church. They went out on a limb to help with the Gulf recovery and God sent an entire tree trunk, branches and all – proverbially – to carry on the work they'd begun.

"When it gets down to the real nitty-gritty," Evan continued, "the folks we help are the ones who teach us the most valuable lesson. It's all about simplistic living. When you become more simplistic in your lifestyle, you can hear God. You may not know what tomorrow will bring, but you know God will be there to care for you."

That quiver of being so close to remembering Jeanne's words stung at her again.

Evan, whom Mary Magdalena saw as the person who had done more for others than anyone she knew left her with, "I'm always telling folks that it's in our DNA to help people. All a body has to do is look at you, Mary Magdalena, and they can see there's some serious DNA going on there!"

She loved the way this man had worded his final statement so that she was able to laugh and get back to her work for the day. Yet it left her with another indicator that her job was not yet finished. ***What is it I'm to do?*** she prayed, as she answered the phone to hear a woman with a young child who needed shelter.

3

Mary Magdalena sat alone in the sanctuary of St. Andrew's United Methodist Church as she gazed at the stained-glass window of Mary of Magdala standing beside the tomb. She'd often found comfort in that window of this octagonal room which had become a source of solace for her. There was nothing unusual about her presence here, for even though she was of a different religious background, two of the church's members had reached out to her at a time of need earlier in her life. Dudley and Cynthia Cunningham had taken her into their home five years before when she'd needed a place for physical, spiritual and emotional healing, much of which had come while sitting in their eight-sided conservatory – the same shape as this sanctuary.

That's how she had come to find this setting as an uplifting respite. The stately limestone building, which so closely resembled the façade of the town's courthouse which initially demanded her attention and admiration, had a beauty all its own. But even as majestic as was its façade, it held nothing in comparison to the grandeur of the inside of the sanctuary. Next to the peace and calm she'd learned to find in Riverside Park, this sanctuary had come to be her retreat of solitary refuge.

Solitary, except for the one man who called me to this town, she mused, sitting in her usual vantage point in the middle of the room. Suddenly, it seemed the stained-glass window spoke to her; or rather the voice of that one man who stood beside Mary of Magdala at the empty tomb in the window was now speaking to her again.

And solitary, except for the one who will hopefully call to me now, she prayed as she sat seeking and searching, with no clue for exactly what, but only a burning desire from within for guidance in what to do. The desire had been constantly gnawing at her since she'd viewed the formless sand upon her return from Mississippi five days earlier. Each time she'd looked out her front window at the site of the sand sculpture, the nameless desire had chiseled away at her conscience a little more until she felt compelled to do something.

That something had been to come here, to this spot with the window, to try to remember the words the woman had mentioned on the airplane. For a reason she couldn't identify, she sensed those words held meaning for her longing, and what she was to do.

The future...no, uncertainty...no...not knowing...close, don't know...maybe. Her mind halted its meandering as she focused on Jeanne's face and her statements about Katrina. ***Today, no...tomorrow, YES! Don't know...tomorrow...don't know about tomorrow...I don't know about tomorrow... That's it!*** she determined, feeling a note of accomplishment.

But what are the rest of the words? As hard as she tried to remember, even picturing Jeanne's round face and eyes that twinkled with radiating exuberance at the mention of her students, her mind drew a blank. ***I remember she said that she only remembered twelve words, and I remember commenting how twelve was a good number, for there were twelve disciples. We even laughed at the analogy***, she told herself, ***that the twelve words represented the twelve disciples, all of whose spirits were with her during that terrorizing time of the unknown.***

Her eyes remained focused on the glass portrayal of Mary of Magdala as she contemplated on whether the words, "I don't know about tomorrow," had rung through that woman's head at the time of the crucifixion, during the days that followed, on the morning she went to the tomb. ***What ARE those other seven words***? Hard as she tried, Mary Magdalena's mind drew a blank as the first five words played over and over in her mind, but certain that could the woman in the window talk, she, too, would have experienced the missing words.

How is it, she wondered, ***that Mary of Magdala was chosen to stand in the likes of all the disciples?*** She recalled the many stained-glass windows she'd observed on trips to Italy and throughout Europe with her grandparents and her father, windows that showed this woman beside the apostles...***the disciples and Mary, the mother of Jesus.***

Out of sheer instinct, Mary Magdalena picked up a Bible from the pew in front of her. As had become her habit, she held it for a moment, as if the words inside would come through the cover and seep through her skin and into her soul like osmosis. She had no idea why she did that; only that it had become a feeling of comfort to her while she prayed that God would give her the words she needed to hear for any given situation. As her eyes closed and she lifted her words to the heavens, she could sense her fingers moving across the pages until they came to rest. She opened her eyes and the Bible at the same time, her thumb resting on a particular spot, and began to read.

All we like sheep have gone astray;
we have all turned to our own way,
and the Lord had laid on him
the iniquity of us all.

She had heard this scripture many times as a child. It was one of her grandfather's favorite passages. Mary Magdalena could even remember one afternoon when he took her on his lap and read that scripture, sharing how it gave him the confidence to feel adequate to go out into the world and serve, and how it gave him the courage and strength to go out to minister to anyone in any situation.

Those words now took on a new meaning as Mary Magdalena heard what the passage really said. "All we...," ***It is ALL of us who have strayed. Not just Mary of Magdala, all of the disciples, the churchgoers, the pastors, everyone...ALL of us.***

She sat there, boggled by the fact that God saw fit to give her certain memories, but not allow her others, which in this case were the missing seven words of Jeanne's song. ***In His time***, she heard in her grandmother's patient and kind voice, ***in His time.***

It must be a red-letter day, Mary Magdalena laughed to herself. ***Both my grandparents are here for whatever is in store for me***, she joked, but fully aware of why her grandmother's prophetic words had come to her. She would remember the words to the hymn when God felt she needed to know them.

It wasn't until that moment she became conscious of the hand on hers, which still lay on the scriptural passage in the open Bible. She looked up to see a familiar face as she smiled at Cynthia Cunningham, the woman who had first introduced her to this sanctuary. A woman whom she had come to dearly love and respect. And most of all, a woman whom she had come to know as "friend."

"Our UMW is having a luncheon downstairs in the Fellowship Hall. Why don't you join us?" invited Cynthia. "There's someone visiting with us who I think you'd like to meet."

"Thanks!" Mary Magdalena accepted. "I like that idea now that I've fed my spiritual hunger for this morning."

She looked down at Cynthia's hand, the hand of friendship. "That's it!" she blurted, scaring Cynthia to the point she jerked her hand back. "Those are the other words to the song. 'And I know who holds my hand.'

"Oh, Cynthia," she said, hugging the woman beside her, "you have no idea the gift you just gave me. Your coming in here had nothing to do with the luncheon. You were an answer to my prayer." Mary Magdalena hastily explained her quandary about the missing words and how this act of kindness had provided them, as well as filling a need for her.

"Does that mean you don't need lunch now?" Cynthia asked, smiling.

"No, never!" replied Mary Magdalena, leaving the Bible open on the pew as she followed her "messenger" to the Fellowship Hall. "The one thing I have learned in visiting here is you never want to turn down a meal prepared by the United Methodist Women!"

I Know Who Holds Tomorrow

"Why didn't you tell me Charlotte Crenshaw was here?" Mary Magdalena asked when the speaker for the program, an upbeat author who had written a series of books inspired by Joshua's sand sculptures, was introduced.

"I thought it would be a nice surprise," said Cynthia, smiling. "She's also the guest speaker for our UMW Sunday. Why don't you come to church and sit with Dudley and me?"

"Are you sure that husband of yours can stand both of us giving him a hard time?"

"He'll be alright. Besides, we won't give him the hard time until after church. Nick and you can be our guests for lunch. We'll wait until he's paid for the meal before we give him a hard time."

"How could I turn down that offer? I'd rather give Dudley a hard time than anyone else I know."

The minute the luncheon was over, Mary Magdalena rushed to speak to Charlotte. "I'm sorry I didn't see you during Holy Week. I was a chaperone for the Alternative Spring Break for the students at U of M. I thought that would be a nice way to support my alma mater, given the alternative way I spent my Easter vacation some years back."

The two women embraced as the author noted the light-hearted way in which her young friend now accepted her mistake of the past. ***It's always hardest to forgive one's self***, she reminded herself of her own mistakes of the past. "I wasn't here for Easter either. I knew Joshua was going to do Noah's Ark, though. We spoke about it after last year's sculpture, and I was certain the Lord would lead his hands in that direction."

"That's what gets me about the two of you, Charlotte. You said the Lord would lead Joshua's hands in that direction, and I've watched you as you write. You say the Lord gives you what you need to say."

"That's right."

"Does God speak to you all the time? Is He always telling you what to do?"

Charlotte laughed. "Ah, familiar questions," she mused aloud, leading Mary Magdalena away from the crowd and off to a corner. "Let's put it this way. God's booming voice has never come out of the sky and said, 'Charlotte Crenshaw, I want you to do this,' or 'I want you to go there.' But the doors around me have opened so widely, and the opportunities have knocked so loudly that I knew God had 'ordered my steps,' as the saying goes. And there are many times when I recognize His wishes and desires for me as clearly as if He had rung a bell to call for my services.

"Ah, yes, He's paged me. He paged me when I first met Joshua. He paged me and put me in the path of every notable person I've ever met." Charlotte's blue eyes gazed directly into Mary Magdalena's with an affectionate smile. "Just like you. I'd never met a person named Mary Magdalena before. I felt most honored having made your acquaintance." She took the young woman's hand. "And I felt God's power running through you and knew that He had great tasks in store for you."

"Really?" Mary's Magdalena's word sounded more like a surprised exclamation than a question.

"Really! I can feel that. It's just like with Joshua. He has an idea of what he wants to do for each year, but he has to wait until the Lord plants the seed and gives him the vision of how to make the shape come out of those huge sand piles. There's not a true artist alive for whom God doesn't provide divine inspiration. As to whether the artist is open to that inspiration, now that's another story.

"People can tell you they don't believe in God, but I'd surely like to know how they realistically think they could live or breathe, much less paint, sculpt, write, and make music...anything, without Him having breathed that gift into their being. I fully believe that God planted a seed inside each person. A seed which can grow into a thing of beauty, if nurtured with the Living Water and the Light of the World.

"But I also believe people can be like that parable of the seeds. Just because that seed is planted in someone doesn't mean it will grow and flourish unless the person takes ownership of it, and cares for it. I've met many people in my life who possessed great talents, but they either refused to accept them, or weren't disciplined enough to develop them. Or worse, they used the talents, but for wrong instead of good."

Charlotte gave a winsome sigh. "Enough of a sermon for today. You're not supposed to get that until Sunday."

"No, wait," pleaded Mary Magdalena. "I have one more question." She waited for Charlotte's inviting nod. "That passage about God knowing us in the womb, do you really believe that?"

"Absolutely! That is one of my two favorite scriptural passages. There's no doubt in my mind that the Word of the Lord actually did come to Jeremiah. That's what I'm saying. Those words in the book of Jeremiah were divinely inspired."

Mary Magdalena took Charlotte's arm and gently led her into the corridor away from all ears. "Do you really think God can still smile on me, after my past, I mean?"

Aware of this young woman's past, and also of her missionary grandparents, Charlotte took both her hands. "Did you ever stop believing there was a God? In those years that you strayed, did you ever once forget your upbringing?" She watched carefully as a solitary tear made its way down Mary Magdalena's cheek.

"It was like I shrouded that part of my life with a veil. I was afraid to see that part of my past."

"Because you knew. You knew God's watchful eye. You knew that He was there with you."

"Not in that place!"

"Yes, in ***that*** place, Mary Magdalena. God is ***always*** with us, not only when we allow Him to be. It's us that tries to keep Him out, that tries to hide Him with a mantle of denial. But, you must remember, God is omnipotent. He's bigger than all of us.

Katrina was big, God is bigger...Katrina was big, God is bigger...Katrina was big, God is bigger. The words haunted Mary Magdalena as she recalled the plywood sign on the coast of Mississippi.

"Charlotte, I think you've answered my question better than you'd have ever realized."

The author grinned. "That's because it wasn't me who answered it."

Mary Magdalena nodded enthusiastically. "So He really does speak to people like me?"

"He speaks to ***all*** of us."

"One last question. Why did you choose the words 'in those years that you strayed?' Or rather, why did you choose the word 'strayed'?"

"It wasn't my word. It was the divinely inspired word from Isaiah. 'All we...,"

"...like sheep have gone astray," Mary Magdalena interrupted, finishing the verse.

"Ah, I see you know the verse, too."

"God gave it to me this morning as an answer to a prayer."

"See, God does speak to the listening heart." Charlotte looked at the face of the woman before her. "You do have a servant's heart, you know. You never fell far from the tree."

"God told you that?"

"No, I have eyes. It's written all over you. Please come Sunday. I think God has something to say to you."

Mary Magdalena nodded, tears filling her eyes. "I think He does, too. I can feel it."

The couple said their good-byes and Mary Magdalena slithered up the stairway, finding her way inconspicuously back to the sanctuary. Charlotte's observation had left her with an even deeper urgency for discovering the answer to whatever was eating at her. She could hardly think, so preoccupied was she in searching her soul, sure there was something God willed her to do.

But what, Lord? she began to pray. ***O Father, I know not what You would have me do.*** Her prayer stopped as the inadequacies of her past ripped at her, like the surging waves of Katrina had done to the coast of the Gulf as they lashed against the sand and all that lay beyond. Her past lashed all the way to the core of her heart, deeming her unworthy to even speak to God, much less do something in His name. Suddenly, the awesomeness of her Maker, the Creator of all things...***who truly IS bigger than even Katrina***...swept over her with even bigger swells than the lashings at her heart and soul.

My child, my child..., she seemed to hear.

O, that God would even lower himself to speak to someone such as I. Mary Magdalena's eyes shot skyward. She had viewed the stained-glass dome of this sanctuary on several prior occasions and admired its splendor. But today, what she noticed was the circle of angels surrounding her and looking down upon her from the heavens as they showered her with the security of God's love, His grace and His ultimate sacrifice that came with the slaughter of the Lamb.

So great was the presence of the Holy Spirit that it seemed she could actually feel the raindrops, not harsh as had been the surging reminders of guilt from her conscience, but as a gentle cleansing rain that washes the earth, that leaves the blade green, and with it a newness, a freshness in the air that allows one to breathe deeply as they sense its aftermath fill the lungs, pervading one's entire being. ***The kind of rain that remained after Katrina, signaling that the end of the storm was near. The kind of rain where the iridescent rainbow shines through, promising God's love is still with His people and His earth.***

The entire sanctuary became a dazzling display of God's miraculous wonders as Mary Magdalena looked around her. Walls, whose pleasing, yet vibrantly, pastel color had comforted her from the very first time she stepped foot in this sanctuary, permeated her thoughts. She'd sensed the calming peacefulness they provided when she'd visited here with Dudley and Cynthia during which they'd opened their home to her as a haven of healing. These walls had provided a serene backdrop for the place she'd come to pray following Sabrina's murder. And now as she, for the first time, realized that their color was a light sea-foam green, she knew why they called to her. The sensation they evoked was the same tranquility one felt when walking the beach following a storm, when waves were little more than soft ripples, and when diminutive whitecaps rose and fell so gently they were barely noticeable.

Her eyes moved to the windows, whose images were so pulsating that they called for their admirers to burst forth with praise and rejoicing. Mary of Magdala, depicted in the first window beside the risen Lord, reminded Mary Magdalena of her own rich heritage that went along with having that shared name. ***A name that has obviously spoken to generations of my family***, she noted, her grandmother's name also being the same.

And the woman at the well, she observed, looking at the image in the second window that was so real she felt she could reach out and take the cup of living water the woman was offering. ***The same Living Water the woman had just received from the man, Christ, depicted beside her... a drink that would never leave her thirsty again.***

The third window showed Jesus as a boy in the temple. Mary Magdalena's mind was a flurry of questions, set in motion by this array of brightly-colored glass which reminded her of the day she'd gone back to visit the Little Italy section of Cleveland, where she grew up. The windows of the Wade Chapel in the nearby Lake View Cemetery had spoken to her in much the same way these were speaking to her now. That was the day she had gone to find closure and make peace with her deceased grandmother, who was laid to rest in that cemetery near her childhood home.

She examined the depiction of Jesus. He had been raised by devout parents. Seeing Jesus in this light, the sun's rays splashing on the walls of the sanctuary in such a way that Mary Magdalena could literally see the Light shining on Jesus' face, and also shining through him as the effect of the sunlight spilled the colors of his image from the window onto all the surfaces in its path. She stood in wonder and awe at the visual truth before her. ***The visual truth that God's light shines through all of those who truly believe in Him, and He allows the light of His son to pass through them to all those in their paths.***

Her days of going to Mass, Catechism classes, and all the reminders that went with growing up in "the temple" – no matter whether that temple was a cathedral or sanctuary or other place of worship – sent signals of both familiarity and differences through her whirling thoughts.

Did Mary of Magdala have devout parents? How many of Jesus' friends, who were also raised by devout parents, turned from the ways of their parents' teachings? Her questions brought her to realize the human side of Christ, allowing her the gratitude she'd never fully appreciated, until now, for family who were grounded in their faith, and who had brought her up in "the temple." The flow of light through the window allowed her to see that her family's faith also had the capability to continue to shine through her, should she allow Christ's light to fully penetrate her heart, her soul, her everyday life.

And lastly was the window which had gone unnoticed on all her other visits here. She'd seen it, of course, and admired its magnificence, but she'd never given much virtue to its meaning. Until today. Today, when the shepherd holding the sheep in his arms could have just as easily been holding her in his arms. The sheep that had gone astray. The shepherd was there to let everyone who entered this hallowed hall be visually reminded that he was there to lift them up, and carry them were they too weak to walk, back to shelter, to a safe haven of rest.

All of the sheep, she uttered silently. ***All of us who have gone astray... everyone.***

Bet Rawlings, the organist who unbeknownst to Mary Magdalena had entered the back door behind the organ, began to play. The notes soared through the air as they escaped the metal and wooden pipes, resembling small people with lips and mouths that had been filled with breath, only the pipes' breath came from the electronic blower housed in a large cabinet that was unseen.

Mary Magdalena mused over the analogy. ***Unseen, yet***

the power, the source of breath that allowed the pipes to speak, to emit such majestic and beautiful sounds. God, the unseen Power who breathed life into the beings of His creation, who gave them the ability to speak, to share his gifts of beauty with the world.

She listened attentively as Bet's fingers glided with alacrity across the keyboards and her feet raced across the pedals adding a strength that balanced all the sound. ***God giving His people the strength to balance their lives between the deep, heavy burdens, and the high emotions of gracious blessings and abundance***, reasoned the listener.

Mary Magdalena was unsure how long she had been there when Bet finished practicing and returned to her office. She knew it was time to go, yet she was afraid to leave, afraid the spirit she had just experienced would be absent upon her return.

My child, my child..., she heard again. She understood. Just as the rushing surges of Katrina had left the Gulf, their aftermath was still there, and would forever be indelibly written on the hearts, the souls and the minds of all who had experienced her mighty power. So was this mighty Power, which was greater even than anything Katrina had held.

Mary Magdalena stood, sure that she would return to this house of the Lord on Sunday, sure that she would again feel the magnitude and the majesty of His love rain down upon her, and sure that she would find the waiting answer for which she was seeking. ***As surely as he has borne our griefs***, she said to herself, looking down at the Bible which lay still open on the pew. She didn't close it, but rather, left it to speak to the next person who happened upon this place.

She had entered this house of worship seeking an answer, which she did not receive. She left it with the assurance that she didn't know about tomorrow, but that she knew who was holding her hand as she slowly strode down the massive limestone steps and walked out to face the world, safe in the sheltered arms of the shepherd.

4

"You're up early," Nick said, coming down the stairs.

"Yes," Mary Magdalena replied, not stirring from her position as she stared out the front window toward the sand pile that was scheduled to be removed that afternoon. "Do you know what my favorite thing about the sand is?"

"You've mentioned it before, but why don't you tell me again?" Nick could tell she needed to talk through this more than she needed simply to share information.

"I love the fact that when it's all said and done, the sand goes to kindergartens or playgrounds where daycares or churches have a need. It has a mission and it continues to be used for a ministry. I love that." She took a sip of her coffee. "It's a visual reminder of how Jesus came here for all of us, and he goes out into the world with a lasting and continuing purpose."

Mary Magdalena finally turned to face her husband as a lone tear rested on her cheek. "I think that was Joshua's greatest accomplishment. Not getting the sand here, not organizing this event and not even crafting the sculpture, but allowing something so meaningful to continue serving others after it has left the volleyball court of Riverside Park. That, to me, is the most important aspect of the sand sculpture."

Already dressed for work, she put on her coat and kissed Nick good-bye. She reached inside her coat pocket and pulled out a plastic bag. "I'm going to bring some of the sand here and make a small flower bed. I don't know what I'll put in it yet, but it will be something to remind me of the spring break I spent in Mississippi."

Nick nodded. "How about magnolia since that's their state flower and their state tree?"

"That's a good idea. It may have to be one of our pink-saucer varieties, but that's a good possibility." She headed back to the kitchen for a larger plastic bag. "Only it will have to be a bigger bed."

"Do you want me to walk across the street with you?"

Mary Magdalena loved the gentleness in Nick's voice. It was a trait she was grateful she learned about him before paying attention to his tall, lean physique. Had she not experienced the help he gave his father with the sculptures, or the endearing way he spoke to everyone who visited the annual event at the park, she'd have seen him as any other acquaintance. It was not until after he had rescued her from a dangerous mistake that she noticed the handsome face of the man who was now her husband.

"No, she answered slowly, looking into his kind face before staring back out the front window. "I feel the need to be alone."

"Mary Magdalena," replied Nick lovingly, "you won't be alone."

"I know," was all she said as she strolled out the front door into the strong April wind that was not uncommon for this area. She knew her husband was not speaking of himself, but of a greater Presence.

She picked up the sand, allowing it to sift through her fingers as she was reminded of the shifting sand along a beach. As the morning clouds opened and rain began to pelt on her face, she envisioned the Gulf's sand washing in, washing out, until what was left was unfit for beach lovers. Suddenly, all she saw was the vision in her mind of the sign in the Gulf standing firmly planted on the soil, "just like a tree that's planted by the water and shall not be moved," bearing the words **KATRINA** WAS **BIG,** BUT GOD IS **BIGGER.**

The sands of time, she thought to herself, thinking of the creation of the universe, the sands of the Gulf and the sand that lay in her fingers and beneath her feet. ***All a part of God's handiwork,*** she mused, each granule together making a huge mass. ***Each of God's children working together to accomplish great things.***

The one gnawing question of what it was she was supposed to be doing to satisfy this longing, this hunger inside her, turned into countless questions – questions which seemed to have no answers, at least in her mind. That is, until she came to one last question. The final question she'd asked the librarian on the airplane. "***What was going through your mind during the storm***?" to which Jeanne's answer came immediately with great certainty and without hesitation, "The only thing I remember is hearing the words to a hymn that I'd learned as a child as they played over and over in my head. I don't recall all the words. In fact, I only remember twelve of them, but they are 'I don't know about tomorrow, but I know who holds my hand.' That's what kept going through my mind the entire time of the storm and I was never frightened."

Mary Magdalena let the last particles of sand fall from her hands. ***I don't know where I'm going from here, but I'm***

not frightened. Her hands, that had moments ago been covered in sand, now felt held by an unwavering strength. ***I have no clue what will happen tomorrow, but I know who holds tomorrow.*** She wondered what thoughts had been going through the hymn writer's mind at the time he penned the words that had spoken to Jeanne and now spoke to her.

Her thoughts drifted to August 22, 2007, the day Findlay experienced the second-worst flood in its history. Blanchard River, which ran right through Riverside Park, had come up her street and all the way up to her front door. She recalled the panic that had filled the city, as well as her own self, at the thought of losing her home and all the meaningful treasures stored within its walls. Treasures which Mary Magdalena had come to realize, during her time in Mississippi, weren't so irreplaceable after all.

Although Findlay's flood crested at 18.46 feet, which was barely short of 1913's record level flood of 18.50 feet, no one was killed, though some homes were destroyed and hundreds suffered damage from the rising waters. Five days and many national media stories later, President Bush declared Findlay a disaster area.

A disaster area, Mary Magdalena imagined, peering at the bland nothingness of the shape in the remaining mounds of sand. ***The figure of the man who lay in this area only a week ago depicted one of history's greatest disasters***, she realized, feeling a moment of silent grief, which was instantaneously replaced by the vision of her first year here.

Suddenly the park came to life in front of her eyes as she mentally saw Jewel, the woman who had been an "angel" in so many ways to her and everyone else there. She envisioned Wayne, who had supported Joshua from the beginning, writing poetry to portray the same images who were in the sand in words. Chic, who had helped with the sculptures from the first and welcomed her so warmly it still brought a smile to her face. And then there was Yogi, the park ranger who kept a watch - along with all the Civitan and other volunteers - over the area at night.

Mary Magdalena gave a chuckle at the idea of the sand sculpture now being guarded by an entire army. ***Actually the Marines,*** she corrected herself, ***but a whole crew of men taking the place of one solitary man. Yogi, the man who reminded me of the Centurion in the story of the Crucifixion. The man who ventured to tell the world and all who read the New Testament that "truly this man*** was ***the Son of God."***

Her chuckle became quiet at the thought of the "one solitary man" who had come to be associated with this volleyball court at Riverside Park. Mary Magdalena stared at the sand for a final moment, again seeing it completely void of shape with no evidence of the many hours of toil and love which had recently gone into it.

The "one solitary man" who took the place of all others on the cross, and whose life of toil and love could never be erased.

Memories of the years she'd been here, witnessing the countless ways in which people's lives were touched by the work of Joshua, flooded her soul. The vision of all the friends she'd met on this same spot - ***this disaster area*** - faded into the same nothingness as the shape in the sand.

Gone, but not forgotten, Mary Magdalena declared to herself as she turned and walked from the spot which, in a few hours, would again become nothing more than a volleyball court. She returned to her driveway, got into her car and drove to work, going out of her way toward Main Street to see the remaining effects of the flood. Miller's, the restaurant that had been there for decades, and where she originally heard of the sand sculpture through one of Findlay's most charming characters in the form of a waitress named Joni, was no longer there. She had feared Dietsch's might not return, but like everyone else in the town, was thrilled that the 1930's establishment was still in business, the brothers that owned it making chocolates and ice cream the same as their ancestors who had founded it, and as their offspring who were carrying on the tradition. Many other places, she observed somberly as she drove through the downtown streets, had not fared so well or had relocated to higher ground. She passed the county jail, the main branch of the library that had come to be a frequent hangout and the Central Middle School, all of which suffered considerable ruin.

She made the turn from North Main Street onto East Trenton Avenue and headed toward Blanchard Street, thinking of all the families or individuals who would be assisted in some way during this day at Findlay's Family Center Agencies, grateful to be a small part of that assistance through her job with the Hope House. Yet, she reasoned, ***thanks to the past two weeks of my life***, that those receiving and those giving were all in the same proverbial boat, none of them knowing what tomorrow held, but some fortunate enough to know who would be holding their hand.

5

Mary Magdalena had shared her feelings with no one, including her best friend Ebony, in her conquest to discover an answer to a question of which she still wasn't sure. There was something about the entire situation that seemed oddly reminiscent of a pirate on a treasure hunt, and she knew the precise treasure map that contained her answer. She had held it in her hand as Nick opened the door for her as they left for church.

Now, seated in the familiar setting of St. Andrew's United Methodist Church between her husband and the Cunningham's, Mary Magdalena turned her head to see the procession of United Methodist Women entering from the narthex as the pipes of the organ filled the air with harmonious praise. ***It sounds even more magnificent***, she observed in contrast to the afternoon before, ***with the room crowded with people***. As she watched the ministers and Charlotte lead the procession, she realized that she'd never "heard" this woman speak to a crowd. She'd only heard the author's voice through her books.

Sure, she'd witnessed her do a monologue of Mary Magdalene at the sculpture a couple of years back, and she'd chatted with her on occasions, but this was a side of Charlotte she'd never seen.

I wonder what she'll say, Mary Magdalena mused, remembering how they'd agreed that God would have a special message for her during the service. Her ears were attuned to anything that might strike a chord within her during the next hour. ***Will it be something out of the ordinary? Will it be so simple that everyone around me notices?*** She glanced at Charlotte, who was smiling at her as they made eye contact. ***Or will I even recognize the words that He sends me through the service?***

Since it was Missions Sunday, the topic selected by the planning committee was "Publish Glad Tidings." Charlotte wasted no time in sharing ways for people to "Publish Glad Tidings" – many of which could be acted out in silence, as well as by audibly telling people about the "Good News" and Christ's love for everyone.

Mary Magdalena listened intently for every word, but what struck her was when Charlotte spoke about the non-profit she'd created for children's literacy, named for the author's children's book character Rudy the Red Pig. The organization not only helped replenish school libraries destroyed by natural disasters, but also provided free cultural arts camps for the children in those areas – a facet of work which caused the listener's ears to perk up just in time to hear Charlotte say, "through Rudy and Friends Reading Pen, Incorporated, we have adopted the South Hancock Elementary School in Pearlington, Mississippi."

I must not be the only one excited about this, Mary Magdalena deduced as she heard a man give a whooping big "Amen!" at Charlotte's words.

"Now there's something you don't hear in a Methodist Church every Sunday," said Dudley, loudly enough for those around him to hear.

"Shhhh!" mouthed Cynthia, resembling a mother ordering a child to be quiet.

"Someone else out there must have been doing some recovery work in Mississippi," noted Charlotte, smiling with the rest of the congregation at the gentleman's response. "You'll understand the significance of my next words. South Hancock will be the first real school to reopen in Mississippi since Katrina. Three schools were combined to be able to build this school, which is going to be the finest facility I've seen anywhere. It's getting a lot of extra attention because it is also the first public building to open that was built from the ground up."

She went on to explain that the organization was placing a rocking chair, each one painted by an artist from around the country, in every classroom of the school so that each teacher would have a special reading center for the children. "Rudy has put nearly 12,000 new books into the library of South Hancock, and the surrounding schools. Middle school students, high school students, community college students and even the teachers have been touched by contributions from people just like you all over the United States who have donated books and time to make this a reality for Mississippi's children."

Mary Magdalena glanced back in the direction from where the "Amen!" had come to see if there would be another.

"Do you want to know the best part?" Charlotte asked. "The best part is that Hancock County, Ohio, was one of the first places Rudy visited. Thanks to the efforts of your own public library, over two hundred books came from this place and now reside in Hancock County, Mississippi. From your own hometown that was struck by its own natural disaster less than a year after that notable contribution. I'd like to share with you how the influence of this county, of the residents of Findlay, affected those children.

"I'd like to tell you about a young guy, a fourth grader who came out of a FEMA trailer being used as a classroom, on my first trip to visit the librarian of that school. He saw me walking toward the trailers, looking lost and confused. 'May I help you find someone?' he asked, stopping me in my tracks. It wasn't enough that he was asking such a perceptive question, but he was also polite about it. I don't know how many of you have spent any time in schools lately, but that's not always the response I see or hear coming from many students.

"When I told him I was looking for the librarian, he promptly asked, 'Are you the author who's coming to read?' I nodded in affirmative, only to get another question. 'You came all the way here just to see us and read to us?' he asked, as if that thought were incomprehensible to him. What struck me through that short conversation was the fact that he was blown away by the simple fact that I was here to spend time with him, with all of the students.

"That's when the power of what we were doing hit me," admitted Charlotte. "Here stood a fourth grade boy, who typically could care less about most things at that age, who was thrilled that I had come to see the students, to bring books and to spend time reading to them. I did nothing, just show up, and you'd have thought I'd handed the boy a great treasure."

With that, she drilled home the point that "your presence is a treasure. You don't have to do anything but show up in order to publish the glad tidings to those children. The message comes through loud and clear."

Charlotte challenged the entire congregation as she pointed to the stained glass window of Mary Magdalene. "Why do you think it is that Jesus first appeared to Mary Magdalena instead of one of his disciples?"

I wonder if the "Amen!" fellow will answer, Mary Magdalena pondered to herself. His silence told her that he must not know the answer either. She'd never heard her grandparents share that part of the Easter story, and she'd certainly never read it.

Charlotte had captured the attention of the congregation as faces turned and stared at the image on the window while proverbially sitting on the edge of their pews to hear the answer. "Tel-e-phone, tel-e-graph and tell-a-woman. Even back then, Jesus knew how to get the message out and around town."

The congregation broke into a round of laughter as Charlotte continued. "The disciples, the men, had seen Jesus in action. They had witnessed his miracles, they had heard him speak, they had dined with him in the Upper Room, and they had heard how he would come again.

"How many times did they have to be told and shown? These were the men who fell asleep in the garden, who denied their Lord. Yet here was Mary Magdalene, a woman who, like all of us, possessed flaws of her own. She was by no means a perfect person, yet she had the will to 'Go and tell.'

"That's all you need. A willingness to accept God's call to go out and publish glad tidings. God will give you the exact words you need to say. And in case you don't hear them clearly, they're all printed out for you right here," she explained, holding up her well-used Bible.

BAM! Charlotte's words – ***God's words through Charlotte***, Mary Magdalena reminded herself – struck her so powerfully that she felt as if she were going to fall out into the aisle from the startling blow.

The whole time Charlotte was speaking, Mary Magdalena sensed the anticipation mounting in her anxiousness to hear what God required of her. After the words of the sermon, she felt compelled to go back to Mississippi, this time to work with the children, but had there been any doubt, it would have all been washed away by the time the choir finished their anthem, ***I Have Felt the Touch of God***.

Not only did the melodious strains convince her that she possessed the ability to show others the face of God, they took her back to a time of reading all the cards and letters received by her grandparents. Letters that she'd found in her father's study and read once again after their deaths. ***After that letter she left for me***, Mary Magdalena mused, remembering how it was that she went from being "Maggie" to using her full name.

She began to name all the persons through whom she'd felt the touch of God, wondering if there were enough hours left in the day to name them all, many – like Bet Rawlings – who had unknowingly touched her through the music as she'd sat alone in the sanctuary during the past week. It was no accident this was the anthem selected for today's service. No matter how well Bet might have planned, she'd had a little help in choosing today's titles. Mary Magdalena wondered if the lyrics spoke to anyone else with the same power as they had to her.

The rest of the service was a blur as she relished in all the ways God had spoken to her during the morning. It wasn't until the notes of the postlude were dancing through the air that she realized Nick was already standing, as were Dudley and Cynthia.

"Planning on spending the day, are you?" Dudley asked in his usual manner.

"No, I was merely waiting for the crowd to clear so I could exchange a few words with Charlotte," Mary Magdalena replied. Her answer was not a lie; she simply saw no need in admitting that she'd been that caught up in the 'face of God.'

Besides, she knew those words would only serve to bring more ridicule.

"Why don't you go downstairs?" suggested Cynthia. '"She'll have to come that way to get her things from the choir room. I have to speak to someone here and by the time I've finished, Charlotte should be down there. We'll meet you down there on the way out the door."

Mary Magdalena turned to Nick. "Do you mind if I go alone? There's something I'd like to say to her in private."

"No." He squeezed her hand as a sign of his support as she exited the pew.

"I suspected you'd be here today."

Turning, Mary Magdalena saw the welcoming voice belonged to C. J. Hartman, one of the church secretaries, who made a point of welcoming her each time she'd come to sit in the solitude of the sanctuary. "Hello, C. J.! I almost didn't recognize you in the choir today. I'm so used to seeing you in the office."

"The choir is a form of therapy for me. I get much more from it than I give."

"I wouldn't agree with that, especially after today's anthem. I doubt there was a single person in the congregation who couldn't relate to someone from their past through those lyrics. Please tell Bet how beautiful it was. I'm still reeling from the message I received from it."

"I'll do that." C. J. extended her arm toward the man beside her. "This is Mike Wolf, a high school friend who happens to be visiting today. He lives in Laurel, Mississippi."

"Ah," acknowledged Mary Magdalena. "You're the one who...,"

"...said, 'Amen,'" he admitted. "I was so excited to hear all the work Charlotte's doing down there that I couldn't help myself. Did you know she's been written up in our United Methodist ***Christian Advocate*** magazine for the state of Mississippi? I remember reading about her last year after the huge success of her first cultural arts camp. Diann, my wife, teaches the Academically Gifted students in the elementary school back home, and she's really going to hate she missed hearing today's sermon. I can't wait to call and tell her all about it.

"I can't believe I actually met Charlotte. It was just a fluke that I was here today. I came up to visit my mom who's in West Virginia now, and at the last minute, decided to come here and visit in hopes of seeing some of my old friends. Not only did I run into some friends, but I actually met someone whom I've read about. This is amazing!"

"It wasn't a fluke," ventured Mary Magdalena. "It was a part of God's plan."

"I'm sure you're right. Charlotte gave me a card to take back for Pastor Wade. We need to have her speak at our Court Street United Methodist Church in Hattiesburg when she comes through Mississippi the next time. They'll love her. At Court Street, we tell people that we're the church between the tracks. We don't know which side of the tracks we're on."

"Then I guess you have the privilege of ministering to the people on both sides, right?" asked Mary Magdalena with a laugh.

"You're right about that. We're actually an inter-city church. It isn't uncommon for us to have people from several countries on a given Sunday. We have members, and visitors, from all walks of life and from all generations. That's why I love our church so much. To me, it's like a rainbow to God when He sees all of us worshipping and working together.

"And our minister, Pastor Bruce, he's great. His mother was actually involved in missions through the UMW. From what I've heard, she also did a great deal of work in the UMW with Civil Rights. That family, as well as our church, has a great heritage. And our choir director, she's fantastic. She's Italian, and if I'm not mistaken, is a trained opera singer."

"Really?" asked Mary Magdalena, whose ears again perked with mention of someone else of Italian descent. "I'm Italian, too, and my grandparents were missionaries from Italy."

"Oh, you'd love our church," Mike continued. "Maybe you can come sometime."

"Maybe I can. I'm on my way to tell Charlotte that I'm going with her this summer."

"Really?" asked C. J. "I wish I could go with her. I've already heard from some of our members who hope to join her."

Mary Magdalena gave a nod and turned back to Mike. "Maybe you can coerce her into making a stop at Court Street. Then we'd both be able to visit your church. Knowing her as I do, she'll say this was God lining up all the details and she'll be right there."

"I agree," added C. J.

"That's great!" exclaimed Mike, leaving Mary Magdalena waiting for another "Amen." "I'll look forward to your visit. The people on the Gulf still need your help and we're all appreciative when they receive it. When you help them, it's like you help all of us." He reached in his wallet for a card. "Here's my information. If you'll let us know when you're going to be down there, Diann and I would love to help, too. I work on an off-shore rig, so I'm gone ten days, then home for several. I sure do hope you're down when I'm at home."

"Mary Magdalena actually just returned from the Gulf where she participated in a building team," C. J. stated.

"Who?" Mike asked, shaking his head slightly to see if he'd heard correctly.

"Excuse me," C. J. apologized. "I didn't properly introduce you. Mike, this is Mary Magdalena Redford. She happens to be the daughter-in-law of the man I told you about who does the sand sculptures."

He obviously missed the last part of the introduction, for he was still turning her name over in his mind. "Your name is Mary Magdalena?"

She nodded.

"For real?"

"According to my birth certificate, it is," she answered, used to the reaction.

"I've never met anyone named Mary Magdalena before. Wait until I tell Diann. She won't believe this. I'm tempted to call her just so you can talk to her and she'll believe me."

C. J. took Mike by the arm. "We'd better go if we're going to catch Dalton." She turned to Mary Magdalena. "That's a guy who went to school with us, too. I want to make sure Mike and he get to at least exchange hellos before either of them gets gone."

"It was a pleasure to meet you, Mr. Wolf," she said as C. J. led him toward the Fellowship Hall.

"The name's just Mike, and it was a pleasure to meet you, too," he replied, still following C. J. "I'll read about you in the scriptures."

"Now there's a real compliment," noted Charlotte, coming up behind Mary Magdalena. "I've heard about reading about people 'in the funny papers,' but in the Bible? That's quite a powerful statement. In order to read about a person in the Bible, they'd have to be following Jesus' examples as followers and disciples to the best of their ability. There's a lot of theology to that."

"Either that, or they were so bad they got written up because Jesus had to pay him or her a visit," Mary Magdalena acknowledged, thinking of the figures in the stained-glass windows. She gave a muffled chuckle as she stared squarely at Charlotte. "So you were featured in a Mississippi magazine because of your work, huh? When were you going to share that tidbit of information?"

"It wasn't about me, remember? It was about the work God accomplished through my listening ears." She looked closely to see whether Mary Magdalena caught on to the words 'listening ears.' "I'm starved. Where are Dudley and Cynthia, or did they tell you I'm joining you for lunch? And I really enjoyed seeing Nick today. I've missed him since I wasn't here for the sculpture."

"That's exactly what he said about you." Mary Magdalena paused as she changed the subject. "So...when are we leaving?" she asked in a teasing tone, ignoring the question about the rest of the crowd.

"Did you hear your answer?" retorted Charlotte's nonchalant response.

"I heard it, Charlotte, and you did, too. I can tell by the expression on your face. You're consciously trying to keep from offering an opinion, but it's written all over you."

"Guess it's a good thing I write fiction, huh? I wouldn't be very good at hiding the truth," the author confessed, giving a brief smile before her expression changed yet again, this time to one of somberness. "It can be quite disturbing," Charlotte warned her. "It's one thing to go down there and work on a house and meet the family who will live in it, or either lived in it prior to Katrina. It's another thing to go down there and meet the children. To hear their stories and see their faces light up at the least little thing...things the children in our circles take for granted."

Charlotte watched as Mary Magdalena stood there, her eyes impervious to the warning as she stood resolute in her decision.

"You won't come home the same," Charlotte continued. "It will be a life-changing experience." She watched as there was still no hint of turning back on the face of the young woman in front of her. "And you'll be determined to go back, again and again."

"I'm sold," Mary Magdalena said simply. "Where do I sign the dotted line?"

Charlotte laughed aloud as she hugged her newest recruit. "If it's that easy to sell someone on something, perhaps I'd better go into the used car business."

"Charlotte Crenshaw," Mary Magdalena replied in a joking manner, yet full of truth in her statement, "if you keep that up, lightning is going to strike us both right here in the church. You know as well as I do whose words prompted me to go."

"Mary Magdalena, you're going to be a blessed addition to have on this trip. It wasn't only the words of this week that drew you to an acceptance of this call to mission. Your role as a chaperone for ASB laid the groundwork as it whetted your appetite to go back and do something for the people. Your role at the Hope House influenced your desire, and your ease in accepting the call. Between that and all of your volunteer work with youth throughout the community, you're already grounded in a ministry of mission, whether you recognize it as that or not."

"Do you really think of my work as a ministry? Sometimes I feel more like I do it out of a sense of guilt because I want so badly for people not to see me still caught up in my past."

Charlotte took Mary Magdalena's hand. "My child...,"

There were those words again. Mary Magdalena focused on the author's mouth. Was it really her speaking, or was it that same voice that she'd been hearing, the one she'd assumed to be God speaking through her conscience, earlier in the week?

"...your efforts may have begun as an effort to consciously change your past. Whether you were trying to convince yourself, or those around you, that you had changed, that is irrelevant because whether you recognize it or not, the ones around you clearly see that you possess a servant's heart."

"Do you really think that?" Mary Magdalena questioned, doubt still evident in her words.

"Hi, Mary Magdalena! Signing up as Charlotte's latest helper?"

The young woman turned to see a man whose face she recognized from the choir, but whom she didn't know by name.

"I was glad to see you here today," he continued. "I missed you at the sculpture this year. You've become almost as much a part of the goings on out at the park as the sand itself." His comment brought a flattered smile to her face. "As I watched you this morning while we sang the choir's anthem, I thought how fitting those words were for you. The way you've moved here, become involved in the community and thrown yourself into those young people through your job with the Hope House, I think a lot of people have felt the touch of God through your hands."

"Thank you," was all she could manage in her surprisingly startled shock.

"That truly was a meaningful anthem, especially for today's sermon," Charlotte commented. "I think everyone in the congregation could look around and see persons who had touched them in a special way. It was obvious from their faces as you sang. What I should have done was challenge everyone to go home and call or write three people whose actions had allowed them to feel the touch of God."

As the man passed to the choir room, Charlotte looked at Mary Magdalena. "I won't say, 'I told you so,' but I did." There was enough playfulness in her voice to lighten the air. She didn't want her young friend to feel too overwhelmed. She understood.

"Charlotte," called a female voice from up the stairs, "I'm glad you're still here. C. J. told me I might find you if I hurried." The woman rushed down the steps, extending her hand as she introduced herself. "I'm the youth director here at St. Andrew's. The whole time you were speaking, I was thinking of how our youth might get involved. Do you think we could possibly send a rocker or two?"

"Absolutely! There are thirty-two classrooms so we'll take all the rockers we can get. And I happen to know an artist in your congregation who is already painting one of the rockers for me. I'll bet she can do another one, or at least point you to some other artists."

"Why don't you ask Joshua and Harry to paint a chair?" suggested Mary Magdalena. "They're both quite the artists."

"Good idea," agreed the youth director. She looked at Mary Magdalena. "A few of us who go on Appalachian Service projects together have already spoken after her message and are thinking of going down with her. Why don't you join us? I'll bet you'd be great as a volunteer with those children."

Mary Magdalena glanced at Charlotte, who gave her a wink, and then back at the youth director. "I'm thinking about it."

"I have to meet some people for lunch, but here's my contact information." She handed Charlotte a card. "I'll talk to the youth this afternoon when we meet and see what we can get going. I'll get back to you sometime next week."

"Great!" replied the author. "I'll look forward to hearing from you. Thank you for your interest and please tell the youth we'll appreciate any help."

The youth director paused for a second as she headed back up the stairs. "Isn't it interesting that we had the visitor from Mississippi today? That seemed to make your words even more powerful."

"It was remarkable," answered Charlotte. "God does have a way of putting us in touch with those He wants us to meet. Sometimes it seems He can open doors for me faster than I can close them."

The youth director gave an understanding laugh and sprinted up the steps.

"Charlotte," Mary Magdalena observed, "I've watched you on many occasions at the park and around town, and it really ***does*** seem that God puts people in your life for a reason all the time."

"I don't think He does that with me any more than He does with others. I think it's merely a matter that I expect Him to guide my steps, and to guide the steps of those around me. At least that's the way Jack sees it, and I've come to agree with him."

"That's right," noted Mary Magdalena. "I remember the first time I met your son, Jack. One of those TV or newspaper people was talking to him at the sand sculpture about how you really do get out of God's way and expect Him to put you where He wants you. Jack called you...what was it...'an open vessel.'"

Charlotte looked reflectively at the woman in front of her. "An open vessel with lots of cracks from falling on my face at times, but those are the same cracks that allow God's love to flow out to others."

Mary Magdalena nodded, the message of the author's

words filtering into her thoughts. "The way they feel the touch of God through you."

"And the way they feel the touch of God through you."

"Hey, you two!" roared a voice from the top of the stairs. "You'd think from the long conversation you're having that Jesus had told one of you something and you're trying to tell the whole world before you get out of here. If I didn't know better, I'd get the feeling that one of you is named Mary Magdalene."

"That's enough, Dudley! Besides, my name has one letter different from hers," Mary Magdalena yelled back. "For your information, Jesus ***did*** tell me something and Charlotte and I had a little unfinished business we needed to take care of down here."

"Someone apparently misinformed me," he said, making his way down the stairs. "I was told we were having lunch together. Had I known it was going to be dinner, I'd have gone home for an afternoon nap."

Dudley, followed by Cynthia and Nick, continued his cajoling chant of, "Tel-e-graph, tel-e-phone, tell-a-woman. That was a good one! I'll have to remember that."

6

There was only one item on Mary Magdalena's agenda for that afternoon, which was to take a good look at the framed photograph from the sand sculpture three years before that Harry, Joshua's right-hand man, had given her. It had been for no particular reason, but was simply a gift he understood would speak to her in its simplistic silence. "The Fallen," he'd called it, was no more than the right side of Judas' face – the only remains when that particular disciple crumpled to the ground in Joshua's portrayal of the Last Supper. Resembling the mask from ***Phantom of the Opera***, it deemed a fitting demise as it lay where it fell during the rest of the Holy Week event.

She reached up and slowly removed the picture from its special place where it hung on the wall at the top of the stairs. Mary Magdalena had chosen that particular spot for it was one she would pass many times each day, at least in her going and in her coming. It was beside where she had seen the plaque that read, "ASK, SEEK, FIND" on her first time in this house. The same plaque which sold her on this house and which still hung in the same location. The plaque had proven to be in a truly auspicious place – one God knew she would see immediately, and she'd wanted "The Fallen" placed beside it.

Giving special attention to every detail of the photograph, she began with the prominence of the frame. It was wooden, so as not to take away from the focal point of the picture, yet there was such a rich quality in the wood and the manner in which it was crafted, it held its own significance in capturing the eye of the beholder. She then realized in all her times at admiring this picture, she had never given a second thought to the mats which enhanced it in the frame. But now, she paid specific attention to how the slate blue mat against the wood gave a stark, yet distinguishing contrast. A contrast suitably symbolizing the two sides of Judas – the one who followed Jesus and then the one who betrayed him. Finally she noted the narrow band of gold-leaf matting just inside the blue one, markedly edging the photograph. Gold, gilded gold which symbolized the disciple in charge of the money bag for his band of twelve, and the one who eventually put a price on the head of Christ.

And then, there was the photograph itself. Harry had managed to capture what was left of the face in such a way it was haunting, as if it were peering straight into the soul of the person looking at it. Only the right side of the face was showing, standing out against the rest of what was left of "the fallen disciple" in a heap of sand, no shape to any of it.

As she stared into the brokenness of the face, Mary Magdalena could sense her own transformation as, from the air around her, she seemed to hear the words, "Mary Magdalena, we are all fallen from grace." Her fingers outlined the face on the photograph, the words, "We have all sinned and fallen short of the glory of God" playing in her mind. She knew the words well. They were the words from Romans 3:23 which the Reverend Talbert had shared during her time in the Blanchard Valley hospital, a time following her own near-escape from death when she'd made a wrong decision. Words which had applied to the minister when, as a star football player for Findlay High School, he made a wrong decision and ended his sports career. Words he said applied to everyone at some point in their lives.

She looked deeper into the face on the photograph, imagining the faces of all the other disciples in that famous scene from Leonardo da Vinci's ***Last Supper***. There was not one of them who had been void of sin. Not one of them who had not been offered God's redeeming love. Not one of them who had not been in need of the saving grace Christ offered. ***Not one of them who, at one time or another, deserted or denied their master.***

"They're not so different from you, my dear child," Mary Magdalena heard from within. This time, the voice sounded like the rich baritone of her grandfather, who had no doubt shared those same words with many in his lifetime of service as a missionary. Her prayer, which had been heard even without her uttering it, had been answered, and all fears of being "unworthy" had been removed from her consciousness. She was aware there would be other uncertainties and trials in her journey ahead, but she stood there, keenly aware that whatever she'd need for each of those situations would be provided in her hour of need.

The last thing she noticed about her meticulous examination of the photograph was the fact Harry had signed the gold mat. He'd used a very distinct signature, one which held special meaning and was full of pride for him. It was his Indian name, Glenn D. Greywolf. To Mary Magdalena, that, in itself, served as a symbol of deep affection and a shared friendship with each other, but more significantly, a shared love for the same Lord. This gift, which bore his "family" name, said he would always be there for her, in times of need and in times of plenty. He was her friend, her Christian brother...***of a different tribe but created by the same Master***, she reflected.

That's it! she thought to herself. This whole time, she'd been trying to decide exactly what it was she was looking for from this picture. She knew it would hold significant meaning for her, as it had on numerous occasions over the past three years, but there was something she'd missed...until now.

Judas had at one time been a friend to Jesus, his brother, his disciple. He'd been with Christ to see the miracles, to witness the healings. But then, whether through change or impatience with Christ's declaration of his Messiahship, he, too, left a personal signature. ***His kiss***, she concluded, ***THAT was his signature***.

"What will be your signature?" There was no doubt in Mary Magdalena's mind the origin of these words which flashed through her consciousness. They were a question from God. She was ready to accept the calling, to sign the dotted line she'd jokingly mentioned to Charlotte. ***But God doesn't expect me to sign my name on a line***, she reasoned, concluding what He expected was her signature to show through her actions, just as Judas' signature had been obvious by an action.

Lord, she began to pray, ***let me leave an indelible imprint on the life of each Katrina child with whom I come in contact. An imprint which bears your example of unconditional love. Let that be my signature.***

Taking one last look at the picture before placing it back on the wall, she wondered whether Harry had realized on how many occasions this visual symbol of "The Fallen" would speak to her. As she positioned it, then stood back to make sure it was level, the photograph took on a whole new appearance. With rays of the afternoon sun hitting it from the windows, the face took on new depth. The sand surrounding the face, forming a naturally matted background of its own, appeared to have been spiced with fools' gold, just like the mica Mary Magdalena had seen in rocks as a child.

Fool's gold? she repeated in her mind. ***Judas' fool's gold was the thirty pieces of silver. Many prospectors have been fooled at first glance by the dull, yellow-brass metallic luster that gave the appearance of being something valuable, something precious***, she pondered. ***Had Judas been fooled by the prospect of shiny silver, thinking it was more valuable, more precious, than the radiant Son of his Father?***

She thought back to all she had read on the disciples and Mary Magdalene since taking on her full name, in an effort to fully understand their roles and how they were chosen. ***Or had Judas, duped by his own feelings of disillusionment and disappointment, been fooled by the belief that Jesus, too, was going to be a Zealot partisan and overthrow the government?***

Sensing the theology of this analogy was headed much deeper than she was able to comprehend, Mary Magdalena gazed back at the photograph, its hidden luster now fully in view. She couldn't decipher whether its radiant appearance came from the sun's rays reflecting off the gold-leaf matting, or whether the granules of sand had possessed a hint of gold from the beginning but had been lost as she held it down in front of her, hidden from the sun and away from the light.

I understand! she determined, instantly aware of why she'd been so consumed by the desire to come home to see the photograph.

She'd had to dredge her way through all the minute details to finally get to the big picture. ***Like people who can't see the forest for the trees***, she reflected. She wondered whether it was like this for everyone who heard a call from God.

Do they try to explain it away? ***Or are they unwilling to serve?*** Do they feel incapable? ***Or are they afraid of personal failure?*** Do they lack or distrust their own faith? ***Or are they afraid to fully trust the Almighty for all their needs?*** Do they second-guess their calling? ***Or do they feel inadequate?*** Do they immediately jump into action? ***Or do they speculate and weigh the situation until the call has faded quietly away into the background?***

Feeling totally overwhelmed, Mary Magdalena longed for her grandparents, or more specifically, for their wisdom and advice, for their own stories of hearing and accepting God's call to missionary service. Had they jumped headlong into it, or had it been a process that developed, over time, into which they stepped gently?

"It doesn't matter, my child."

Her inclination was to call Ebony, not only to share the news of her decision, but to also engage her services for Charlotte's return trip to Mississippi. However, as badly as she wanted to pick up the phone, she knew her first duty was to discuss the matter with Nick. She had no idea how she would tell him, nor what his reaction would be, but she was sure the words would come to her in due time. ***Why am I concerned?*** she asked herself. ***God will take care of that in His own way, too.***

As she walked away from the photograph, it dawned on Mary Magdalena she was at last following in the footsteps of her grandparents. Although she had often been intrigued by her grandparents' stories as a child, it was not a path she had sought, nor one which had ever held an interest for her.

What have I to worry? she asked herself, this time almost jokingly. ***God ordained these steps even before I was born***, she thought, recalling the scripture from Jeremiah 1:5. ***He chose this path for me***. What she now recognized as her first step into "the mission field" was one she was sure would not be the last in her lifetime.

The time had come to discuss her calling – ***and my answer to that calling!*** – with Nick. Hearing his footsteps coming up the stairs alerted Mary Magdalena she would have no time for preparation. ***The best thing to do is get it over while I still have the courage***, she convinced herself.

"Nick, would you mind," she began tentatively, but getting no chance to finish her question.

"No," he answered.

She looked at him quizzically. "Do you think,"

"I don't know, but I'll ask him."

Again she appeared puzzled.

"Would,"

"Yes."

"Wait a minute," she called behind him as he walked toward the upstairs office, as if their conversation had been quite ordinary. "How did you know what I was asking you?"

"Do you think you're the only one who can dream?"

"What?" Mary Magdalena stared at him, befuddled by his question.

"Don't you remember when an angel came to Mary in the Bible? She had her own personal message from God. But then an angel also came to Joseph because God needed to make him aware of the situation in His own way."

She saw nothing but total compassion and understanding in Nick's eyes. She imagined it being the same compassion and understanding Joshua had seen in Lynn's eyes on the morning at three o'clock when he awoke his wife to share the news that he was going to do a sand sculpture for Holy Week in Findlay, Ohio. ***In a place where there was no sand.***

'We won't," Mary Magdalena began, but then stopped for him to finish the sentence.

"We'll find out when we get there," he verbally assured her, while taking her in his arms as a sign of assurance that he would be there for her.

"I keep hearing something Charlotte shared as we were leaving lunch. You'd already reached the parking lot with Dudley when a man from the congregation stopped her in the restaurant. He asked if she didn't think it was more important to be building houses for all those people still in FEMA trailers and tents, rather than spending time babysitting the children. He went on to say he'd been to the Gulf on three mission trips in an effort to put families back in a home."

"And her response?" Nick asked.

"It was really quite odd. She responded in much the same way Jesus did when he was often questioned by the Pharisees. She tossed him a question of her own and allowed him to chew on it for a minute or so before she said anything else. She simply asked, 'What good is it to build all those homes, schools and churches if you don't rebuild the lives of the children who will go in them?'

"I watched the perplexed look on the man's face as he weighed her words in his mind. You could actually see the wheels churning, so deep was he in thought. Then when you could see him begin to understand the depth of the meaning in her challenge, she continued, 'There are some of us who are unable to swing a hammer and carry stacks of 2 x 4s, but we are able to offer the children resources to vent their own feelings, fears and frustrations in a positive, creative way. Didn't you see when you were there how parents are so stressed and bogged down with simply finding work and keeping food on the table, they have no time to talk to the children, much less do anything constructive with them? Their minds are so caught up in trying to keep up, on top of merely surviving, there's no time to read to the children, to let the children write their own stories, to work out their emotions in a healing and therapeutic manner. If you still see our work as babysitting, I'd love to invite you to participate on our next trip to the Gulf.'

"She then shook his hand and left him to reflect on her words, shaking his hand and telling him how good it was to see him again. There was nothing curt about her at all, just that sincere love she has for everyone. You could see the sincerity in her demeanor when she said she hoped she'd see him on her next visit to the church. It was amazing to watch."

Mary Magdalena paused, recreating the scene in her mind. "All I could think about on the way home was how akin that seemed to the way Jesus handled situations which could have become confrontational. He had a way of saying, 'In your face,' yet it was done in such a kind, gracious manner the Pharisees, or the disciples, or whoever he happened to be talking to didn't realize what had just happened before their very eyes."

"His gracious way was called 'parables,'" Nick replied. "I don't think he meant it at all with an 'In your face' attitude."

"I don't either, but when you look at the many times it happened with the same groups in the Bible, it continually backfired on them. Jesus taught so many people who had no idea of the lesson they were learning."

"Don't you think that's exactly what Charlotte's doing with the children?" he asked. "If she announced she was having a learning session or a therapeutic healing, how many people do you think would come? As it is, she's having so much fun simply in spending time with them that it's contagious. It's like the story she told of working in Cambodia when teens and adults sat far back on the path leading to where she shared stories of Jesus with the children. Each day the teens and adults inched their way a little closer until on the last day of the week, they were in the circle, learning, singing, and praising God with the children."

"It's almost like a Pied Piper effect, isn't it?" Mary Magdalena asked, getting her own big picture.

"It is, and I know a beautiful young woman whose very presence is a proverbial flute."

"Do you really think I'll do a good job with the children?"

"Are there many grains of sand in the sand sculpture each year?"

"You did it!" Mary Magdalena exclaimed with the excitement of a small child. "You answered the question with another question which relayed your point even more clearly than if you'd given a one-word answer."

Nick looked into his wife's exuberant face and wondered whether her grandparents ever had an inkling that their granddaughter would one day be walking in their shoes.

7

Mary Magdalena had been so preoccupied with getting back into her routine at the Hope House and the preparations for the annual Hope House fundraiser she'd practically forgotten what day it was. It wasn't until she stopped by Coffee Amici the following Friday morning, and ran into Charlotte, that she realized the week had already come to an end.

"Why don't you join me?" Charlotte invited, enjoying an Amici Mocha Chiller before leaving for home.

"Are you sure? This is one of the rare times when I've seen you alone. Wouldn't you rather enjoy the privacy?"

"I can enjoy my privacy all the way back to North Carolina. I relish my privacy so much I don't turn on the radio or CD player all the way home. That's my down time, my time to get all my thoughts together after what's gone on, and my time to give God the thanks He deserves for putting me in a place where I so love the people."

She put away her writing tablet to make room for Mary

Magdalena. "Besides, God obviously wanted us both here at the same time, for here we are."

"Right," Mary Magdalena replied. ***There must be some truth to that "open vessel" business with "listening ears,"*** she observed.

"You'll never believe what happened," she began, taking a seat. "Oh, never mind, I forgot who I was talking to for a minute. "Yes, you would believe." Mary Magdalena looked at Charlotte with a mischievous eye. "And you probably already know, but I'm going to tell you anyway."

Charlotte laughed heartily. "See how much fun it is when you let go and let God direct your steps? There's never a dull moment."

"I'm seeing that," nodded Mary Magdalena. She explained how Nick answered all her questions before she finished them. "It was amazing how he knew exactly what I was going to say."

"Did you think the fact he perhaps received his own calling might have influenced that? In the department of signs from God, you're not a privileged character."

Mary Magdalena's face scrunched up in her moment of consciousness. "I thought it was because he was such an understanding husband. All week I've been making his favorite foods in appreciation of him being so attuned to my needs."

Charlotte laughed harder. "Sorry to burst your bubble! Don't go thinking he wasn't being attentive, and whatever you do, don't stop making his favorite foods. Those ideals make for a healthy, lasting marriage." Her laughter resolved to a smirk. "But should you stop making his favorite foods, don't tell him it had anything to do with me. I'd like to remain a friend of the family!"

"Understood," Mary Magdalena said with a nod.

"So, what was it God sent you in here to tell me?"

"Nick has agreed to go with us to the Gulf, and I had him ask Joshua and Harry to go make a sculpture of a dolphin for the students since you said they're the South Hancock Elementary Dolphins. Not only did they agree, but they're going to enlist a couple of other guys who volunteer with Findlay's sand sculpture each Holy Week. I can't tell you how gratified I am to see all this happening before my very eyes. It's like seeing God work the puzzle right in front of you."

"Would you like to hear about a couple more of the puzzle pieces?"

Mary Magdalena again nodded, her expression resembling a teenager about to hear the biggest secret of the entire school.

"Remember how interested the youth director at St. Andrews was about the Hancock County to Hancock County effort? When she presented it to her youth Sunday afternoon, they voted to sponsor an offering next Sunday where people can bring their loose change to purchase rockers for the classrooms."

"Similar to the model of Souper Bowl Sunday?" Mary Magdalena asked, referencing the mission project supported by most congregations on Super Bowl Sunday.

"Exactly!" exclaimed Charlotte. "I take cans of soup and all my loose change to church every year for Souper Bowl Sunday. That practice has made great strides in stocking the local food pantries and helping feed the homeless people." The author paused for a second. "You know, I hadn't thought of it in that way, but this town surely ought to be able to relate to the Super Bowl, given Big Ben is from here. No matter where I am, I make a point of finding out how Ben Roethlisberger and the Steelers are faring." She gave a smug grin. "That is, right after I find out how my Panthers are doing," the author teased.

"In all seriousness, though, I think those youth have a

great idea. Perhaps they should call their effort The Rocker Bowl. Maybe I should pass that tidbit along to the youth director at St. Andrew's." Charlotte's serious expression returned. "On second thought, perhaps a Rock-a-thon would be more fun. Who wouldn't enjoy a couple of uninterrupted hours in a rocking chair?"

"I agree, to all of the above," Mary Magdalena replied.

"Do you remember the man from St. Andrew's who approached me Sunday at the restaurant?"

Mary Magdalena nodded.

"Can you believe he's already called me to find out how much each rocker costs? He wanted to give the first one from Hancock County, Ohio to go to Hancock County in Mississippi. I was amazed."

"Charlotte Crenshaw, I can't believe that amazed you. You, the open vessel who continually experiences God's intervention in your life. I'm not surprised. I heard his question and I also heard the way you opened his eyes to a different way of thinking. That was pretty amazing."

"I can't believe that 'different way of thinking' amazed you. You know the source of the words I shared with him as much as I do."

Mary Magdalena smiled knowingly. "Okay, we're even."

"Why don't you contact the youth director the next time you're at St. Andrew's? I'm sure C. J. can put you in touch with her. I'd love to see if all of us could get together and go as a convoy to Mississippi. If not, we'll meet up once we get there. One of the churches in the Gulf, Diamondhead United Methodist, allows us to stay in their facility while we're in the area. There are also other churches in the area that open their doors to volunteer teams. Both Heritage United Methodist in d'Iberville and Bethel Lutheran in Biloxi have provided lodging, making it possible for me to do work in the Gulf, but

Diamondhead has become a great hub for the kind of work we do. It's much closer to Pearlington and has adequate space for us to work and plan each day's activities. With a project such as the one we do, there are tons, ***literally***, of supplies that have to be shipped down."

"Diamondhead...what an interesting name," observed Mary Magdalena.

"You'll find it even more interesting once you get there," Charlotte noted.

"I'd better be going," Mary Magdalena said, suddenly drawing the conversation to a close as she caught a glimpse of the clock. "Ebony will wonder what happened to me. She's helping organize auction contributions for the fundraiser at the Hope House today."

"Tell her you had some unfinished business from the weekend. I think she'll understand. By the way, did you think of asking if she'd like to join us?"

"I did, but she may be in summer school at the university. She only needs two more classes to graduate after this semester, but she's really considering the possibility."

"Give her my best." She hesitated for a moment before adding, "You know He'll work out a way for her to go if it's His will."

"Yes," Mary Magdalena replied, "I do know that, as does she. We've had this discussion and are awaiting His answer."

Charlotte watched as Mary Magdalena drove away, feeling privileged to have met this person whom she was sure God had placed in her path. Something told her that during the course of this young woman's lifetime, she was going to touch many others. ***Just as her grandparents did***, the author thought.

Sipping the last of her drink in silence, she wondered what changes would transpire in Mary Magdalena between now and July, in preparation for her second tour of duty to the

Gulf, and what changes would transpire while in the Gulf, in preparation for the rest of her life.

In your time, Lord…in your time…she prayed.

I Know Who Holds Tomorrow

8

Mr. Wolf wastes no time, Charlotte concluded, returning to her office the following week to face the hundreds of messages accumulated in her web mailbox. One in particular caught her attention from the Reverend Austin Wade, the name she recognized as the minister of Mike's church in Hattiesburg, Mississippi.

"Reverend Wade, please," she requested when the secretary of Court Street Church answered the phone.

"Austin Wade here. May I help you?" A pleasantly vibrant and welcoming voice brightened the air all the way from the other end of the line.

Certainly not the kind of voice to put you to sleep from the pulpit on a Sunday morning, noted Charlotte. "I'm calling in response to your e-mail," she explained after introducing herself.

"Yes, Mike Wolf called me the day he heard you and was insistent that you come to our church in Hattiesburg while you're in Mississippi this summer. He was most enthusiastic about having met you."

"He strikes me as the type who is most enthusiastic about anything, at least if it's something he likes."

"You're right," Austin replied. "Therefore, I hope you don't think me impudent for asking you to call so we could chat a bit."

"Not at all. I understand totally," said Charlotte. "I get this all the time. Someone hears me at an event or conference and immediately returns home all 'on fire.' You're certainly not the first pastor to call me and you certainly won't be the last. I'd expect my own minister to make certain a speaker is reputable before extending an open invitation to the pulpit."

"After speaking with you, I can understand Mike's enthusiasm," replied Austin. "Even through the phone, I can sense the gusto with which you approach things for which you have a keen passion."

"Ay! I must admit that's a part of my nature. Like Mike, my zeal for people and life isn't exactly discreet."

"I also suspect that's what makes you so successful at what you do."

"I'm not sure I'd call it successful. Let's merely say 'listening for God's will and walking through lots of doors.'"

"I'm going to be in Europe on a sabbatical for a month this summer," Austin explained. "We're lining up guest speakers for each of those Sundays. Would you be available on July 22nd to speak at our church? It's the only date I still have open."

"That's the Sunday I'll be leaving the Gulf to come home," she informed him. "Perfect timing! I could go north through Hattiesburg and then head east, rather than going to Mobile to head north. Our entire group could come with me."

"Why am I not surprised? That's great! I'll have the secretary call Mike immediately. He wanted to know the minute I received an answer from you. And look at it this way, going home that direction will bring you out on the north side of Atlanta. You'll avoid lots of traffic."

"That, in itself, makes it worthwhile," she observed. "Have you ever tried taking buses and vans through there and keeping them together? Especially in a rain storm so severely blinding you couldn't see in front of you?" Charlotte gave a muffled sigh of experience. "We plan our trips very carefully to dodge the heaviest flows of traffic in Atlanta."

"Tell me about what you do in the Gulf," Austin requested. "I read the article in our ***Christian Advocate***, but I'd like to know more."

Charlotte explained in detail the work of her non-profit and how it had begun as a means to help the Gulf's children. "You see, my mother was a librarian. I well remember when she volunteered for two years in a small bookmobile to help get a real branch of the library in our area. I guess it's because of her passion and dedication that I believe every child should have a book in their hands.

"I was listening to ***The Today Show*** one Sunday morning, which stands out in my mind for three unusual reasons. First, I seldom watch television; second, especially on Sunday morning when I'm typically in church; and third, I was with my dad because he'd just come home from a massive heart attack and quadruple bypass surgery. I wasn't paying any particular attention to the show, it was merely on immediately before some show my dad wanted to watch. However, when one of the hosts made the announcement about how many children and students in the Gulf were still without books, I literally felt God reached His hand right out of the television and grabbed me, saying, '**Do something!**'

"Their announcement, which came as part of a drive Scholastic Books was holding to raise books for the Katrina children struck a chord within me. During the next week, I spent much of my time researching the situation. It was odd for I was scheduled to fly into New Orleans and drive to Mississippi for a benefit concert ten days later. My son, Jack, was with me and suggested we take our own tour to assess the state of affairs for ourselves. It was Jack's pleading voice, after getting a firsthand look at the area, with the words, "Mom, you've got to do something to help these children," which prompted my decision.

"It wasn't his voice, you know."

"Yes, I know that very well, for it wasn't the first time he'd served as my messenger. Anyway, thanks to a son who's as compassionate about God's hurting children as I am, the rest is history," she ended, after sharing the details of their first visit to the Gulf following Katrina with Austin.

"I believe both Jack and you will enjoy worshipping with our church family. You see, a part of our Court Street Creed reads, 'We are a church that reaches out with deep compassion to help hurting people.'" The phone was silent on Austin's end for a moment before he added, "It's too bad you couldn't come for one of our Wednesday evening meals to work with our children. I think you'd love them as much as they would love you." Within a couple more minutes, Reverend Wade had persuaded Charlotte to bring her group for a second program, on the Wednesday evening before the Sunday she was to speak.

"This will be a meaningful opportunity for the youth of my congregation. They're used to seeing the mainstream of middle class folks in their church. I want them to experience a downtown inter-city church. It will be quite a culture shock, if there's anything left to shock after their work with the children in Mississippi's Hancock County."

"You're right," Austin seconded. "Being from North Carolina, you'll appreciate the significance of the fact we were selected by the Divinity School of Duke University to serve as a Teaching Congregation for their students."

"I understand that more than you'd know. I may serve at a Lutheran Church, but I'm their 'token Methodist.' You see, I was one of the few Carolinians who chose to attend SMU rather than Duke. Don't ask me why. I'd always had an affinity for that university in Texas, even back in high school. But I'm very well aware of that program at Duke, and the fact they recognized you is commendable.

Charlotte again thanked Austin, this time for both invitations, as she left him with one request. "Make sure you inform Mike Wolf the only Sunday I could come was the same one you needed someone. That should rock his boat."

Austin laughed.

"And while you're talking to him, tell him Mary Magdalena is coming with me. He should have loads of fun explaining that to the congregation of Court Street."

The author hung up the phone and immediately looked up the church on the internet. She found the church, in the downtown Historic Neighborhood of Hattiesburg, most interesting as she read about its long-standing history "between the tracks." But the comment which most impressed her read, "Somehow, through our 100+ year history, we have survived – sometimes flourishing, sometimes hanging on like a stranded mountain climber with fingernails dug into the ledge on a cliff."

Well, Charlotte said to herself, referencing what she'd witnessed on prior visits, ***I see this attribute of "resilience" is nothing new to the people of Mississippi!***

PART TWO

From the moment Mary Magdalena drove into the state of Mississippi on I-59, she sensed a change in the air. She wasn't sure whether it was really there, or whether it was an internal indicator warning that she was now in war-torn territory, a region annihilated by the blasting of nature. It was a view she missed during spring break, when she had flown in from Ohio's Port Columbus International Airport. The huge blue tarps hanging where walls had once been in the Gulfport-Biloxi International Airport were disturbing, but they didn't affect her with the same impact as being amidst the terrain did now.

Within seconds of reaching the state line, she began to notice remaining signs of a changed environment. Pine trees, which once stood straight and tall, now all leaned and were chopped off, giving the appearance of broken matches sticking up from the ground. Barren land stretched in front of her, with debris scattered and laying amuck, just as it had since August 29, 2005. As drastic and dramatic as the change that had taken place on that day had been, it was obvious there had been little or no change since that time, at least in this area. Neither she nor Ebony uttered a word until they reached Exit 16, marked Diamondhead, after passing through the vicinity that was to be their temporary home, their "fertile field" of love for the next fourteen days.

Mary Magdalena longed to go beyond this long stretch of four-lane interstate, to see the people, the homes, or what was left of them, to experience the lives that had been forever changed. But she knew it was not yet time. She understood Charlotte would give her a private tour before the day was over, allowing her an unobstructed view of everything, without thought of driving in unknown territory. ***And with a veteran's eye of progress from the storm until now.*** That's why she'd planned to arrive early in the afternoon on this hot July Saturday, a full day before the rest of the volunteers.

Turning up the exit ramp, Mary Magdalena knew not why but she instinctively felt a rush of tingles, carrying an accompanying message that she was here for more of a reason than "doing something special for the children" for the next two weeks. She sensed a greater raison d'être, with no indication of what. As she pulled into the parking lot of Diamondhead United Methodist Church and saw the familiar van with the North Carolina license plate, she knew emphatically and irrevocably that Charlotte Crenshaw held the key to whatever door she was to unlock on this Gulf coast.

"Well, I'm certainly glad the two of you heard the same voice I did," Charlotte said, rushing out the front door of the church to greet both Mary Magdalena and Ebony as she welcomed them to their new "home" for the next couple of weeks. She wondered how long it would take them to ask the question, the first question she ever heard from anyone, when they arrived here to help her with one of her projects. The author didn't have to wonder long.

As soon as Ebony carried her belongings inside the building, she stood staring across the driveway into the fenced area, only yards from the front door, with its short white picket border giving the appearance of a well-manicured flower garden except for one thing - the white PVC-pipe crosses that stood in place of flowers. A large, white angel statue stood with her wings outspread at one end, and a lone, young tree sapling guarded the grounds at the other.

"I noticed a dog bowl as we turned in the drive. Does the church have a dog?" asked Mary Magdalena.

"As a matter of fact, it does," Charlotte answered. "It appeared here after the storm and the church members put food out for it. It's been here ever since and the volunteers who come keep it fed. It's rather pitiful looking, but it's a moving visual reminder of the fact that neither man, nor beast, was spared the torture of Katrina."

She noticed Ebony's dark-brown eyes still glued to the crosses. Ebony Hand, who at Northern Exposure had been known as "Bubbling Brown Sugar" still fit that description in Charlotte's eyes, only for a very different reason than her perfectly-flawless and creamy golden-brown skin and shapely figure. She was a sweetheart underneath her layer of irony which sometimes rose its blunt head in her dry-witted come-backs, and you could expect a touch of spice in any circumstance in which she was involved.

To Charlotte, this was a woman whose spiritual leanings ran deep, which she assumed was what drew Ebony and Mary Magdalena together. Secretly, she suspected their shared days in that dreadful environment of Northern Exposure would benefit them in their upcoming days in this dreadful environment. They were strong individuals who had learned, through a hard-core education, to take care of themselves in practically any situation.

"So who's minding the store this week?" Charlotte asked, referring to Ebony's job of tutoring the children and youth at Hope House, in an effort to alleviate the young black woman's attention. She was aware there would be plenty of time for Ebony's reflections later, ***after*** she'd gotten "the big picture" of Katrina's wrath.

It worked, for Ebony let out a rollicking cackle. "Joni! Can you believe that?"

"Joni?" Charlotte repeated questioningly. "As in my favorite waitress from Miller's?"

"Yes," answered Mary Magdalena. "You know, after Miller's had to close down following our flood in Findlay, she went to work at the McDonald's right across the street from the high school. She loves all the teenagers, you know."

"Yes, I do know. She's given her entire life to being a Girl Scout leader and her husband teaches at the high school. I've always been amazed at the wonderful role models and mentors they both are for all those adolescents, a feat which has obviously not gone unnoticed, given all the awards they've received for their outstanding service."

"You're right. All the students know her, and would jump hoops for a chance to go each day and see her at breakfast or lunch. Huh! Some would go at both meals if allowed."

"I shouldn't be surprised. I've never seen her lacking something to say to everyone, nor seen anyone not humored by her spontaneous comebacks. She's a great people person. I missed her this past year in Findlay since Miller's wasn't there. Guess I'll have to start eating breakfast at McDonald's when I'm in your area. I'm sure it would be the best Egg McMuffin I've ever had!"

They all laughed as the three of them hastily unpacked Mary Magdalena's car and "set up camp."

"The sanctuary will be the bedroom for the females," Charlotte informed them. "Our Methodist Disaster Response Center provided air mattresses for all of us. Grab one," she instructed, pointing to the stack on the floor. "Take it to where you want your space to be, and I'll have your beds ready by the time you freshen up a bit. You'll be living out of your suitcase, so put it beside your bed like a footlocker. There's a hanger for your towels on the rack across from the shower in the women's restroom. All the food goes on the kitchen counter and the supplies go in the Worship Leader's office, which has been converted into a supply closet for the volunteers. Once everyone gets here tomorrow, we'll sort all the supplies and get them ready for each day's activities. Any questions?" Without giving the two young women time to reply, she finished with, "Good!"

"When you said you were Charlotte's latest recruit, you weren't kidding," observed Ebony with a grin.

"Any comments from the side lines and we'll begin drill practice," Charlotte shot across the room with a grin as she pumped up the air mattresses.

"You know this routine well, don't you?" Ebony asked, this time completely serious.

"Unfortunately, yes," admitted the author. "I am most grateful for having been allowed the opportunity of working with these children, for it is indeed a privilege. But it's regrettable they've had to experience what they have." She stopped the electric pump for a moment. "I say 'unfortunately' lightly, for you'll see something in these children that you don't see in the children back home. They've developed a resilience which will allow them the capability to handle anything thrown at them during life." Her head dropped. "It's just too bad some of their parents didn't learn the same lesson."

"What did she mean by that?" asked Ebony as they headed to the restroom and shower area.

"I'm not sure," replied Mary Magdalena. "But what I am sure of is that we'll find out well before these fourteen days are over."

"Okay, ladies," declared Charlotte once both women had showered, "your beds are ready and so are we. Let's go. I'm taking you to Biloxi to the Hard Rock and then the Beau Rivage."

The two young women peered at each other questioningly, and then back at Charlotte.

"We're going to the casino?" ventured Mary Magdalena, hesitantly.

"Somehow, with all you're always doing and giving to others, I never pictured you as a gambler," stated Ebony.

"No, and I'm not, in that order," replied Charlotte with a smile, glad to see her scheme was already working. "I'm taking you to lunch at the Hard Rock Café and after that, we're walking down the block to my favorite ten-dollar store in the country, which happens to be in the Beau Rivage, where I'm going to pamper each of you with a present."

"Ten dollars and lunch," noted Ebony jokingly. "So that's all we're worth?"

"Hey," cautioned Mary Magdalena seriously, "don't complain. That's better than you got some nights at Northern Exposure."

Ebony's cynical face immediately changed. "Yeah, but sadly, not many nights. That's the kind of place that should have been leveled to the ground."

Charlotte knew it wasn't going to take long for these two astute women, who'd seen that side of the world, to recognize the measure of contrast between the opulence of the Gulf's casinos on the one hand and the obliteration on the other.

Charlotte's tour of the vicinity did not include the unexpected crossing of an alligator as the threesome drove through what was left of the back roads between Waveland and Bay St. Louis. It was smaller than what she'd imagined one to be, and much quicker, as it sped across the lanes more swiftly than she could retrieve her camera from its case.

"Are those everywhere down here?" asked Ebony precariously.

"No," answered Charlotte, acting as if this occurrence was nothing out of the ordinary, "just mostly in our sleeping quarters, and only at night." Her comment drew precisely the shocked look she'd anticipated. "No," she then admitted with a laugh, "to tell the truth, that's the first one I've seen down here, other than the big ones several times that size on the Alligator cruises."

"Remind me not to go on one of those," Ebony responded without haste.

"Oh, didn't I tell you?" Charlotte questioned. "We're taking all the campers on one of those cruises at the end of the second week. That's when we'll be in Pearlington, which is near all the swamps, you know. We've already ordered shirts so we'll all be dressed alike that day, and one of the most distinguished bakeries in Picayune is making a life-size alligator cake for us to eat when we get back to camp."

"In that case, you'd better remind me to be sick that day," warned Ebony.

The three women spent the rest of the afternoon and evening laughing and talking, unhurriedly walking the streets of New Orleans after backtracking from their visit to Biloxi, as they caught up with each others' lives. It was one of those rare and wonderful occasions when friends, who haven't seen each other in years, are reunited and all is as if they were never apart. Charlotte knew this light-hearted, laid-back moment in time was important, for come the morrow, they'd be facing situations that would drain them mentally, physically and emotionally. There was no way to prepare for it but she wanted to make sure, when the time came, these two women would know they weren't there alone. ***And neither are you, Charlotte***, came the familiar reminder on which she so often counted.

"The streets are much cleaner here than I'd imagined," Mary Magdalena commented, as they strolled New Orleans' famed French Quarter.

"That's because they were totally flooded in this whole area during Katrina," explained Charlotte. "All the dirt and trash washed away."

"It's kind of like us, isn't it?" asked Ebony.

Charlotte simply nodded, allowing the two women to see the scene before them, each in their own way.

"So many businesses are still closed," noticed Mary Magdalena. "Will they ever re-open?"

"That's hard to say. There's still so much clean up that has to happen. What you see here is totally different from what you're going to see when I take you through Hancock County's worst areas of destruction tomorrow morning," said Charlotte. "The damage the various areas suffered came from different means of destruction, although it was all from the same natural disaster.

"This area suffered flooding due to breaks in the levees. In Bay St. Louis, where you have the Gulf coming in at you from two different directions, the swells were so great they literally demolished and obliterated everything...***everything***... in their path. And then you have Pearlington, where the Gulf took over the Pearl River, and everything remotely near it. You'll begin to envision the unfathomable vastness and magnitude of the storm when I take you along Mississippi's coast line in the morning. It will be a stirring Sabbath." Charlotte stopped, biting her own lip. "Bring tissues," was all she could manage.

10

Twenty-three volunteers sat at four connecting tables where they'd met to commune at Barnhill's Buffet in Gulfport, Mississippi, upon their joint arrivals from their various locations. "Thank you for making this trip," Charlotte began, making sure everyone had gone for dessert, "which for most of you has encompassed the entire day. As you're finishing your meal, I want you to be aware that you're eating the foods you like, in a manner quite comparable to everyday life at your own homes. The first reason I chose Barnhill's for our meeting spot is because you were all able to eat anything you wanted, and plenty of it. You've traveled 'from afar' and needed a chance to sit and relax, not to mention building up your strength for the next two weeks.

"The second reason I wanted you to come here is to make you aware of the fact that there are still families here who have no stoves, other than a camp stove in a tent. They have no refrigerators, only coolers. You have just enjoyed a meal which is, for many of the children you will meet, a great luxury. For the next two weeks, you will see life quite differently from what you're used to in your corner of the world. And you will leave here at the end of that time with a greater appreciation for all 'the little things' you take for granted at home.

"The third reason I wanted us to come here is that Jesus always ate with his disciples, and at the home of persons such as Mary and Martha, and Zaccheus. Dining together was a big part of meeting, and getting to know each other. We are all disciples here, so from this moment on, we'll dispense with the last names. Who ever read Matthew, Mark, Luke or John's last names? They weren't important. What is important in the next two weeks is the fact that we are all one big family, and we'll learn to work, love, pray and yes, play, together."

After greeting the collective group, Charlotte spread her arms to include every volunteer as she said, "Each of you has come because you've experienced the awareness and felt the need of these Katrina children. You all possess different talents, all of which God will use to rebuild many young lives this week. Thank you for answering the small voice that called you here.

"This is going to be a busy two weeks," she continued. "It has been a chore simply getting you all here from various locations." She'd picked up her son, Jack, at the airport earlier in the afternoon, who in turn had waited for the arriving flight of a teenager from Findlay. A whole troop of volunteers had arrived in a mini-bus, bearing the name of their church in bright blue and orange letters, from St. John's Lutheran Church of Concord, North Carolina, shortly before a car carrying a mother and two daughters pulled in the restaurant's parking lot from Fort Mill, South Carolina.

"The first day will go fairly quickly, as we'll spend much

of the day getting used to the children, and they to us, learning names and setting guidelines and boundaries. The next day will go slowly, the third day will begin to pick up, and the last two days will literally buzz by. Then we'll move on to the Pearlington Recovery Center and start all over again.

"In some ways, this will seem like the longest two weeks of your life." Charlotte looked each person in the eyes before adding, "But I can promise you, it will also rank among the most rewarding two weeks of your life."

She loved the enthusiasm and spirited energy she saw written on the face of each volunteer. This was nothing new for her. It was the same every time she greeted persons new to the ministry of mission work. Experience had told her there was only so much she could do to prepare them for the approaching lessons. The real tests would come with the actual hard knocks of seeing the children and their environments first-hand, like Mary Magdalena and Ebony had gotten a taste the day before.

"Each of you will be assigned a group of children. There will be an adult, with one youth helper, for each group. Should you see a need in another group at a time when things are quiet within your own group, then you may help the other volunteers as you are needed. But, remember, your primary goal and concern is the social welfare and stability of the children within your group.

"There may be some children who have not spoken a word since the hurricane, when several of them returned to find their homes twenty feet under water. There may be some who are 'suicide' children, meaning their parents for whatever reason – whether drug-induced or due to lack of emotional stability – left the children to fend for themselves. Some of those may or may not have had older siblings, and some of them may have been separated from their siblings. The bottom line is every single child you meet will have been dreadfully traumatized.

"The more stories I hear, the more venues of trauma I hear about. I can't even begin to imagine what these children have seen or experienced. All I can imagine is that we are not alone in this mission. I know each of you individually and there's no doubt God has placed us together for a unique mission nor that He will equip us for whatever we are dealt.

"There should be no crisis here, for one of our main goals is to have rules and make these children abide by them. Most of them have spent the last two years in a make-shift school, which unfortunately meant regular rules and discipline were not enforced with their usual vigor. Teachers have had enough trouble merely trying to teach with the limited resources they had, not to mention the added emotional issues. We will set rules the moment the children gather tomorrow morning, and we must all abide by them. We will set the example as well as the rules. There will be ***no*** variations in this, yet I ask you to be extremely cognizant of the fact that unconditional love must first be shown through our enforcement of these expectations."

"I'm beginning to feel like a policeman," said Brice, an eleventh-grade ROTC cadet from the Concord church.

"No, don't feel that way at all. Our goal is, in a nutshell, to be courteous and respectful in everything we do, and do it in such a natural way that the children simply follow suit." Charlotte glanced impishly at a couple of the youth. "For some of you, I know that will be difficult, but do it anyway!" Her words received the giggles she sought as she tried to lighten the mood a bit.

"You need to understand there is no way to know who or how many will show up for the camp, even though we've had registration through the area churches and through the Boys and Girls Club." Charlotte gave a "That's all" sigh. "This is one time you will literally have to go with the flow."

"When you told me you were Charlotte's latest recruit, you weren't kidding, were you?" Ebony's comment was not a question, but a statement of seeing exactly how regimented this act of love was.

"It is a mission, Ebony," answered Mary Magdalena. "You can't simply jump into a project of this magnitude without lots of planning and advance work. It took a lot of people brainstorming and pitching in to make what we're about to do a reality."

Charlotte, overhearing the conversation, agreed. "Exactly right!" she exclaimed energetically. She took a deep breath before flashing a big smile, strengthened by her serious eyes, which interviewers said "spoke to people." "Before we all call it an evening, there's only one last item of business." Her head turned from side to side as she nodded at each person. "I do want to share with you my thankfulness. You have left your homes, your families and your comfort zones to give the most important gift a person can give, and that is the gift of yourself.

"As Mary Magdalena just stated, numerous people have contributed to our cause. Their donations, through your various fundraisers, have helped to get you here. Much generosity is represented through what we will be doing with the children this week. I think the act that made the biggest impression on me during all these efforts was seeing children take an envelope off our Gulf tree at church and place pennies and nickels from their own piggy banks into it. Some gave thirty-eight cents, some forty-three cents and some a whole dollar. But whatever their gift, it hit a soft spot in my heart each time I saw one of them approach the Gulf tree with his or her fist balled, tightly holding their savings before sharing them with another child.

"Children helping other children," she said resolutely. "That's what this entire project is all about. Children donating their favorite book or their money earned from doing chores to help children in need. Children whom they've never before seen and may never see.

"Just so you know, there has been a release form signed by parents so that you may snap photos of all the children to take back and show your own children. A Pen Pal, if you will, except in this case, it's a Photo Pal."

Charlotte placed both hands on the table as she asked, "Any questions?" After getting no response, she instructed, "Then it's off to bed for all of you. Morning will come early as we have lots to set up when we get to Main Street United Methodist Church in Bay St. Louis which, by the way, didn't escape their own damage. When the minister was able to get to the church following Katrina, the steeple was lying sprawled across the front yard. You'll see remains of needed repair, yet this is another example of victims sharing what they have left with others less fortunate. As you'll note during our tours of the coast, their congregation fared better than some.

"Thanks again!" She hugged each volunteer as they passed her, thanking them individually for sharing of themselves for this most worthy cause – "the children."

"I'm going to nickname Charlotte 'Boomerang,'" said Ebony as they headed for the women's shower.

"And why is that?" asked Mary Magdalena. "I'm sure there's a reason."

Ebony laughed. "There is. They say what goes around, comes around. From where I'm standing, it appears she's got a whole lot going around. She's surely getting something in return for all of that."

Jack passed the two women as he exited the men's shower area. "It wouldn't matter whether she got anything in return, or whether she didn't, Mom would be right here doing the same thing as long as there were children to help. It's a part of who she is." He chuckled. "The big joke between my brother and I is that our mother doesn't have anything, but she surely doesn't lead a boring life. We may not inherit 'things' from her, but we'll certainly have lots of 'brothers and sisters' from around the world."

"What else do you need?" asked Ebony.

"Nothing," answered Jack. "She's taught us that what you have cannot be measured by the things you can see."

"By faith, not by sight," said Ebony. "One of my grandmother's favorite scriptures. She lived by those words, too."

"Looks like it didn't hurt you any," observed Jack.

"Well, then," stated Mary Magdalena, "that makes three of us. My grandparents were also fond of those words and how much power lay in them."

Charlotte instructed the volunteers to line the entrance to personally welcome each child who entered the facility at Main Street United Methodist Church. “Talk about uncanny,” she whispered to Mary Magdalena, “take a look at this little girl coming in. She looks exactly like I did at that age, except her hair is longer than mine was. My mother always kept mine cropped off around my ears.”

Mary Magdalena leaned down so her face was on the same level as the girl’s whose long, curly bright-red locks were as bouncy as her exuberant spirit. “How are you? My name is Mary Magdalena and I live in Ohio.”

“I’m fine,” replied the child, whose head tilted sideways with her neck scrunched against her right shoulder, and her eyes meeting the floor, reinforcing the bashfulness heard in her tiny, yet spry voice. “My name is Lena Camden and I live in a FEMA trailer.”

A lump formed in Mary Magdalena's throat. ***Great! I've only encountered one child and I've already stuck my foot so far in my mouth I can't get it out.*** She watched the child walk toward the volunteer giving out name badges. Her demeanor, though quiet and shy, gave her the appearance of being a perfect candidate for a commercial. ***If the talent agencies got a load of her, they'd be lining her door step and front sidewalk to offer her a contract.***

"Hey!" exclaimed a young lad, looking all of eight or nine. "You're pretty. Can I be in your group?"

Mary Magdalena turned her focus back to the line of children suddenly backing up in the door. "Thank you," she replied, shaking his hand. She had no idea what else to say.

"It looks like the bus has arrived," said Ebony.

"Yeah, I hope I don't blow it with the rest of the children as badly as I blew it with that first little girl. How insensitive could I have been?"

"Don't take it so hard," replied Beverly Harding, their liaison from Disaster Response Center whose words of expertise did not go unrecognized, nor unappreciated. "They're a lot tougher than you think. What matters is your presence. Your words are secondary, trust me."

Mary Magdalena turned in time to see an older boy bolt in the door and take off toward a corner. She watched as Charlotte went to him and tried, with no avail, to get him to join the other children in a game while waiting for all the registrants to assemble. He made his own game of dodging anyone who came near him, giving out a moan which sounded somewhat like a wounded animal. Within a few minutes, several of the adults had taken a stab at attempting to engage him in the activities. They finally left him in the corner, under the table where their quilting center – complete with a sewing machine and ironing board – had been set up.

Pamela Jones, the quilter who had come from South Carolina with her two teenage daughters, and was a kindergarten teacher, had not been assigned to a particular group. Her role was to have each child create a quilt square, which in some way would bear – through picture or word – their remembrance of Hurricane Katrina. The goal was to work with each child individually by Wednesday afternoon. Come Thursday, she would be finishing the quilt on her machine so the children could see the fruits of their combined labor. She set about her task, looking busy as she lay out fabric squares from which the children could choose, but mainly keeping an eye on "the strayer" – since no one had caught his name any better than they had him – to make sure he didn't get hurt with the iron or the sewing machine.

"Looks like it didn't take long to figure out which one was going to demand all our attention," Mary Magdalena said softly.

"Figure, phooey!" exclaimed Ebony, not so softly. "We didn't have to figure at all. He announced that coming in the door. Why, he couldn't have done better if he'd come in with a sign."

Charlotte smiled at the two young women. "I would think you two would feel right at home with this child, given your work with at-risk children and teens back home."

"Yeah, and I thought we left all of them there," replied Ebony, trying to sound jovial though unsuccessful in her effort. "I thought this was going to be a vacation."

Mary Magdalena gave a small chuckle. "So much for that idea. This is going to be about as much vacation as the one when I headed for Florida and landed in Findlay."

"Look at it this way," Charlotte said lightly. "At least on this vacation, you can look out the front door and see the water and the sand." She glanced over her shoulder at the boy.

"And he may be small, but I get the impression there's enough of him there for both of you."

"Very funny, Charlotte!" Ebony replied sarcastically.

"I didn't mean for it to be funny," stated Charlotte. "I'm completely serious. There's enough of him for not only you two, but for every single one of us." She looked back at the child again. "Look at his eyes. They're telling a story so deeply buried within him that I'm not sure he even knows it. And it's my goal to make sure he finds it before this week is up and will hopefully release it."

She took a slow breath, her mind clearly lost in thought. "Do you remember when I said last night there would be one child who would get the most impact out of this week?" She waited a moment for their response of nods. "That's the child. It isn't always so easy to spot which one it is, and sometimes you never know, but he'll glean more than you think from this week. Trust me."

Charlotte linked her arms through the elbows of the two women and led them toward the stage. "Besides, he isn't going to hurt anyone. At least no one besides himself, and that's doubtful. From the looks of it, he's actually a big wimp when it comes to physical pain. That's already obvious."

"How can you tell that?" asked Ebony. "I think you've been watching too many of those FBI profile shows."

Charlotte laughed. "Didn't I tell you? All those years I was on an organ bench, I was doubling as an undercover agent."

Her comment made Mary Magdalena also laugh. "Under choir robe is more like it!" joked the young woman as she looked across the author to her best friend. "You know how it is with the teens we have come into the agency at home, Ebony. You get a read from some of them instantly, while others take much longer."

"You're the two who read. I only do the 'between the

lines' work," replied Ebony.

The author dropped their arms and turned to face the young black woman. "Think about it. Where do people come when they're hurting so badly they have nowhere else to go?"

Ebony's expression indicated she got the point. "Well, I guess after they try the bottle or places like Northern Exposure, they hit the church."

"Exactly," Charlotte responded, hating to admit to herself that in many instances, people did have to go the long, hard route her friend had just described. "C'mon. I think it's time to get the children and all our volunteers into a big circle. It's showtime."

Time flew as the children sat in a circle, the volunteers intermingled among them, and each person shared their name and one thing about him or herself. It didn't take long to break any proverbial ice, but then, given the warmth of the Gulf on this July day, ice didn't stand a chance. Besides, had there been ice, it would have melted by the time they watched the boy in the corner dart from place to place trying to be seen, yet refusing to join in the activities.

Charlotte's years of teaching showed as she refused to be daunted by his antics. She tried a tried, and true, method to get his attention. Pamela's older daughter, Dani, was a percussionist in her high school band. Her role was to work with the children on the African drums that Charlotte had brought.

Pamela had spent years in Charlotte's children's and youth choirs and traveled the country with her, so she knew the routine well. She'd explained the drill to her daughter prior to their arrival in the Gulf. "They only play the instruments if they're participating in the other activities. She won't budge on that. Never has."

The minute Dani brought out the three drums and placed them in the center of the circle, children waved their hands wildly to get a turn to play. Charlotte led the campers in a rhythmic song, explaining the drummers were selected by virtue of their behavior and participation. She brought out other instruments so each child would get a chance to play something, explaining that before the day was over, every participant would get an opportunity to beat one of the hand-crafted drums, whose ornate wooden designs and fur-trimmed skins begged for attention.

Ebony lightly elbowed Mary Magdalena. "The Pied Piper's at it again," she said while motioning to the older boy, "the strayer."

He had moved closer and closer until he stood right behind the children, his eyes glued on the drums. When it came time for the children to change drummers, he slid into the circle as if he'd been there the entire time. Not to be fooled, Charlotte purposely ignored him, calling on the other children.

"Oh, would you like to play the drums?" she finally asked.

Jack winked at Mary Magdalena and Ebony as a signal to pay attention to his mother's actions.

The boy nodded his head and began to move toward the drums.

"Then you'll have to join us in the rest of the activities," Charlotte informed him.

"Obviously Jack has seen his mother at work before,"

Ebony noted.

"Shhh," whispered Mary Magdalena, sure the boy would bolt and again run to one of the corners, if not the door. But all she saw was him look at the author, his eyes so dark they nearly matched his black hair. The look on his face showed he wasn't dumbfounded. In fact, his expression said this was exactly the reaction he had expected.

After a short silent showdown, Charlotte asked his name.

"Levi," he said slowly, his eyes still peeled on hers, as if there was a showdown between them.

"Levi," she said, extending her hand, as if offering a truce, "I'd love for you to play the drums after lunch. Would you like that?"

"No, I want to play them now," he answered.

Mary Magdalena was surprised to hear the total lack of emotion in his voice.

"Do you think she's being too hard on him?" Ebony inquired with a whisper.

Jack's elbow in her side was an indication to be quiet. His expression told both of the young women this was not his mother's first rodeo.

Or obstinate child, concluded Mary Magdalena.

"I'm sorry, that is not an option," spoke Charlotte. "You will get a turn after lunch." She paused. "***If*** you've taken part in some of the other activities." Her eyes spoke of concern for the boy as he sulked back to the quilting corner and sat down, making noises and gibbering in an effort to be disruptive.

She went to him. "You're a great percussionist. I like your noises. Perhaps you'd like to do those at music time instead of playing one of the drums." Her words were soft, but loud enough to be heard by those who were listening.

The sounds immediately stopped as the astute author

went back to the circle of children, who were now singing along with Jack and Pamela, and the rest of the volunteers who'd learned the songs prior to the trip. "After lunch, we'll have another chance to sing and play the instruments. I want to teach you some motions and steps to put with the songs. Levi will be helping me demonstrate the motions."

Mary Magdalena glanced back to see a quiet and completely still boy in the corner, his face not quite as harsh as it had been earlier that morning.

Charlotte pointed out lines on the floor. Each group, with a leader at each end, sat as instructed on the appointed lines. "Levi," she called, "you're in Jack's group. It's on the back line." The children, loud and rambunctious at first, heard one of the female teen leaders begin a stomp-clap pattern. Slowly, they began repeating her pattern until they'd all gotten quiet as they listened for her to change patterns.

"That's great!" exclaimed Charlotte. She took a roll of tickets, tore one off and placed it in a bucket on the stage. "At the end of the week, we have a surprise for you. The more tickets you earn for good behavior, the more rewards you'll get. Tiffany," she said, pointing to the attractive teenager who'd led the stomp-clap, "will become your leader whenever you begin making too much noise. Any time she has to give you more than three patterns, you lose a ticket. If you get through an activity with no patterns, you earn a ticket."

Once ground rules were explained, she then read one of her children's books, with the life-size mascot of the book's character making an appearance and acting out the story. Having their undivided attention, she told how authors came up with stories, going on to explain that, "Each one of you children has a story inside you. A very unique story that the world is waiting to hear," she explained, "and no one can tell it better than you. During the course of this week, we're going to allow you to be the authors of your own stories. I'll write them down on this big chart tablet as you tell them," she instructed, pointing to a large spiral pad on an easel, " and we'll make copies for you to keep."

The author pulled a worn leather book from an oversized tote which looked like it could have easily belonged to Mary Poppins. "Can anyone tell me what this is?"

Hands shot up throughout the rows of children, but Charlotte waited until one particular child, his hand flailing wildly at first, found his place on the back row. "Yes, Levi?"

"It's a Bible."

She smiled and put a ticket into the bucket. "Yes, Levi, it is." Charlotte didn't ask if he had one at home. It wouldn't have mattered. His answer indicated that he'd seen someone use a Bible in his young lifetime, but chances were that it, like everything else he owned, washed away in the hurricane.

"Have any of you ever heard of Noah?" the author asked.

Again, hands shot up throughout the room.

Mary Magdalena understood what Charlotte was doing. ***She's engaging the children in a discussion of a familiar character, who also lived through a flood***. She watched intently as the discussion moved to a catchy song about the animals going on the Ark, two by two. Complete with motions and animal sounds, the children were soon so involved that they'd lost all inhibitions and nervousness about being with strangers.

The emphasis of the discussion then turned from Noah to their own memories, allowing them to open up and spill out months of pent-up anger and fear. Charlotte was opening the door for the youngsters to share their experiences as a means of positive therapy. ***It's working***, she observed as the children, one by one, stood at the front of the stage and told how their lives had been affected by the hurricane.

At first, some of the children were hesitant, but then as they watched others venture forth, they began to speak out about the trauma they'd endured. Instead of hurtful pain, their memories began to take on the face of battle scars, of which they'd earned the right to be proud.

Mary Magdalena glanced around the room to see if the volunteers were following Charlotte's instruction of not allowing themselves to get so caught up in the stories of destruction and horror that they became basket cases, balling their eyes out. She saw tissues surfacing, but no visible tears, at least for the moment. ***Those will come later***, she determined, remembering the author's exact words from the evening before. "You're going to feel your heart rip into, but you absolutely must ***not*** cry in front of them. We're here on a mission. A mission to help them. A mission to help them grow. A mission to allow them to void themselves of masses of hurt and pain, and a mission to help them grow in strength and resilience that will allow them to fully recover, holding onto their experience as a way to help them cope with other difficulties that will come at them in life. Your tears, and there will be many, can wait until you get on that bus each afternoon after camp."

She noticed the expressions on the faces of each of the volunteers which proved Charlotte's words. Their eyes showed the heartache with the tears welling up behind, yet they were managing to hold it together, now comprehending the merit of the author's advice, until they could get out of sight from the children.

Mary Magdalena sat motionless, amazed at how intricately the stories were etched on the children's minds. Many of them had been just three or four at the time of the storm, yet they recounted every single detail as if it had only been the day before. They were not details which could have been learned and memorized, but details which were lived first hand. She had been so engrossed in the encounters given by each child that she failed to notice the next child who'd raised her hand was the young girl with the bright-red curly locks.

"Yes, Lena," said Charlotte, inviting the young child to share her story.

The girl tilted her head to one side, her bashfulness showing, just as she had done when she arrived to a building full of total strangers. Now, though, a broadening smile spread across her face indicating her growing sense of trust as barriers of fear were being broken. She spoke so quietly and deliberately that no one dared move, including Levi, as they struggled to hear her story.

"My daddy came home from work and took my mommy and me away until the storm was over. We didn't get to come home for several days, but I was okay because I got to take my favorite stuffed animal with me. When we did get to come home, there wasn't a house there anymore. It had washed away."

So much for the talent agents lining her door steps, Mary Magdalena surmised.

Suddenly, Lena's head straightened as her face lit up with excitement. "But our front steps were still there." She turned and looked directly at Charlotte, her blue eyes beaming. "That was a good thing, wasn't it?"

Bring on the talent agents! Mary Magdalena exclaimed to herself, more assured this child had the ability to easily sell an Eskimo an air conditioner.

Lena's "Shirley Temple curls" bounced veraciously as she shrugged her shoulders forward and then dropped them, a sign of how proud she was she'd braved getting in front of a group of people and telling her story. You could have heard a pin drop as she stood there, her body twisting from one side to the other as her feet remained firmly planted.

Charlotte swallowed hard and bit her lip so sharply she

was afraid it would start bleeding. The fact that Lena reached up and threw her arms around the author's neck, then squeezed as tightly as she could, didn't help matters in regards to the volunteers following the advice from the evening before. Warning or no warning, tissues abounded, along with sniffles.

The children watched with interest, each of them having a similar story. Because they'd all endured the same natural disaster, it seemed none of them had bothered to share their stories with anyone prior to this day. They were the only ones, at the end of the storytelling session, whose eyes weren't red and throats weren't hurting from swallowing such huge lumps.

"I think that's enough stories for one day," Charlotte declared, after a five-year-old told how his family left their house and came back to find a different house sitting where they'd lived before the storm, and another child telling that all eleven houses on his street were gone when they came home after Katrina. "Time for lunch."

Levi charged to the front of the line. No one was surprised when Charlotte instructed him that his group was last and he could go to the back of the line. She said no more, for his face showed he knew why. He jumped and mumbled in his attempt to create a scene, but he stayed in the back of the line, Jack at his side.

It wasn't until the children lined up for lunch that Mary Magdalena noticed nearly every child was either holding onto a backpack or had one strapped onto them – including Levi. ***How touching***, she thought. ***They were so excited about the things they'd be making they wanted a way to carry them home. Wait until they see the bags we've brought for them to carry all their loot home on Friday.***

"Wouldn't you like to put your backpack in the corner while you eat?" she suggested to a young girl, about the size of Lena, whose face had been a virtual ray of sunshine from the instant she'd arrived.

The child's lips immediately began to quiver as her excited smile fell to a look of horror.

"Don't be pinching the kids," whispered Ebony as she passed behind her friend.

"It's okay. You may keep it," Mary Magdalena hastily added, offering the little girl an assuring smile. Thinking perhaps the child had brought a favorite toy to show the volunteers, she asked, "Did you bring something special with you today?"

She watched as the child clung tightly to the backpack, struggling to carry a plate and drink at the same time as she went from the food line to a table. The girl's small body was still trembling. "Here, let me help you." Mary Magdalena took the plate and drink, making sure she didn't touch the bag. "May I sit with you at lunch?"

The small girl nodded, but fledging tears were still on the horizon. She found a seat where Mary Magdalena could be beside her, but where she could keep her hands firmly on the backpack. Neither of them said a word as they sat amidst a roomful of children who were indistinguishable as to whether they'd come from parents who were government officials or parents who had no education and barely made minimum wage, if that much. ***That's what I've missed***, Mary Magdalena told herself. ***There's no distinction of classes here. They're all bound by the same disaster, the same set of circumstances. Everyone suffered...no one was spared.***

She became instantly aware that every one of these children was in the same boat. They had all lost everything...***all they owned***, she sympathetically determined.

"Would you like to see what I have in my backpack?" the little girl asked once she'd finished her dirt cake dessert with gummy worms on top.

Mary Magdalena nodded, grateful she'd not totally destroyed the rapport she'd developed with the children during the morning. She watched as the child, still clinging tightly to the canvas bag, unzipped it and took out the terrycloth-covered remains of a stuffed animal. "Is this your pet?" she asked.

"No," said the girl, her lips beginning to tremble again. "We didn't find my pet after Katrina. My daddy said my kitty would be alright until we got back home. This was the only toy we could find and it was stuck in a tree limb."

A boy seated nearby came over with his backpack. "Want to see what I have in mine?"

"Sure," replied Mary Magdalena, unable to count the number of times she'd put her proverbial foot in her mouth thus far for one day and fearful of how many more times she would before the afternoon was over. She could hardly believe her eyes when all the boy retrieved from his backpack were a chipped piece of ceramic tile, a rusted nail and a thick piece of pop-bottle glass.

"They're not really anything special. It's just I wanted something and these were all I could find after the storm that weren't so covered in muck I couldn't get them loose."

"I love to color," said a little girl, who identified herself as the little sister of the boy who'd just shared his belongings.

She reached deep into a side pocket of her small backpack and brought out three well-used crayons and a tiny tablet, most of its pages filled with writing.

Her brother reached his hand back into his bag. "This is something really special, though," he said as he pulled out a clear plastic sandwich bag containing something that resembled Jesus with his arms outstretched on the cross.

Mary Magdalena had no idea what it was, but she could tell it was something of great value to the boy, and it was something of nature.

"Have you ever seen one of these before?" he asked.

"No," she said, still staring at its unique shape.

"It's a catfish bone," he explained.

"Do they all look like that?" Ebony asked, bringing her group to join Mary Magdalena's group.

"Every one that I've ever seen," answered the boy.

By this time, all the children had finished their lunch, provided by gracious donors, and gathered around the circle to share their treasures. It wasn't long before Mary Magdalena realized, through their stories and their 'show-and-tell' time, the reason for the backpacks. ***This is all they have. If they leave their bags at home, they're afraid someone will steal them. These small trinkets are all they have left to show for their short, yet turbulent lifetimes.*** She turned her head and gazed at the children who stood around her. ***They'll never have their baby pictures to show their grandchildren. They'll never have a lock of hair from their first haircut, or their first lost tooth. They'll never have the first picture they drew, or their baby books filled with memories.***

She put her head into her hands, sweeping away the wisps of hair that outlined her face, and struggling hard not to let the children see the despair written all over her. "***You cannot cry,***" she told herself, repeating the words Charlotte had instilled in the volunteers the evening before. "***Not in front of the children. We're here to support them, hold them up. Save the tears for the bus.***"

Suddenly, Mary Magdalena felt her grandparents were looking over her shoulder, enabling her with some of their strength. She removed her hands and held her head high, sensing the legacy her ancestors had bestowed on her. ***Just as the legacy Katrina has bestowed on these children. They are strong. They are resilient. AND, they have a story that can never be washed away.*** Her eyes focused on "the strayer" with his backpack firmly strapped to him. ***Even Levi.*** A smile formed on her face. ***Especially Levi.***

"It's time to get back to work. We have a lot of projects and activities for you to do so we'll be ready for the big surprise on Friday," Mary Magdalena announced. "We only have time for one more."

A timid fair-skinned, blonde-haired boy stood beside her. He raised his backpack onto the table and reached inside, making a huge production of displaying his "wares" – not purposely, but merely by virtue of his preciously adorable persona, as he held up his hand for all to see.

Mary Magdalena stared at the two small items in his hand. One she recognized immediately. It was a large, clear glass marble, filled with lots of tiny air bubbles, giving it the appearance of a crystal ball. The other object looked hauntingly strange, so much so she couldn't even tell from what kind of substance it was made.

The boy placed the second object in her hand. It wasn't until after careful observation, turning it from side to side and over and over, that she realized the tiny object in her hand actually ***was*** a hand. A small miniature hand with the four fingers together and the thumb outstretched. It was so worn she still couldn't decipher from what material it was made.

She looked at him questioningly.

"It's the wizard's hand," he explained. "He was my favorite thing. It was really a candle my grandmother had brought me for Christmas one year. It's the first present I ever remember getting." He flashed Mary Magdalena such an endearing smile she found it hard not to pick him up and squeeze him. "She gave it to me because I loved ***The Sorcerer's Apprentice*** so much."

"Was it Mickey Mouse?" Mary Magdalena asked.

"No," answered the boy. "It was a real wizard. He was dressed in a black cape and had a long, white beard." He was quick to add, "But he wasn't scary. He sat on my dresser and I felt safe every night when I went to bed."

Mary Magdalena's curiosity was raging wildly, wanting to know what happened to the rest of the wizard, but she didn't dare ask.

She was delighted when another child inquired, "Where's the rest of the wizard?"

Tears came to the boy's eyes as he explained, "We found his long, white beard and we found a lot of chunks of his black robe. I looked all over for the little wooden stick he had in the other hand, but we never found it ***or*** the other hand. My daddy said it must have fallen against something with a fierce force to make it break all into pieces like that. I wanted to pick up all the pieces, but there was too much muck to get near them. I was only able to reach these two pieces."

Mary Magdalena looked over her shoulder to see the memory of her grandparents wasn't the only thing there. Levi, his head stretched high in an effort to see the two objects, was standing on his tiptoes to get a better view and hear the story.

I wonder if it has anything to do with his story, she said to herself as she stared at the boy's treasures with different eyes. The marble no longer resembled a crystal ball, but the world. The hand, sculpted from wax, reminded her of the hand of God stretching out to Adam in Michelangelo's famed painting in the ceiling of the Sistine Chapel. ***God reaching out to man.*** She was certain the boy had no idea how many sermons could be inspired through his two small objects, easily conceivable as trash to the rest of the world, but worth the entire world to this precious child.

The world, the hand...the world, the hand of God...the world, His hand. Mary Magdalena began to sing. The words were familiar to all the volunteers and obviously to most of the children as they joined her with "He's got the whole world in His hands, He's got the whole wide world in His hands, He's got the whole world in His hands, He's got the whole world in His hands."

She stood from her seat at the table and pointed to different groups of children as they yelled out "brothers" and "sisters," "mothers" and "fathers," and all the other words of the well-known spiritual, ending with the verse about the "wind and rain."

That's right, Mary Magdalena, she sensed from within. ***The wind and the rain. The mothers and the fathers. The brothers and the sisters. All these precociously pure children.***

She stopped singing and looked at the children, their backpacks containing all their belongings in their hands. The words "KATRINA WAS BIG BUT <u>GOD</u> IS BIGGER" played through her head. ***God is bigger,*** she said to herself, singing the chorus of the spiritual one last time with the children. "We'd better get back to our groups. I think Charlotte wants to bring out the drums."

I wonder what makes him feel safe at night now, she wondered as she carried her plate and cup to the plastic garbage bag, all of which had been provided through donations, and led the children back to the circle.

"What a great song," said Charlotte, as the children found their places. "We're going to play a game with that song. This time, you're going to call out the name of the child beside you instead of using all the other words to the song. God has every single one of us in His hand."

"Not me." Everyone turned to see the words, which were spoken clearly and distinctly, had come from Levi.

"Yes, and you, too, Levi," replied Charlotte.

"Hun-uh," he uttered adamantly.

"I think it's your turn to play the drums, Levi," said Jack, following his mother's lead. "You were great during lunch and you listened quietly as others showed their treasures."

"Good timing, hoss," Ebony mouthed as Jack passed her, Levi following his steps.

"Do you hear that?" Mary Magdalena whispered to her friend shortly after the music began.

"I sure do," Ebony answered. "Those children all did exactly what they were supposed to do. Not one child has missed a name so far."

"No, not that. Listen to Levi. He hasn't missed a beat. That child's got great rhythm."

Ebony tuned her attention to the beat of the drums. "You're right. And not only is he doing it right, he's got the other two drummers doing it right."

Mary Magdalena nodded excitedly.

"I think he's found his niche," noted Ebony, her eyes resting on his unspoken leadership. "Do you think Charlotte knew that when she bribed him with the drums?" The gaze she received in response from Mary Magdalena was all she needed. "Forget I asked that!"

"Was that good?" asked one of the campers after they'd gone all the way around the circle.

"No," answered Charlotte teasingly, and then adding, "that was better than good. That was ***splendiferous!***"

"Is that a word?" asked another child.

Charlotte cackled with enthusiasm. "It was *so* splendiferous that you each earned an extra ticket for Friday."

"Me, too?" Levi sat staring at the author in disbelief.

"You, too," she nodded as she walked over and gave him a big pat on the back. "Are you ready to help me teach them the motions to the song about the animals getting on the ark, Levi?"

To the shock of all the volunteers, the boy stood from the drum and walked to the front of the stage with Charlotte. He didn't say a word, but stood beside her, waiting for his next cue.

"Did you know he'd be like that?" Ebony asked as Jack came back around her.

"Like what? Rhythmic?"

Ebony nodded.

"Yes," Jack replied simply.

"How did you know?"

"Because I could tell my mother knew. That boy has no idea she's got him wrapped around her little finger right now."

"Do you think that's the end of the problem?"

"No," he said, still watching Levi on the stage. "The minute the music is over, he'll go right back to doing the same thing he was doing before lunch. You missed all the fun during lunch when I had to chase him all over the church. I know this place from the attic to the basement now, thanks to him. He even found a piece of broken stained-glass that had obviously been lodged in a corner ever since Katrina."

"What did you do with it?"

"I'm going to give it to Mom. It can be her treasure. I'm even going to find her a used backpack down here to put it in." He looked at the two young women. "Do you know why they all have backpacks?" he asked.

"To keep their treasures in," was Mary Magdalena's solution.

"Did you ever wonder where they all got the backpacks, given they lost everything else? Don't you think it a bit odd that these kids, who have nothing, all have canvas backpacks? And not only do they all have canvas backpacks, but matching canvas backpacks?"

"Somebody must have given them the backpacks," said Ebony, thinking aloud.

"After Katrina," added Mary Magdalena.

"While Levi and I were spending our lunch chasing through the church," Jack shared, "I learned something. The only way I caught up with him was because his backpack got hung on the nail of a board which must have blown loose during the hurricane. When they replaced the steeple on the roof, the board appears to have gone unnoticed.

"Levi wasn't about to leave without that backpack. That's how valuable those bags of canvas are to these children. And do you want to know why?" he challenged, taking the inquisitive eyes of the two woman as his invitation to continue. "It isn't that warm, cuddly sweet reason of carrying their special little 'treasures' around. In those bags are contained all they have. *All* they have."

Jack gave them a moment to digest his words before he explained, "If they leave their things in their FEMA trailers or tents, their belongings are gone when they return. They carry their clothes, their toys, the only memories they have in those backpacks."

"So that's why they're not putting their backpacks in a corner during the activities," reasoned Mary Magdalena.

"They're afraid someone here will walk off with all they have left," Ebony deduced.

"Exactly," confirmed Jack. "What's worse, do you want to know what Levi has in his bag?" Once again, the two women simply glared at him, waiting for an answer. "Nothing. Not one thing."

"You're kidding," said Ebony. "He gave up the chase for an empty bag, but only because the bag was all he has?"

"He as much as admitted that to me," stated Jack. "I really think he wanted to get caught, only he didn't know it. If I hadn't known better, I'd have thought that board with the nail was planted."

"Maybe it was," Ebony speculated.

"I've heard of stranger things," agreed Mary Magdalena.

"So have I," declared Jack. "Many times. I've grown up with my mother. She's always walking into situations like that."

"And when you came back with him must be when I felt his presence over my shoulder," decided Mary Magdalena.

Jack nodded, noticing Levi had again retreated to his corner. He left him there as he gathered the rest of his "brood" to make puppets, complete with hair, hats, clothes, and anything else their creative minds could imagine.

As the campers laughed and showed off their handheld friends, some fashioning them after themselves, some after a sibling or parent, and some after a favorite star, Levi stealthily slipped a white tube sock off the table, along with a piece of fabric, a few buttons and a bottle of glue. Jack watched quietly as the boy made a new friend from the materials and hastily threw it into his backpack.

"Was that only one day?" asked James Charles, a friend and choir member of Charlotte's who'd taken off from work to be the designated bus driver for the St. John's crew. "I feel like I've been gone for days. That was more exhausting than driving through Atlanta during the peak of rush hour traffic." His playful assessment received several laughs as volunteers loaded the bus.

"Now you see why Mom asked James to be the driver," Jack shared with Mary Magdalena and Ebony. "His jovial spirit can 'drive' a threatening mob right into a babble of laughter. She knew he possessed the ability to lighten any heavy load that would come from working with these campers."

"And his lightening of loads usually involves stopping somewhere for ice cream," added Paula, a math teacher of several of the St. John's youth and another of Charlotte's choir members.

"You know what I like most about James?" asked Jack. "It's a virtue Mom shared about him, but I've seen for myself. James is probably the only person I've ever met who begins every conversation with 'How are you doing today?' and really cares how you're doing! I've seen people ask that as a polite nicety, but before they get a truthful answer, they're already off and running with whatever item of business is the basis of the conversation. Not James. He genuinely cares about people more than anyone I know, and they can feel it."

"That must be why he was able to pull so many stories from the children today," noted Ebony.

"One thing's for certain," Mary Magdalena said as she took a seat. "These children aren't lacking for stories."

"I'd think they had made up all those stories, but even ***their*** creative imaginations couldn't fathom the kinds of tales they shared with us today," stated Dottie, an elementary school music teacher who, besides being active in the role of music at

St. John's, was a parent of one of the youth helpers, herself a well-trained musician.

"Even after retiring as a writing teacher in a magnet arts school, I've never heard the kinds of real-life adventures the children shared with us today. It's inconceivable anything that horrible could happen," said Marjorie, a reader of Charlotte's who'd recently moved to North Carolina and become an instant friend.

"I'm not sure had Katrina happened to me when I was their age, I'd still even think there was a God," shared Tiffany. "I can't believe they all lost everything they had and still seem to believe in the Bible stories or that there is a God. I'm afraid I'd be belligerent about losing everything. I fear I'd be mad and angry at God."

The rest of the trip back to Diamondhead was quiet as all the passengers laid their heads back on the seats, grateful for a few minutes of rest and silence as they digested the events of the day.

And the teen's words, judged Mary Magdalena from the troubled looks on their faces.

12

"Dinner is here tonight," announced Charlotte, as James turned into the church's parking lot. "One of the ladies from our Concord contingency's church prepared spaghetti sauce, froze it and sent it with us. She was going to send pecan pies, but since a certain bus driver can't pass ice cream without stopping, I informed her we'd find our dessert here. Considering the Dairy Queen is less than half a block away from our "home" here in Diamondhead, we're good in that department."

She looked down the aisles of the bus, wanting to say something prophetic, but all she could manage was, "Great work, ya'll." She looked at the volunteers from Ohio. "And yes, we're in the south. I can get away with saying, 'Ya'll.'"

"Yeah," seconded Brice. "We'll have 'ya'll' saying it, too, by the time you get back home."

As giggles filtered through the bus, Charlotte sensed the air of anticipation and insecurity hovering over them the evening before now dissipating. "You're free to do whatever you wish for two hours. We'll have the salads and spaghetti ready by then. By the way," she added before the bus door opened, "my best friend's husband is in Biloxi doing recovery work through his job. I've invited him for dinner. Afterwards, he'll get on the bus and give us a private guided tour of the area. Since he lives here year round until their big job is finished, he knows much more about this place than I do."

"He lives here?" asked one of the teen males. "Where did he find a house?"

"A very insightful question," noted Charlotte. "He didn't ***find*** a house. He lives in a FEMA trailer park, filled with other workers."

"He left his family and the comfort of his own home to stay in a FEMA trailer park?" asked Tiffany's sister, a diva whose good looks were matched by a mind that led her high school's 'Odyssey of the Mind' team. She was aghast. "How long has he been here?"

"For nearly eighteen months." Charlotte made careful note of the expressions on all the faces in order to compare them to the faces of the day when they would leave the children.

"I'd never do that," volunteered Brice's sister, a Girl Scout whose passion was horses.

"You're here now," challenged the author.

"Yes, but that's only for fourteen days. Eighteen months and still counting? I couldn't take that," stated Tiffany.

"It does take a special person," Charlotte concluded. "One who puts others before himself. One who is devoted to a life of serving others."

"Sounds like a preacher, except your friend gets paid for it," said Brice.

Charlotte snickered. "And your minister doesn't?" She opened the bus door and allowed everyone to exit, leaving them to digest those words as an appetizer before dinner. It was obvious they were getting a lot of food for thought, "spiritual food," in addition to their feasts of meals.

"Do you know what I noticed?" asked Paula, stopping on the sidewalk to speak to Charlotte. "The children were not at all what I expected."

"My thought exactly," chimed in Dottie.

Marjorie paused to join their sidewalk chat. "I don't know why I suspected we'd have poverty children, or slow learners, or lots of nationalities, but there were no Hispanics. Only five African-American children and the rest were from Caucasian families, mostly middle class. They were basically no different from the children in one of my gifted and talented classes when I still taught in Vegas."

"That's exactly what struck me," said Paula. "They were all bright, eager to learn anything we taught them."

"They were all starving for what we brought," added Dottie. "I couldn't tell if their rowdiness stemmed from excited enthusiasm, or lack of behavioral skills."

"A mixture of both," Charlotte explained. "One of the things that came out in the brainstorming session when I first met with teachers, ministers and members of the Disaster Response team was these children had been totally void of direction on many fronts since Katrina. Teachers have probably had less materials with which to work than we've brought with us. Most classes are crammed into FEMA trailers, with few or no books or supplies and told, 'Here. Have school.'

"I regret that, for many teachers, the time since Katrina has been spent more as babysitting sessions than giving children a quality education. There were no libraries, no resources. You're all three teachers. Go figure."

Charlotte saw the empathy written on each of their faces as they began to comprehend how devastating the roles of the teachers here had been. As that continued to sink in, she went on to describe their home life. "Parents have been so busy trying to keep their families together, a roof over their heads and food on the table that no one had time to devote to the children. Many children were left to care for themselves after the school day. The agencies had no spaces for them, persons who might at one time have watched over the children were now obsessed with simply trying to find their own food, clothing and shelter. All of the basic needs vanished, wiped away in one fell swoop. Or in this case," she relayed with great agony, "a thirty-foot high surge.

"One of our toughest goals to reach during these two weeks is to instill an appreciation for discipline back in these children's lives as we prepare them for a new school year. For most of them, they've had no *real* school since Katrina, only a makeshift trailer. They've had to sit on the floor with the absence of chairs. Luckily, school supplies have come in from many sources, and the federal government is at least making sure they all have paper and pencils." She sighed. "And a lunch."

The teachers hung their heads and walked toward the PVC-pipe crosses, as if that were the only fate worse than what they'd just heard. No one knew the story behind the crosses, or the story of the persons buried there, but the presence of the white circular tubes seemed a visual remembrance of the souls and bodies which were lost during Hurricane Katrina.

Jack hung around until the rest of the volunteers had gone their separate ways before approaching his mother. "Mom, before we call it quits for the day, I have a comment."

"Yes?" she asked invitingly, aware this son was the one person who kept her in tow when she got in way over her head.

"That one boy, Levi...he needs a keeper."

"A keeper?" she repeated.

"Yes. I think you're going to have to devote someone to

be one-on-one with him for the entire week. From what I've observed today, he's manageable, but he cannot be expected to interact with the other children. At least, not without some repercussions."

"Do you think he's autistic?"

Jack lowered his head. "Yes, but more importantly, I think he's an artistic autistic."

She weighed his words, her eyebrows furrowing as she listened more intently.

"You know how I told you about my best friend's girlfriend having a younger brother that was autistic?"

"Yes," she said, following his train of thought.

"In many ways, he's like Levi, except that he's much worse. I attended a meeting of their support group one evening, just to be supportive myself, and I saw a boy there who was extremely artistic. There were several who possessed abilities totally out of line for their behavior otherwise."

"So you're thinking I should put one of the men with him?" Charlotte asked.

"I'm thinking I'd like to be his keeper," volunteered Jack.

"You? You're always telling me how you don't like children."

"I know. But I don't see Levi so much as a child. I see him more as someone who has a need."

"Are you sure you're equipped to deal with him? If you really think there's a problem, we can alert his family that we have no one capable or trained to work with him."

"I think that's the problem. I'm not sure his family is capable or trained to work with him. I get the impression he's there because they want a break from him."

"What makes you think that? Did he give you any indication pointing to that?"

"No, it's a gut feeling."

Charlotte peered at her son, appreciative both of his concern and his willingness to accept such an unpredictable responsibility. "You're sure about this?"

"No, not really, but I can't let him disrupt the rest of those kids. And I certainly can't bear to watch him cowered up in a corner, moaning like a wild animal."

She looked at the sincerity in his eyes and found herself reminded of a day more than a year before. "Do you remember that day in Denver when we flew to New Orleans?"

"Very clearly," he answered with a grin. "It's the day we were nearly killed by that guy who pulled straight into our path from an entrance ramp, inches in front of us, and then stopped on that Mississippi interstate, seconds after we crossed into the state. That's the day I thanked God you'd recently taken a lap around the racetrack in Concord as a part of your research. There's no doubt God was riding with us that day."

"I'd forgotten that part," she said with a grin of her own. "What I remember is renting a car at the airport and touring the entire city of New Orleans and then coming to Mississippi. We were here to do a benefit concert, but it turned out to be the most meaningful turn of my life. All because you saw a need and made one comment."

"I do remember," he said, looking down.

"You looked at me and said, 'You've got to do something to help these children, Mom.'" Charlotte noticed the tear in her own eye matched the one in her son's. "That's why we're all here today." She reached out and gave him a hug. "This is to say 'Thanks' and 'I love you.'"

As they turned and walked toward the door of the church, she stopped in place. "Just promise me one thing. If Levi gets to be too much, please tell me."

"It's a deal," he replied, opening the door for her.

Charlotte gave her son one last hug. "I'm going to have

to be careful the next time you tell me you have a comment, Jack. You get me every time!"

13

"Looks like word of your camp spread through the FEMA trailer parks," stated Beverly as the volunteers arrived on Tuesday morning. "You have more children today."

Charlotte nodded excitedly. "It would suit me if every child in Harrison ***and*** Hancock Counties showed up before the week's over." She paused a second. "I thought the FEMA parks were called 'Renaissance Villages.'"

"Only by the media and government officials who want to make them sound like more than they are. They can call them anything they want, but to the people who live in them, they're still FEMA trailers. And," she added, "there's not one thing wrong with that terminology. For the families who've lost their homes, what they're called isn't important. Having a roof over their heads is."

"I see your point."

"Whatever you call them, there are still far too many

people who need trailers but can't get them. Word is leaking out all over the place there are hundreds more sitting in fields in other states which never made it here, lined up in rows with no one living in them. It breaks my heart every time I hear of a family who is still in a tent or struggling to find a place to live."

"Do they ever consider moving since they have to start over anyway?"

"Some have moved. They've either gone to live with family members elsewhere, or with persons and churches who had the means and have offered them places to live until they could get back on their feet. It's not that simple for everyone, though," Beverly explained, her voice full of woe.

"Many people have elderly family members who either refuse, or are unable, to move. For most of the ones who stayed, the Gulf is all they've ever known. They either worked in the fishing industry, on the banana barges, or some other occupation that centered around the Gulf shores and water.

"Look at it this way. It would be like the mountain people of your Appalachian mountains. Those mountains are a part of who and what they are. They are their heritage, their culture. The mountains are actually a part of their DNA."

Charlotte gave a perceptive nod. "You say that as if you know that area."

"My husband's family is all still in the Appalachians."

"My grandparents came from the Appalachians and you're right. I can still hear my grandmother saying, 'You can take a man out of the mountains, but you can't take the mountains out of a man.'"

"There's a similar saying for the people of the Gulf. I guess it doesn't really matter where you live. If your family's spent generations there, as most of these people have, it's the only home you know. The home is not the dwelling, but the people, the way of life...,"

"Even if the way of life is suddenly 'nothing,'" Charlotte said, finishing the sentence for Beverly, as she looked over the crowd of children that had multiplied.

"I'm here to report that the second day of camp is off and running," Mary Magdalena told Charlotte, a huge gleam in her eye. "The children who were here yesterday are explaining the rules to the 'new kids on the block' and all we have to do is put them in groups and get out more materials for them. I can't believe it."

"They obviously retained a lot more from yesterday than some of you non-believers thought," replied the author, showing no hint of surprise. She gave Mary Magdalena an appreciative squeeze on the arm. "Just wait until tomorrow!"

"Jack and Levi aren't the only notable pair here," said Ebony, darting her eyes toward the door. "Look at those two guys that just walked in and tell me who you see."

Charlotte peered at the new boys. "They look exactly like all the pictures of Huck Finn and Tom Sawyer."

"That's what we all thought," agreed Paula, coming over to make sure the other volunteers had seen the pair.

"Are you sure they didn't escape from one of the books I brought?" joked Charlotte.

"Watch how well they work together," noted Ebony.

"Speaking of working well together, and notable pairs, where are Jack and Levi?" questioned Charlotte as she looked around the room. Ignoring her instincts, she moved to the stage where she greeted the campers, congratulated them on doing so well on their second day, and then read their story for the day while her volunteers acted it out.

"Now it's your turn," she instructed Tiffany.

Charlotte stood back and smiled as Tiffany called on her sister and three friends for assistance. She was rightfully proud of how each of the volunteers had managed, in only one day, to find his or her strength, and was beginning to take on leadership of the various activities.

"Today, you're going to make up your own drama," said Tiffany, herself playing the role of the "Drama Queen" as she spoke. "We've brought a box of fabric for you to use for costumes and scenery." She pretended to think, already knowing the plan of action. "Why don't we do the story of Noah's ark since we learned a fun song to go along with it yesterday?"

Heads nodded as the children's excitement grew.

"What characters do we need?"

As children rattled off answers, Tiffany invited them to come to the stage and choose a costume. Once Noah's story was finished, she then prompted the children to make up their own drama. None of the volunteers were surprised their production revolved around the hurricane. What did surprise them, however, was how the children grabbed a piece of blue fabric and, holding the four corners, threw it up and down fiercely as they managed to recreate the raging wind, the violent waves and the brutally relentless rain, using their voices to produce such vivid sound effects that an eerie feeling swept throughout the entire room.

It was then Charlotte noticed a figure, completely covered in black, slide along the wall to the quilting corner. Had she not known better, she'd have perceived it to be the children's interpretation of the angel of death, walking in right on cue.

She wasn't the only one who saw the dark apparition, for Ebony punched Mary Magdalena and nodded in the direction of the movement. That's when all three women saw Jack walking behind the figure. He lifted an index finger, signaling them to turn their attention back to the stage show.

"What did Jack do?" asked Ebony. "It looks like he tied Levi up like a mummy."

"I guess that's one way to take care of him," snickered Mary Magdalena. "At least he's being still and quiet."

"You'd be still and quiet, too, if you had a piece of fabric wrapped around your face. All you can see are the whites of his dark eyes against all that black."

Following the drama session, Pamela and her two daughters brought out the drums and gathered the children in the circle for music time. Levi walked to the circle, Jack behind him.

"What did you do to him?" Charlotte asked, at first fearful of the answer.

"He's a Ninja," grinned Jack. "What boy doesn't want to be a Ninja? Don't you remember that get-up I had?"

"Aren't those guys vicious?" inquired Mary Magdalena. "Do you think that might be a little dangerous?"

"No, far from it," Jack assured them. "He picked out the fabric himself and I told him as long as he was quiet and did everything the others did, he could be a Ninja. If he doesn't cooperate, he loses the privilege."

Charlotte had to admit there was definitely method to her son's madness.

"Can I play the drums, Fonz?" asked Levi, approaching them.

"***Fonz***?" questioned Ebony as the boy walked back to the circle after receiving an affirmative answer.

"He wanted me to be a character, too," explained Jack,

rolling up the sleeves of his T-shirt.

"But Fonz?" repeated Mary Magdalena.

"That's his favorite character," replied Jack, taking a comb from his back pocket and running it through his hair, his other hand smoothing down the strands behind it.

"I hope this isn't catching," teased Ebony, while glancing at Mary Magdalena, "'cause if it is, tomorrow we're going to be Laverne and Shirley!"

"That's enough," sulked Jack, walking to the circle to keep an eye on his "buddy."

"Would you get a load of that?" asked Ebony. "Levi's moved up from being 'the strayer' to being 'a buddy.'"

"Let's hope they all make that much of an improvement during the week," said Pamela, who overheard the comment as she took another child to make a quilt square.

Charlotte watched admirably as the volunteers worked with their groups. She could actually see the bonds being made, not only between the children and volunteers, but between the volunteers. They worked together in teams and as a unit, finding a need and filling it.

She observed the children. Yesterday they had come in not knowing who or what to expect, void of any organized discipline, each doing their own thing. She'd not bothered to explain that to the volunteers. Charlotte was more interested in the volunteers realizing a change, within themselves and in the children, at their own pace and in their own way. For everyone, including her who'd been on numerous missions around the world, it was a learning experience, but more than that, a spiritual growth of "brothers" and "sisters" working together.

Her trained and experienced eyes easily spotted the two children of suicide parents. They were the ones who'd found a "safe" face the day before and had clung to it. The older of the two, a girl of only six, was a beautiful child who was doing her best to be a mother figure for her younger brother, who was four. He was actually too young to be attending the camp, but in his case, Charlotte and the Disaster Response liaison made an exception. He'd spent most of the first day under the table for whichever activity his sister was involved in at the time. He didn't participate in anything, but at least he stayed out from under foot.

Today, Charlotte noted, he was watching Jack and Levi from underneath the table. Then, she noticed him quietly slip out from under the table, hurriedly grab a piece of fabric from the costume box and take it to Jack. She watched a short exchange of words before Jack and Levi went to the middle of the room, after scrounging up four metal folding chairs from around the church, and secured the fabric to the chairs so that it made a covering. The young boy darted underneath - or rather, inside his tent - and sat on the floor, his knees crossed.

"Don't say a word," Jack said as he approached his mother. "At least now he will be in the midst of things." He stood there a moment as he watched the older sister go to the young boy and speak to him. Once she was satisfied he was content, ***and safe***, she went back to her group and continued making a writing journal, which she'd chosen to decorate with a pink and purple foam cover and lots of flower and butterfly stickers.

Jack, with Levi following him like a shadow, went back to "the tent." "Hey, little fella," Charlotte heard him say, "would you like a special book, made just for you, so you can be like your big sister and draw pictures and color?"

The young boy sat motionless for a moment and then whispered something in Jack's ear. She saw Jack shake his head and point to the table, and then point to himself and pat Levi on the back. In a matter of seconds the boy was practically attached to Jack's side, but walking toward the table where his older sister was finishing her journal. He stood quietly as Jack picked up foam covers, stickers, and different colors of papers, allowing the young boy to nod or shake his head as a sign of how he wanted his "special book" to look.

Charlotte's eyes moved to other tables and other volunteers, other children and other activities, as she stood mesmerized by all the interaction. The one thing which amazed her, as it did any group of people in any place, was how God took all the combined talents and wove them into a beautiful tapestry of his children working together and living in peace, which bore His signature.

Baptists from Fort Mill, South Carolina, Lutherans from Matthews and Concord, North Carolina, Methodists from Charlotte, North Carolina and Findlay, Ohio. Charlotte tried to imagine this particular tapestry as it appeared to God. ***Add those denominations to the Pentecostals, Catholics, and Presbyterians represented in the children.***

An elementary music teacher, a high school math teacher, a locksmith, an insurance agent, a retired gifted and talented teacher from an arts magnet school in Las Vegas, a kindergarten teacher, a mechanic, a secretary, the owner of a cleaning service, a bookkeeper. The author uttered a prayer of thanks for the volunteers who had taken time from their busy schedules to make a difference in the life of a child, several of them who spent the days at their real vocations making a difference in the lives of children, and others who never saw a child in a day's work, but all whom God had equipped for this special mission.

Then she gazed at the adolescents who had taken a step in faith, not sight, never having been on a mission trip before. ***An athlete, the president of the her school's student government, an ROTC cadet looking into the Air Force Academy, a clarinetist, a percussionist, a burst of energy excited***

about anything, an Odyssey of the Mind scholar, a horse lover desiring to be a vet, a drama enthusiast who wanted to be a Broadway actress, a young home-school graduate who'd already begun a career of music and children's books. These were the ones caught in the middle, not a child though not yet an adult, having great ideas though not proven, having a desire yet lacking experience, the conduit between the Katrina children and the adult volunteers.

As Charlotte watched the children energetically and creatively releasing nearly two years of pent-up living horror stories and nightmares, she beheld a loveliness radiating from them, pouring love and appreciation from an overflowing cup. The vision before her was the extended effect of all the recovery efforts and teams who had planted seeds there before her.

Enjoying the unadulterated joy on their young faces, her mind drifted to the pallets of books she'd watched leave the rented warehouse near her home which stored all the donations from around the country. It had been the day before she left to come here. Time was running so short that even long-lost friends came over in the hour of need to help her, and her sons, secure and tightly pull the shrink wrap around each pallet. Charlotte recalled the prayers she offered over each stack of boxes as she wound her way around them, making sure the gifts from children around the country would arrive safely to their destination. When all was said and done, they'd sealed just over 12,000 new books with love for their recipients, seven-hundred miles away. She then stood there, reliving the sensation of heartache from her first trip to the Gulf following Katrina, combined with the exhilaration she'd felt each time a child placed a donated book into Rudy's book trough. Waiting alone for over an hour that afternoon, on a freightliner to haul the pallets away, the author entrusted all her efforts of the past two years in the truck driver's hands.

They weren't the hands of the truck driver, Charlotte. They were My hands, she heard as her thoughts returned to the imaginary tapestry which had grown in size and richness of color, now with many intricate designs. ***The same hands that are holding your hands now, and the same hands that are holding the hands of each volunteer and youth here.*** Her lips pursed with the reality, ***And the same hands that have been holding those of all these children from the day of Katrina.***

She mentally named off each school, church, daycare, library and convention she'd visited over the past two years as a part of her non-profit literacy campaign for children. She recalled each flight, each step in a new city, as she visited twenty-eight states in her plight to raise books for the Katrina children. The same children in front of her eyes, the same children she would see next week, and the same children who would darken the doors of practically every school or children's facility in Hancock County, Mississippi. An image of tiny hands fluttered through her mind as she pictured hundreds of children with a book in one hand, and their Father's hand holding the other.

Charlotte slipped out the side door unnoticed and walked the few steps it took her to grasp a full view of the Gulf. She turned and peered behind her at the streets, for miles farther than she could see, which had been flooded by these mighty waters. And she thought about the flood of love that had poured from thousands and thousands of persons all over the United States to shower these children gathered in the fellowship hall of Main Street United Methodist Church, the children who would next week be gathered at the Pearlington Recovery Center, and the children who would soon occupy the newly-built South Hancock Elementary School in Pearlington.

The power of that love is mightier than any wind

and waves, she said to herself as her own flood of tears swept down her face.

Charlotte took slow, laborious steps back to the church, allowing her tears to run their course as she envisioned the completed tapestry, which now included the threads representing the individuals rebuilding lives inside the fellowship hall, and the young children adding their own spice and color to the woven creation of God's love.

"I don't know about tomorrow," she sang softly, remembering the song Mary Magdalena had mentioned, "but I know who holds my hand." Charlotte tiptoed through the back door to find Levi and the young boy from the tent, each holding one of Jack's hands.

"I don't know if there were less hours today, if they were better behaved, or whether we're getting the hang of it, but today seemed half as long as yesterday," said James as he closed the door of the bus and headed back to Diamondhead.

"Too bad you weren't the Fonz," shouted Jack. "You wouldn't' say that." His comeback sent a wave of laughter through the bus.

"Look at you playin' all big and bad," said Ebony. "I could tell you enjoyed every minute of that."

Jack had to admit it was definitely much easier playing

along with Levi than chasing him. "And a lot less tiring," he added. "If I'd had another day with him like yesterday, I was catching the first plane back home come this afternoon."

"Okay," announced Charlotte, "take a quick siesta because we're heading to d'Iberville as soon as you get cleaned up. There's a great Chinese buffet there which also serves American food, southern-style, the way ***most*** of you like it," she said, joking with her mid-western friends.

"If we're not careful," said Mary Magdalena, "you'll have us all drinking sweet tea by the time we get home." She pointed to the teen from their home town. "One of us has already gotten addicted since last night!"

"At least one of you knows something good when you taste it," teased Brice. "We'll share some of our Sun-Drop and Cheerwine with you tonight. You can't get any better than that!"

Family, mused Charlotte with great delight as she began to sing ***We are Family,*** everyone on the bus joining her.

"After dinner," she shared, once the entire crew was sufficiently wound up, "we're going to the Hard Rock Café and the Beau Rivage."

"My first trip to the casino," blurted Brice's sister with great enthusiasm.

"No, ***you're*** not going into the casino," corrected Charlotte. "You're only going to get a peek inside to see the extravagant expense. I want you to focus on the fact the Hard Rock Café was scheduled to open only a day or two after Katrina. Graham Mandell, a friend of mine, was here for a conference and got to see it when it was finished. He has pictures of it ready to open, only a couple of days prior to Katrina, but then he got called back home two days early due to the hurricane. The next time he saw a photo of the Hard Rock, on the television after the storm, there was only one of the front four columns and the gigantic guitar sign left standing.

"Graham's coming down next week to help us in Pearlington," she informed the group. "I'm anxious for him to see it and compare the 'then' and 'now' appearances. After you see the Hard Rock this evening, I'm sure you'll have lots of questions for him. There are a lot of clothes, guitars, and the 'same old-same old' you see in all the Hard Rock Cafes, but some of these washed into the ocean during Katrina and were found during the aftermath of the storm. It's interesting to see the effect of all the salt water on them."

"I've heard there's an outfit of Madonna's that was found and put back," volunteered Tiffany.

"You heard right," Charlotte responded. "There are lots of cool clothes, instruments and pictures of the musical stars for you to see and enjoy. And be sure to look closely in the restrooms next to the ***ice cream shop***," she instructed, putting lots of emphasis on the last three words for James' sake, "or rather, the mirrors in the restrooms. They're my favorite part of the Hard Rock.

"I want you to pay special attention to the 112-foot guitar that welcomes guests. If you know anything about Hard Rock Cafés, you know that Peavey guitar symbol well. This is the tallest one of any of their locations, but get this...it survived the storm. Every time I look at it, I find myself more amazed. And while I'm sharing trivia," she added, "you might like to know that Peavey is a Mississippi-based company. That might have something to do with this guitar being the largest.

"My final note about the Hard Rock is that it's located at 777 Beach Boulevard in Biloxi. Any idea why?" Charlotte watched as hands shot up all over the bus. "Well, after all the damage they endured from the ravage of the storm, their 'official' opening date then became July 7, 2007."

"I get it," yelled Brice's sister, "07/07/07."

"Well, aren't you the lucky one?" teased Charlotte. "If

you're into superstition and luck, then I guess that means something to you. As for me, my good fortune comes from a greater source than some lucky number, and my belief runs much deeper than seeing three sevens in a row.

"Now, back to the important things, my favorite shop down here is inside the Beau Rivage," she continued. "There are lots of expensive stores, but there's one where they have purses, jewelry, scarves and accessories for only ten dollars each. You ladies, from young to old, can shop there and still have money to eat on the way home."

"Have you ever gambled in a casino?" Dottie's daughter inquired of Charlotte.

The author stared directly into her face with dire frankness. "Yes," she admitted. "It was actually here in Biloxi several years ago when I was coming home from seminary. I'd had a bad wreck on the way to Dallas and could only drive a couple of hours at a time due to the concussion I'd suffered. We had to stop here for the night because it was too far to the next town. That was back when there were only a few casinos, before their big boom, and there was one with a Western theme. I don't even remember the name of it, but I sure do remember the giant, age-old trees that sat next to it.

"Anyway, Jack begged to see a 'one-armed' bandit, to which I quickly informed him it was strictly against our denomination's beliefs to support the gambling industry. He was so fervent in his plea that I finally decided to teach him a lesson. After getting some dinner, during which I explained dinner was so cheap because gamblers had already spent the rest of their money, we went back to the casino. I walked to the first slot machine inside the door so he could stand outside the carpeted entrance of the casino and see me waste my money.

"I put a quarter in, pulled the long arm, and turned back to look at Jack. Just as I was about to say, 'See, I told you so,' I heard *CHINK, CHINK, CHINK, CHINK* until eighty dollars landed in the metal tray which held the winnings." Charlotte paused for the laughter to die down and Jack to make a smart remark. "I turned back and stared in disbelief at all the tokens landing in the tray as people came over to watch. After the last token had fallen, I took one of the red plastic cups and retrieved all of them from the tray. When I turned around to see Jack's face, it was brighter than the lights in the casino. He was thrilled and already planning all the ways we could spend the eighty dollars.

"I immediately scolded him, saying, 'it is ***not*** our money and we don't believe in gambling. The only thing we can do with this money is give it to the church when we get back home.' He looked at me as sincerely as he could in his pure innocence and asked, 'You think God wants dirty money?'" She was surprised the bus wasn't rocking and rolling from the passengers bouncing from laughter.

"That boy has always had a knack for throwing out some comment which would get me every time." She smiled. "As it turned out, though, I was actually grateful we stopped. There was a huge arcade for children, so I was thankful Jack had something fun to do, in light of the length of the trip home. Since we'd both determined God didn't want 'dirty money,' I gave him twenty dollars of the money. He had the same good fortune on the Skee ball machine I had on the slot machine, and we drove all the way back to North Carolina with a stuffed Harley-Davidson hog bigger than Jack. It was so big that part of it had to hang out the back window. Jack's favorite part of the trip home was all the truckers blowing at us when they saw the big hog."

Charlotte laughed jovially with all the rest of the passengers. "And that, my dear friends, is my casino experience." She looked at the teenage girl who'd originally asked about her gambling and added, "I have learned an important lesson about casinos since then, and since you Lutherans use real wine in communion, I'll share it with you. You've probably all heard the old joke that the only difference between a Baptist and a Lutheran is a Lutheran will speak to you in an ABC store. The only difference between a Baptist and a Methodist is a Methodist will speak to you in a casino!"

She turned to the bus driver. "Oh, and by the way, James," warned Charlotte, "make sure you don't park the church bus right next to the casino. All I need are incriminating photos getting back to the church."

The author laughed heartily and shared the story of one of her other Gulf mission trips. "Everything down here was still closed and we were trying to get directions to a particular place where friends lived. We wanted to look them up to make sure they were okay. The only place open was the liquor store, so we parked the church bus right outside the front door and in went the driver. You should have seen the people inside the store lining the windows to get a peek and take photos. I was sure one of the pictures was going to land on the news or something horrible."

"Isn't it ironic," asked one of the teens, "that the first places to open were the casinos and the liquor stores?"

Her insight worked, concluded Mary Magdalena, watching how Charlotte had effectively opened the door wide enough to allow the youth and volunteers to make their own assessments of the recovery process.

14

"So how was it, ***really***, to be Levi's keeper?" Charlotte asked, after everyone else had gone inside the church at Diamondhead to get ready for their big night on the town.

Jack's eyes met hers and she immediately recognized the pain written on his face, the pain he'd hidden from the others, riveted throughout his entire body. "Mom," he began, appearing to be in a far-off daze, "you've taken me all over the world with you and I've acquired an education that books and school could never give me, but I was nowhere near ready for what that boy taught me today."

Charlotte led Jack out to a vacant corner of the church lot where they sat under the trees.

"He lives in a FEMA trailer with ten other people. ***Ten other people...,***"

"Eleven people in one trailer?" Charlotte uttered in disbelief. "I can't imagine living in one of those things with four people for this long a period, much less eleven. I look at these people and wonder how they stay sane. I sometimes wonder if all these survival skills they've had to endure aren't worse than the storm itself."

"His grandparents," Jack continued, as if oblivious to his mother's words, "an older sister in her twenties, her live-in and their child, a father, two other sisters in their teens, a boy cousin the same age as Levi and a nineteen-year-old brother."

Charlotte counted on her fingers as her son went down the list as if that would lessen her anguish over this depressing story.

"It gets worse," he said sorrowfully. "The nineteen-year-old brother is on house arrest. Seems he got caught for breaking and entering. From the impression I got, Levi is his punching bag whenever something doesn't go his way."

Charlotte's face was aghast.

"It gets worse. Levi stays locked in the closet most of the time by his grandparents."

"He what?" the author screeched, shaking her head. "No wonder he bolted in the door the way he did on Monday and cowered in the corner. It sounds like the only life he knows."

"It gets worse," Jack said a third time, sounding like a broken record. "Did you notice that in the roll call of family members, I didn't mention a mother?"

Charlotte went down the list again on her fingers. "Dare I ask where she is?"

"Levi hasn't seen her since Katrina. None of them have. Can you imagine witnessing a storm of that magnitude, and then not being able to find your mother? What's worse, having no idea whether she's dead or alive?"

The pair sat silent, their minds filled with tons of questions, all with no answers as they both stared in the direction of the white PVC-pipe crosses.

"You've been out here a long time," Mary Magdalena stated, concern in her voice as she neared the mother and son.

"Is everything okay?" asked Ebony.

"That depends on your definition of okay," Jack answered languidly.

"I take it your day with Levi wasn't as happy-go-lucky as you let on during the bus ride," Mary Magdalena speculated.

"Let's just say it was a day of learning." Jack didn't feel comfortable sharing Levi's home situation with anyone else, but he did choose to confide one last tidbit of information with them. "Do you remember yesterday when I said Levi had nothing in his backpack? I was wrong. He does have something in it. Something, I dare say, more valuable than most of the objects kept by the others."

He disclosed that Levi's mother had been missing since the storm. "What he carries in his backpack is nothing more than a memory of her. Or rather," he corrected himself, "a memory of something which belonged to her. It was a strand of beads. When he saw her the last time, she was holding them."

"Were they rosary beads?" asked Mary Magdalena, reaching in her purse to show him the ones her grandmother had left her. "If so, they could have been something she was holding onto as she prayed about the approaching storm."

"I don't know." Jack paused, trying to remember the child's exact words. "From what I gathered, they were more like Mardi Gras beads. He did say they were silver."

"Then chances are they weren't rosary beads."

"I'll bet they weren't real silver either," conjured Ebony. "Probably those plastic things they sell in all the shops down here."

"Levi told me today when he opens the bag and reaches inside, he can see her face and feel her presence," Jack added. "It's like, in his mind, she never left."

"Any chance we could contact the local police and see if they couldn't begin a search for her?" asked Ebony.

"And give them a description of silver-colored Mardi Gras beads?" Jack responded cynically. "Who down here ***doesn't*** have Mardi Gras beads? There's not a town anywhere near here that doesn't have Mardi Gras parades. The only thing they have more of down here than New Orleans Saints' jerseys is beads."

"Trying to locate her would be next to impossible," answered Mary Magdalena. "I heard so many stories of missing family members in that week I was here at Easter. They could never acquire enough manpower to track down all of those people. Besides, she could have gotten washed out to sea, or hitched a ride, or been picked up by anyone. That was a tragic time and, sadly, this is not an uncommon occurrence that resulted from Katrina."

"With the rest of what I learned today," shared Jack, "she may have used it as an excuse to say, 'Good riddance!'"

"That bad, huh?" Ebony braced herself for an unpleasant answer.

"Worse."

"You mentioned yesterday afternoon you thought Levi might be autistic," said Mary Magdalena. "Do you still have that inclination?"

"Even more so."

"Do you think maybe there was anything genetic in his

mother which may have prevented her from having the mental ability to get home, should she still be alive?" Mary Magdalena inquired, utilizing the sociology skills she acquired from her public policy major.

"Quite the contrary," answered Jack. "That was my first thought, too, but in listening to him speak about his mother, I quickly ruled out that option. She was apparently very intellectual and, from all indications, took very good care of him. He was certainly closer to her than anyone else in his family." Jack's expression showed a sudden tinge of brightness. "Levi did say one thing that keeps eating at me. I'm sure it's totally insignificant, but it's one of those things that is unsettlingly haunting, and I have no idea why."

"What is it?" asked his mother. "Maybe if you talk about it, something else he said will jump out at you, or perhaps you'll see it in a new light."

"Levi mentioned the beads were all twisted and gnarled and she was trying to untangle them. The last vision he has of his mother is her working her fingers around the beads, but he said it was like her fingers simply wouldn't work. Why would anyone with any intelligence sit and knead their fingers around plastic beads when a storm like Katrina is about to descend on them? None of it makes any sense to me.

"I don't know, but for whatever reason, I can't get that image out of my head. It's like I see this portrait of a woman sitting in a chair, similar to ***Whistler's Mother***, except this woman's head is down and her hands keep moving. It's really weird." Jack looked at his watch, ready to forget the image. "I'd better run inside and change."

"Why?" asked Mary Magdalena. "I thought you liked being 'the Fonz.'"

"You make a cute Fonzie," taunted Ebony. "I think you should stay that way."

"I'm not sure he has a choice," said Charlotte, pointing to the others getting on the bus. "Looks like it's time for the one-armed bandits!"

For the first time since their return to Diamondhead, Jack gave a slight hint of a smile.

"Maybe you can win Levi a Harley-Davidson hog," teased Mary Magdalena. "You know the Fonz did have a bike!"

"He wants a basketball," stated Jack, in a tone that told the three women they would not return from Biloxi without a stop at the Wal-Mart sporting goods department.

15

By request from Charlotte, Mary Magdalena introduced the major project for Wednesday morning. Since she was now officially a Findlayite, not to mention she was the daughter-in-law of the sand sculptor and had taken an active role in the slate of volunteer helpers, she was voted the expert on the activity involving the campers shaping objects with their hands. Using poster-sized pictures of some of Joshua's creations, she explained how much work, time and talent went into his famed artistic renderings each year at Holy Week.

"Could he come and do one here?" asked one boy. "We have lots of sand here."

"You do have a lot of sand here, but it's very different from the sand the sculptor uses back in Ohio."

"I thought you said it was in Hancock County, too," stated one of the older girls.

"I did say it was in Hancock County, but it's in Ohio

and that's very different from your state of Mississippi. Your weather is different, your plants are different and your soil is different. That means the sand has a different quality about it."

"Can't your father-in-law do a sculpture in our sand?" questioned another boy, disillusionment in his voice.

"Yes, he can make a sand sculpture here," she answered, "and if you'll listen very carefully, I'll let you all in on a little secret."

The children all sat upright, craning their necks toward Mary Magdalena as if that gesture would help them hear better, as she leaned her head toward them and spoke in a whispered tone. "The Sandman, as Joshua is called in Hancock County, Ohio, is coming here to Hancock County, Mississippi, to make a very special sand sculpture just for all of you as a part of the celebration of getting in your new school."

Gasps of animated "ooh's" and "ahh's" floated throughout the room as the children clapped and cheered.

"Can we help?"

"What will he make?"

"Is your husband coming?"

"How big will it be?"

"Can he use our sand or is he bringing his own?"

"Where will he do it?"

"Can I invite my grandma from California?"

Mary Magdalena fielded question after question, trying her best to inspire the children with each answer in preparation for their own creations they would soon make. "And now," she explained, getting them psyched up for their surprise activity, "we're going to let you do what Joshua did when he was your age which helped him be able to do sand sculptures. But first, we have to get ready." She pointed to the boy who had shown her the wax hand and marble. "I need you to help me lead our song."

Pamela and her younger daughter put the drums in the center of the room as the children moved into a circle with no more instruction. Levi, who'd been quietly seated on his assigned line beside Jack, waited until Dottie gave him the 'okay' signal to take his place at a drum between the percussionist and her. The "brood" – who had resembled an unruly mob on Monday – moved in tandem like a well-oiled machine.

Mary Magdalena had her "leader" point to different children to yell out whatever word he or she wanted to be in God's Hand, which held the whole world. As each one took a turn, Tiffany jumped into the middle of the circle beside the drummers and began to demonstrate motions to put with the words. Within less than five minutes, the room was filled with the glorious sound of music, accentuated by the sounds of clapping, the tambourines and the movement of dance.

"It's hard to believe these are the same children, isn't it?" asked Paula, moving next to Charlotte.

"Yes, it is," the author answered, never taking her eyes off the children, "but this gets them every time. And do you want to know why? Music is the same in every language, all over the world. It speaks to the soul in a way words can't." She looked at Levi. "I can't explain it, really, but it's like God took language to a whole new level when He created music." Suddenly she gave an unwarranted snicker. "Too bad someone didn't do this with Joshua. No one dares let him sing at the sand sculptures!"

"Maybe these children can teach him to sing when he comes here," suggested Marjorie, who had joined the other two.

"I don't know," Charlotte replied with hesitation. "They say 'you're never too old to learn,' but they also say 'you can't teach an old dog new tricks.' I'm not sure where Joshua falls in that equation. Since you're the math teacher," she said to Paula, "I'll leave you to figure out that one."

James stepped in the back door and signaled Mary Magdalena that one-pound blocks of clay were cut and ready for distribution. She in turn gave Tiffany the signal to do a stomp-clap pattern with the children to get their attention.

"Today we need you to spread out and give each other lots of space," Mary Magdalena instructed. "Your group leaders will show you where to go. One of the volunteers will then hand out brown paper bags. Leave those flat on the floor, for James and Jack are going to bring each of you a square block of clay. This is the same kind of clay Joshua used as a child to make his creations. You see, there was a dentist in his hometown who did ice sculptures every year. Joshua would go see them and then go home and take his modeling clay, trying over and over to make the same things the dentist did. After lots of practice, he was able to take over doing the sculptures for the town after the dentist was no longer able to do them."

"Does this mean that one of us will do them when Joshua is no longer able to do them?" asked one of the boys.

"I hope so," answered Mary Magdalena, "but I'd like to think that some of you could do it right here in your own Hancock County before that time."

"Can't one of us girls do it?" whined one of the older girls. "Why does it have to be a boy that gets to make the sand sculptures?"

"It ***doesn't*** have to be a boy who makes the sand sculptures," explained Ebony, stepping up to help her friend. "Joshua's first helper was a woman who'd been a friend of his for a long time. His sculptures have become so large, and attract so many people, he now has lots of volunteers to help him. Mary Magdalena has helped and so have I."

"That's right," confirmed Mary Magdalena. "And," she added, "I'll bet you girls can make a sculpture just as great as anything you boys can make."

"No way!" yelled a few of the boys.

"Way!" retaliated some of the girls.

"Does Joshua ever let children help him?" asked the young boy who'd come out from his tent, surprising everyone, and most especially his sister, with his question.

"He has a small sand pile around the back of his sculpture where children can come and make their own creations," Mary Magdalena explained. "This next year will be his 10th anniversary of doing a sand sculpture during Holy Week, and he's planning a special time when children can come and make an original sculpture with him."

"I wish I could go," said one girl.

"Can we help him when he comes here?" asked another of the girls.

"Absolutely!" blurted Ebony. "I might even come and help you help him." Her answer, ***and*** her enthusiasm drew a large round of laughter from the children. "It looks like you all have your clay now." She took a piece of clay from James and demonstrated how to "feel comfortable with the clay," explaining that the first thing one had to do was become one with the clay.

"Is this what God did when He made Adam and Eve?" asked the boy with the catfish "Crucifixion" in his backpack.

Charlotte caught Ebony's coaxing glance, asking for help on that one, as she stepped forward to the stage. "God shaped and molded each and every one of you into a very unique individual and He wants to become one with all of us. He wants to be a part of our lives, and for us to look to Him for all our needs."

Suddenly Levi began to rock back and forth, moaning softly.

The author, ignoring his actions, tried to think how to break down this complicated explanation in a way all of the children could understand. "How many of you prayed, or saw your parents pray, when you heard about Katrina?"

Every child raised his or her hand. Every one of them except Levi, who moaned louder and rocked harder.

"How many of you prayed, or saw your parents pray, when you returned to where your home had been after Katrina?"

Many of the children raised their hands a second time. Again Levi became more agitated.

"And how many of you pray, or see your parents pray, every day?"

A few of the children raised their hands for a third time as Levi jumped up and ran toward the hallway where the restrooms were, Jack following him.

"That's what I mean when I say that God wants to be one with you," Charlotte continued, while uttering her own prayer to give her son what was needed for Levi's needs. "He wants you to be with Him ***all*** the time, not just when you're afraid or need something."

"How can we find Him?" asked the young boy who'd earlier been under the tent.

"Oh, boy!" gasped Ebony in horror, her words directed at Mary Magdalena. "When that boy decided to speak, he didn't have to become some great philosopher. The next thing you know, he'll be looking under his tent for God! I didn't mean to open this can of worms."

"It's alright," her friend assured her. "They need to know that God is all around them. Even in the tent with them."

Charlotte managed to divert the children's attention back to their blocks of clay by walking around the room to see how they were doing. "Making things with clay takes a lot of thought and concentration, and a lot of work with your hands. I'm going to be quiet now so you can all focus on what you want to make. And don't be afraid to try something besides a simple ball or worm. You can make anything you want, just keep working at it. You've got lots of time, for this is not something you can do in a hurry."

She watched as Levi and Jack walked back in the room, side by side as the Ninja and "the Fonz." ***I wonder what the two of them will make***. Secretly, she placed an addendum on her prayer that molding the clay into some tactical object would be a very therapeutic activity for this hurting child.

"I can't believe them," seemed to be the common observation among the volunteers as they walked around the room admiring the clay masterpieces. Even Charlotte had to admit she'd never encountered such creative or intricate specimens of artwork from children in all her travels.

"Do you think there's a reason for it?" asked Tiffany.

"I do," answered the author. "These children have lived through the worst natural disaster our country has ever seen. They've seen things which I've never seen, and things which many people who've been in war-torn countries have never seen. The impressions of what they witnessed are so articulate in their minds I suspect there's no end to the things they could create. What amazes me is the ability they have to do it. Look at them. Some of these children are incredibly young. They were only two or three at the time Katrina struck, yet their work is as detailed as anything I've seen from adult sculpting students."

Charlotte had been so occupied with admiring all of the sculptures she failed to notice a couple of the boys had taken off to the restroom without permission. Apparently their group leader had missed it, too, until another camper came running from the hallway, shouting that someone had destroyed the boys' restroom. She hastily sped toward the hallway where the restrooms were located, with James fast on her trail.

Jack met her at the door of the restroom. "Levi and I have everything under control," he assured her.

"What did he do?" she stormed. "I thought he was doing so well and seemed to be enjoying the clay."

Jack opened the door to the restroom just enough for Charlotte to peek inside and see the boy washing the mirrors with a paper towel.

"Thank goodness, you've made him clean his mess."

"It wasn't his mess," Jack said to his mother's surprise.

"What do you mean?"

"He asked if he could go to the restroom and I gave him permission. When he didn't come back after a few minutes, I went to check on him. That's when I found him cleaning up the big mess in there. It wasn't him that did it. There was too much clay thrown around the room to have come from only one block. I've already discovered the two culprits and they know they're in hot water. I've also explained they'll tell their mothers when they arrive this afternoon, and I've given them the ultimatum they may not be able to come back for the big surprise on Friday."

Jack gave a satisfied smirk. "I think it's important you understand our Ninja took it upon himself to clean up their mess. The place was so wrecked they'd even thrown clay in the toilets. Levi took care of getting that out, too. I haven't said a word to him about what to do, and when I asked if he needed some help, all he did was shake his head and keep cleaning."

James patted both Jack and his mother on the back. "You've taught him well, Charlotte."

The mother and son smiled at each other, then at James.

"I do have one request," said Jack.

"What's that?"

"I think Levi should get a special reward by receiving a few extra tickets for the surprise on Friday, and I'd like to present them to him before lunch."

"And I think that's a grand idea," replied Charlotte, signaling her agreement with a broad smile. "Sometimes I don't know what I did to deserve you."

"You prayed a lot!" Jack shot back, giving her a wink before pulling out his comb and pantomining his best "Fonzie" imitation.

"Today's lunch is pizza," called one of the youth, receiving lots of cheers and applause.

"It's a good thing my daddy isn't here," shared Lena as she sat beside Charlotte.

"And why's that?"

"He said if he ate one more piece of pizza, he'd turn into a pepperoni."

"Doesn't he like pizza?" asked Mary Magdalena.

"He used to," said the small girl, taking a petite bite of her own slice.

No one got a chance to ask Lena for more information before the church secretary came around the corner. "I hate to interrupt," she apologized, tapping Charlotte on the shoulder. "There's some woman on the phone from the Chamber of Commerce. It seems she's just left Diamondhead United Methodist Church where she'd gone for some civic group meeting. While there, she overheard a truck driver attempting to deliver something for the schools. The secretary at Diamondhead knew nothing about it, so this woman took it upon herself to call the central office for the school board. Someone there told her Charlotte Crenshaw must be in town, and suggested she call here, saying they'd heard you were having a camp for the children."

"Now that's what I call a roundabout way of getting hold of someone," said Ebony.

"That's what I call having a reputation," stated Marjorie. "Something shows up here for the schools and they think Charlotte's in town. Think about it. Why would they assume that unless she's sent things here for the schools before?"

Mary Magdalena, chewing on the words of the volunteer, watched as the author came back to the table acting as if nothing were out of the ordinary. "A truck comes to make a delivery to the schools here and everyone in town seems to think you're involved." Her questioning tone didn't receive a reply. "Is there something here you're not telling us?"

Charlotte glared at her, trying not to make an issue out of the call. "It's only the supplies we need for next week in Pearlington, that's all." She took a bite of her pizza and turned to Lena. "How is it?"

"It's as good as all the pizza we ate after Katrina."

"That your daddy doesn't like anymore?" Charlotte asked, seeing her questions were getting no clearer answers than those of Mary Magdalena to her.

Beverly, overhearing the conversation, asked, "Did you

get to eat pizza at the Yankee Stadium after Katrina?"

Lena nodded, her blue eyes twinkling as she continued to eat.

"Yankee Stadium?" questioned Ebony. "You went to New York during Katrina?"

Lena shook her head, politely keeping her mouth closed while chewing.

"Let me explain," offered Beverly.

"I wish somebody would," replied Ebony. "I'm totally confused."

"That's easily understandable. You see, the Salvation Army has a Yankee Stadium in Biloxi. At least that's what they call it. The whole thing was really bizarre. The Salvation Army, through a huge contribution, bought all this land near their facility in downtown Biloxi the day before Katrina. The purchase had nothing to do with the storm coming, it just happened to fall on that particular day. When the storm cleared, the military helped the Salvation Army get the facility back into shape, taking advantage of the space they'd just bought to take care of all the residents left homeless and without power.

"Papa John's Pizza was the only place around with elements on which they could cook, so they started making pizzas for everyone. They made so many pizzas that the U. S. Army had to bring the dough from other Papa John locations two or three hundred miles away and fly it in by a helicopter, which was able to land in the ball field on what had just been purchased for the Salvation Army. The original intent for the use of the land was the capability to set up lots of tables and tents to feed the homeless people and people in need. Seems God was a step ahead of them."

The woman nodded and smiled at Lena. "Through the combined efforts of the Salvation Army, the Air Force and the Army, Papa John's was able to feed five hundred people every day at each meal. They made breakfast pizzas, lunch pizzas and dinner pizzas. That's all some people got to eat for days."

"I love pizza!" Lena exclaimed, her bright-red curls bouncing with each word.

"And I love Papa John's," Ebony responded. "From now on, they're gettin' all my pizza business!"

Her statement was resounded by every volunteer.

"It's time for show and tell," pronounced Charlotte. "We're going to let those of you who want to show off your creation do so. Then we'll line them all up against the walls where they can dry. Don't touch them after we put them away or they may break. Mary Magdalena and Ebony will help you carry your pieces to the drying area. Be very careful with them as they each have a voice...your voice.

"By the way, I think you all deserve an extra ticket for Friday because of your superb work. All of you except for Levi, who received his extra tickets before lunch. As for the two who made the mess in the restroom, we'll watch your behavior for the rest of the week and then decide about your tickets." The names of the culprits had not been shared by Jack, even to her, and she didn't inform the campers they could deduce their identities since they'd be the only two without a clay creation.

All of the children, including Levi, were anxious to share their work. The boys who resembled Huck Finn and Tom Sawyer had put their two blocks together to make an alien bird, complete with an intricately-woven bird nest with lots of alien baby birds cracking out of eggs. Levi had rounded the edges of his square block and then used a marker to make indentions so it appeared to be one large "Half of Paradise."

"For those of you who didn't catch that," explained Jack, "that's half of a pair of dice."

"I get it," said one of the girls. "There's only one of them."

"You're right!" congratulated Jack. "You did get it."

"No fair," whined one of the campers. "Levi cheated. You helped him."

"Nope," Jack replied, shaking his head. "He did this all by himself while I was with my other buddy under the tent. See what he made."

The little boy stood from under the tent and showed off a teacup, complete with a decorative handle and a saucer. Beaming with pride that he'd been recognized, and forgetting he was suddenly the center of attention in front of a big crowd, his tiny voice burst with pride as he declared, "I made it for my mommy."

Charlotte's heart was crushed, for she knew this was a suicide child. His real mommy was gone, but the mommy who had taken him in, who cared for all his needs, and who loved him was the woman who brought him in each morning. She fought the flood of tears that tore at her, ripping her apart, exactly as the waves of Katrina had torn at the world as these children had once known it. ***A world that will never return,*** she said to herself, feeling only an inkling of the pain these children had felt.

From that moment, she observed the works of clay with different eyes as she tried to envision the sculptures through the eyes of the children who had created them. Their masterpieces ranged from a teapot – made by the other suicide child to match the cup and saucer of her brother, a chair, a van, a car, a superhero and a whole array of other creative designs. But it was the last two pieces which left the most poignantly powerful impressions on Charlotte - impressions so powerful it was as if God, Himself, had imprinted them on her mind.

One of the older girls held up something which at first appeared to be in the shape of a horseshoe. As Charlotte examined it more closely, she saw it was a rainbow, with half-circle lines etched on it to signify each of the different colors. A puffy cloud, with scalloped edges, was placed on each side at the ends of the rainbow, as a huge sunburst sat atop the familiar symbol that had come to mark God's "promise."

"Did you see a rainbow after Katrina?" asked Mary Magdalena.

"No, but I didn't have to," answered the girl. "I knew God loved me and was with me. I could see the rainbow in my head, just as I saw it when I made this."

Charlotte noticed the heads of several of the volunteers lower as they pretended the tears behind their eyes weren't really there. She knew they now perceived what she'd meant when she warned them they had to be strong for the children.

As the last child walked onto the stage to show her work, Mary Magdalena denoted something more salient than a work of clay. ***That's odd,*** she thought, ***this is their third day here and this is the first time I've noticed how much this little girl looks like me as a child.*** She stared momentarily at the uncanny resemblance to a photograph that still hung in her parents' den of her as a first grader. Looking back to see which group the girl had come from, she noted immediately it was the first graders. She was mesmerized by the child's brown hair, with the matching dark brown eyes and olive skin. ***She's even missing the same tooth as me in the picture.***

Mary Magdalena suddenly realized there was a hushed lull on the stage and all eyes were on her. "And for our final exhibition," she proclaimed, giving an imaginary drum roll, "let's see what Alexis, who looks like I did as a child, has made." She looked down at the clay model made by an exceptionally young girl who was now beaming for two reasons. "It looks like you have a boat there."

"I do," replied Alexis, her voice possessing the same confidence and composure as her young body, all of which were much too advanced for a child of her age.

"That's a very beautiful boat," stated Mary Magdalena admiringly. "It looks like Peter Pan's boat with Wendy standing atop the bow. Is that what it is, a picture from Peter Pan's 'Neverland?'"

"No, it's the boat we were in when we escaped from our house."

"Is it your boat?"

"No, it's a boat my father grabbed when he saw the water coming down our street. He put all of us in it and we were in it for a very long time."

"I love the little people you've put in the boat," Mary Magdalena observed. "You've even put little arms and legs on them."

"They're us!" shouted two boys, who were Alexis' older brothers, from the middle of the room. "We were in the boat with her."

"She's really good with art," boasted one of the brothers, proud that his sister's work was receiving so much well-deserved attention. "I'm good with art, too. We're like our father. He's an artist."

Mary Magdalena gulped hard. ***She's not making this up***, she realized. ***This is really what happened to her family during the storm.*** "Which ones are your brothers?" Her questions had gone from pointing out the girl's mature artistic abilities to pointing out the reality of the horrific aftermath of the storm. She watched with increasing interest as Alexis' tiny fingers pointed to two of the small "people" in her boat.

"And these people on the other side of the boat...are they other family members?"

"No," Alexis answered without hesitation, "they're the three dead people who drowned and were still hanging in the branches of the trees as the boat floated through the water."

Mary Magdalena's jaw dropped, a reaction matched by her entire body as she suddenly felt weak-kneed and totally helpless, to the point of being almost nauseous. She took in several slow breathes, exhaling even slower until she was able to speak again. "What about the girl at the bow of the boat, the one I thought was Wendy? Is that you?"

"No, this is me," said Alexis, her fingers moving to the smallest clay "person" in the boat. She held the clay miniature up, so no one in the room could miss the figure at the front of the boat. "This is the angel who saved all of us."

The burning sensation in the pit of Mary Magdalena's stomach began to subside, sensing an unseen healing – along with the rest of her body and soul – through the faith, and the eyes, of this young child. ***And Charlotte wanted us to be strong for them? They're the very ones holding us up!***

"And see this?" asked Alexis, now taking over the role of the spokesperson, as she had just done as the tower of strength.

It was then Mary Magdalena noticed a tiny object in the angel's hand. An object so tiny she could hardly believe the girl was able to form such a minute entity, much less with such delicately scaled details, making it clearly distinguishable as a bird.

"That's the dove," stated Alexis, with the same confidence and composure she'd displayed when she stepped on the stage with her "square block of clay."

No one budged as the volunteers shuddered in sheer disbelief and the children relived their own encounters with Katrina in their own minds. Charlotte sat dumbfounded, realizing Mary Magdalena had not been far off-base with her perception of the boat looking like Peter Pan and Wendy. ***Even though Scottish author Barrie's novel was spiced with pirates, Indians, mermaids and fairies, his story of "Peter and Wendy" has nothing on Alexis' story***, she surmised, looking at the mass of youngsters who were all characters in Alexis' real-life story. ***And the story of these children has its own gang***, she solemnly deduced looking at the boy under the tent and his sister, ***except instead of being the "Lost Boys," they're the "Lost Parents."***

"And you were ***how old*** at the time of Katrina?" Mary Magdalena slowly asked, not really wanting to know the answer she'd already conceived in her mind.

"Three."

The earlier drum roll and pronouncement had been unnecessary, for the child's work and memories spoke for themselves. Her piece of clay truly did possess a voice. ***A voice***, decided Charlotte, ***which needs to be heard by the entire world.***

They really are ***in the same boat***, Mary Magdalena said to herself, recalling her assessment from the day before. Just as the disciples had been in the same boat, no matter whether they had come from a trade of fishing or tax collecting. ***They are all equal in God's sight. Whether their father is in charge of beautification for the city, whether he works on the banana barge, whether he is a fisherman, whether he took his life...***, she mused mournfully, ***as in Alexis' boat, where their fathers can be either dead or alive.***

"How do you prepare for this?" she asked of the author, after the children had gleefully and giddily moved on to their next task.

"You don't," was Charlotte's painfully honest answer. She looked at the groups of children, all now making a rainbow fish mobile that would sparkle with the colors of the rainbow when the sun hit it. "You have to be like them, like the girl's story about the rainbow and how she knew, and still knows, that God is with her everywhere she goes." The author looked lovingly at the roomful of children, already portraying a different bunch from the ones who'd come in two days earlier. "These children are ***our*** rainbows." She paused. "And we, in turn, are their rainbows, and through their brilliant colors radiating into us, we can then go out and be rainbows to the world." Although she tried to evoke a façade of confidence, the heartache and sorrow in her eyes was evident to the volunteers gathered around her.

Jack stepped forward and placed a supporting arm around his mother, his action spreading through other volunteers who had come to listen as they joined hands in unity of faith, strength, hope and love. "Do you know what hurt me most about that?" he asked.

Charlotte shook her head.

"None of the other children saw that as odd."

"That's because, unfortunately, they were in the same proverbial boat. They saw way too many things which should have been disallowed by their young eyes."

An eerie silence, the same one that had surfaced when the children reenacted Katrina with the blue piece of fabric, fell across the room.

16

Charlotte watched as each child left with a parent. When Alexis ran to the door and hugged a tall man with dark hair, the author rushed to catch him as he waited for his two sons.

"Excuse me," she said, "I'm Charlotte Crenshaw."

"You're the author," he replied.

"Yes."

"My children are excited about being here. They remember when you visited the school back in the winter and read to them and brought all the books. They've been telling me all about you and all the things all of ya'll are doing with them this week. Thank you for coming down here. The children haven't had a lot of cultural arts kinds of activities since the storm so they're having a good time."

"Thank you... from all of us," Charlotte accepted, extending her arms to also recognize all the volunteers, "but it is us who owe you parents the praise. It is our pleasure to meet and work with these children." She wasn't sure how to begin this conversation, but she started with, "May I speak privately with you for a moment?"

"Sure," he answered, a bit puzzled. "Alexis, why don't you go round up your brothers? You can stay with them until we're ready to go." The man looked back at Charlotte. "I hope there's no problem."

"No," she hastily assured him. "There's no problem at all. In fact, your children are incredible and you should be extremely proud of them."

"I am," he said, looking across the room in their direction. "They're good kids, although sometimes the boys can be boys."

"Tell me about it," she responded with a chuckle. "That's my son over there, and he's still all boy."

"Your son is 'the Fonz?'"

Charlotte laughed aloud, reminded of the time Jack had gone with her to Graham's house where there was a framed photograph of "The Church Lady" from ***Saturday Night Live.*** Jack noticed the picture as they started inside and grabbed his mother's coat sleeve. "Please tell me Graham is ***not*** related to 'the Church Lady.'" She had assured Jack that Graham and the character were not related; now she was assuring this father her son was not typically that character. "Yes, he's dressed like 'the Fonz' for a special reason. He doesn't always dress that way."

"The children told me about the dramas you did with them yesterday. They're enjoying dressing up, too."

And folks say we North Carolinians have a Southern accent, she thought as she listened to his words, admiring the combination of the dialect of the Deep South combined with the Cajun tones as the long, slow vowels rolled out in his words. They had a charm and rhythm all their own which she'd never heard anywhere else, and was her favorite accent in the entire world. Thus, Charlotte was enjoying her conversation with this man, not as much for their words as for the charm of his voice. "You were born and raised here, weren't you?"

"Yes, ma'am, I've been in Pearlington all my life."

"Your children tell me you're an artist?"

"I did a lot of sketches before the hurricane. That was when there was still an art gallery. It was demolished like everything else. Since that happened, I only have two sketches left, and one of them was destroyed, too. Now I have a job over in Louisiana until I can go to my artwork full-time."

The brother was right. No wonder Alexis is so artistic. "We made models from clay today. Your daughter's was most impressive. It was of the boat and she even had people in it. She made the angel and the dove on the front of the boat. I've never seen that kind of work from a child before. She's incredibly talented, especially for her age."

"Yeah, I don't guess they'll ever forget that boat."

So it was real. "Do you mind sharing your story with me? Being an author, I love stories. The one she told is the most powerful one I've heard yet."

"Yeah," he said again, taking Charlotte back to the afternoon of hearing Alexis' version of their plight. "I went outside thinking the storm was over. There had been torrential rains and tornadoes all over the place. It looked like a war zone from all the trees, power lines and debris down everywhere. There wasn't any wind or rain, but that was because the eye of the hurricane was over us right then and we didn't even know it. Katrina's eye was so wide the wind and rain had been stopped for about twenty minutes. It was long enough that we'd already gotten the emergency generator set up and had power. We were even fixing something to eat. What we didn't realize was what we'd seen was only the first half of the hurricane. And what the first half didn't tear up, the second half did."

Charlotte listened in awe, not sure she wanted to hear the rest of the story. She'd been in a hurricane, and had three tornadoes in her yard or over her house, and the thoughts were not something she was eager to remember.

"I walked out the front door of my house to check on my grandmother's house, which was right down from mine, because we'd managed to get her out of the area. When I stepped into my yard, the water was about ankle deep. Before I'd gotten six feet from my house, I saw this huge wave coming. What had happened was the water from the Gulf had come up into the Pearl River and the waves were coming right at us. We all live on the Pearl River, you see, and my house is at the end of a long road. The first wave washed up over the riverbank and into the yards. The second wave literally came up over my grandmother's house, which was on blocks, and shredded it right into. I looked out and saw a wave, which they told us later was a 35-foot tall tidal wave. I'm sure that's right because there were these two-story camp houses along the river which were up on pilings. That wave went right over the top of them and when it came down, there was nothing left of the houses."

The author braced herself. She was sure the idea she had of this story was only an inkling of what was coming next. All she knew was it was going to be worse than any fictional story she could dream up in her worst nightmare.

"I ran back toward my house yelling for everybody to get to the attic. By the time I got to the steps, the water was chest high and I'm a tall person. When I reached the top step, the water was up to my neck. I saw a neighbor's boat coming right toward me and managed to grab it. I've always been an athlete and pretty strong, but it took every ounce of energy I had to hold onto the boat, and now looking back, there's only one way I did it.

"My wife helped me get my older daughter and the boys out the attic window. She had to climb out the attic window with Alexis and I had to pull her into the boat, but by then the water was all the way up in the attic. I couldn't get hold of Alexis and she was drowning. I had to get out of the boat and grab hold of a tree limb with one hand and get her with the other. The water was pulling me so hard I couldn't get her in the boat. My sons had managed to get their two dogs and we had a bird that they got, too, but it bit me so hard while I was trying to get them out of the attic that I was bleeding pretty bad from it. That didn't help with all that water lapping at it as I was grabbing for Alexis. I was afraid I had lost her, but I kept struggling with all my might and I finally managed to get a hold on the boat and got both of us in it, with the rest of my family pulling us both in. She grabs for me every time I come to pick her up anywhere now and I always wonder if that has anything to do with it."

"Like she did just now as you arrived."

The man nodded and looked in his daughter's direction.

"She mentioned the dead people," Charlotte said, hoping that part had not happened.

"Yeah, there were three people drowned from the water coming up so high. We weren't expecting anything like that. I don't even know how long we were in that boat, but it was hours and hours. We finally saw a house we now call 'the Barbie house' because it was three floors high. Whoever lived in it wasn't there, and the water was all the way up in the top two floors and covering the floor of the third floor. It was the only house still standing that wasn't completely under water."

At this point, Jeremiah gave a laugh. "The first night's sleep I got after Katrina, I was wearing a woman's pink nightgown. It was the only thing I could find in the dresser. Our clothes were completely ruined from the filth and stink that came from all the muck, not to mention the heat and humidity. It was sweltering hot with the sun beating down on us after the storm, and we could do nothing except stay in the boat until we found that house." He saw the look on Charlotte's face. "It was a split-second decision. All I could see was water and I knew it was deadly. And all I could think about was saving my family. When I saw the boat, it was like magic. I grabbed it and didn't even think about the fact it was someone else's. I don't know whose it was, but they'd have never seen it again anyway. The water would have washed it to who-knows-where. As for the house, it was a matter of protecting my family. It was the only place around. And even with that, we didn't have anything to eat or drink for three days."

Charlotte saw this conversation was like the hurricane. He'd only gotten through the first half of what happened, and it seemed eminent round two of his recount would hold just as much action. She motioned him toward the door and the benches beyond.

"I really felt bad about wearing someone else's clothes, Jeremiah continued, not missing a melancholic beat and his voice still laced with that Cajun charm, "but I knew from the devastation this house would never be lived in again. The bottom two floors were completely ruined, and by the time we were able to get outside again, the mold and mildew had already come up the walls of the top floor. Since the water had hit the floor of the third floor, loose things were floating around and we knew nothing from the bottom two floors could possibly be salvaged." He shook his head sorrowfully. "The way it turned out, the house was so full of mold and mildew the owners had to tear it down...what was left to tear down. I don't even know how long it was before the owners came back to check on it.

"You see, Pearlington only had twenty-two hundred

residents to start with. There were nine hundred homes and out of all of them and all the businesses, only three remained without suffering great devastation. A goodly number of them were just like my grandmother's, shredded in two from the force of the water."

"What about your house?" Charlotte inquired. "Did you lose it?"

"Yeah...,"

She looked at Jeremiah's forlorn expression and immediately wished she could retract the question. "I'm sorry," she hastily apologized. "I shouldn't have been so forward."

"It's alright," he assured her, "I don't mind. I was actually in the process of building a house when Katrina hit. I'd bought some land in 'the Kill' and had a trailer on it while I was working on the house. They didn't get any water damage from the hurricane right there so I thought it was safe. But then there were tornados all over the place caused by the winds from the storm.

"One of my neighbors there saw a tornado turn the trailer upside down and rip right through the middle of it. Thank God, my family wasn't in it. We were at our house in Pearlington during the storm, but that was the house which was completely under water and totally ruined."

A slight shake of his head told the author it was still hard for him to believe. "After all this time, it's still so surreal. Even though I saw it firsthand with my own eyes and lived through it, there are some days when it's hard to realize all that happened.

"It's tough. It's *real* tough. I'm building a house again on my land in 'the Kill.' My dad was a general contractor, so I learned a lot from him about building during my life. I'm able to do a lot of the work myself. The problem, and the same problem we're all having, is it's taking so long. Right at first, it was because we had to wait for building materials to get down here. Everything of that nature…***everything***…in the entire area was ruined. It was days before roads were passable enough for trucks to get the materials to us. There was one spot on the road where a boat literally slammed up next to a tree in somebody's yard and capsized on its side on top of a car. There was another boat right down from there that was actually ***in*** the road."

"I've seen them," acknowledged Charlotte. "I saw them on my first trip down here after Katrina, and then again last year when I took my volunteer helpers to see them. I couldn't believe that one boat was still sitting along the highway going from Mississippi into Louisiana."

"The strange thing was," Jeremiah explained, "neither the boat nor the car belonged to the owner of that yard. Needless to say, that yard was all the person had left, for the house washed away. I wonder if the owner of the yard made himself a house boat."

Any other time, that comment might have been funny, but in this instance, Charlotte understood Jeremiah was completely serious. Her face took on a dismal expression. "I've even heard some of the children this week telling how they came home and saw a house in their yard, but it wasn't their house. One child told me he lived on a street with eleven houses and when they returned, there was not one house within sight. He said his dad couldn't even tell where their street was. One girl told me the only way they found where their street used to be was by the Veteran Monument that was still on the beach. It was there, but the street and houses weren't. All she saw when she returned were some piano keys scattered along the way, where flowers had once been." She gave a weighted sigh. "What really gets me is how people came back, and in the midst of the rubble and destruction, they couldn't even find where their house was. It still tears at me when I drive through some areas and see those street numbers on little pieces of wood scraps, nailed to small stakes stuck in the ground, the numbers written with a black marker – just so the landowner can remember where his or her lot was.

"As painful as those sights are," Charlotte concluded, the dampness in her eyes evident, "there's a part of me that's glad there is still so much evidence of Katrina. It makes us who come here realize the vastness of the devastation, and the length of time it will take for the area to make a come-back."

"One of the reasons it is taking so long for people to get back on their feet is how long it took to get back in the area following the storm," shared Jeremiah. "I told you Pearlington had twenty-two hundred residents with nine hundred homes at the time of Katrina. Eight weeks after the storm, there were still less than eighty FEMA travel trailers in the area. There was no place for the people to live, many set up camp with tents, the businesses were wiped out...," he paused, placing himself back in the picture, "and all the while, you're trying to pretend that there's some sort of normalcy in all of this for your children's sake, if not for your own."

Jeremiah pictured in his mind the flat land where the Charles B. Murphy School his children once attended had stood. Land where, since Katrina, huge tents stood, the medical tent still looking like something from a MASH unit, and the other tents where hundreds ate and camped for countless days. There was one other building which had been converted to a supply house for the residents and had been renamed "Pearlmart" - its shelves holding everything from diapers to toothbrushes. It had been a place where trucks brought in supplies, which went out at a rate of twenty tons a day for the first weeks after the hurricane. He looked back at Charlotte who was patiently and supportively waiting as he worked his way through the pain.

"My dad has spent his time since Katrina working with a lot of the building teams who come here. You'll meet him next week," he noted. "Aren't you going to be working in Pearlington at the Recovery Center?"

"Yes, as a matter of fact we are."

"He'll be there. He works with the Recovery Center to help people get into their houses and back on their feet. There's a woman there now, whom you'll also meet next week. She's finally getting a house after three years."

Charlotte wondered what the woman's living conditions had been during that three years, but didn't ask. She wasn't sure she could handle any more than what she'd already heard.

"You'll know her, because they'll have some sort of celebration for her. It's gotten to be a thing here that when one of the building teams, or the community or Recovery Center gets someone back into a home, it's a big deal. At least as big as we can make it down here. All the money goes to getting people back into a place which can be their own home again. The news and media have been good about covering that. It seems a renewal of hope for those still waiting. I guess for some, though, it could be depressing as they see they're still in a tent or FEMA trailer, and they can't see past that for the moment. Sadly, about half of the children you'll see at the Recovery Center next week are still in that same boat."

That same boat, she said to herself reflectively. ***That same boat as Alexis' boat.***

Jeremiah smiled. "Those children will be glad for you to come. They've only had one other group of people come and do any kind of planned activities with them. If you do for them what you've done for these children, you'll touch a lot of young lives. My children remember you from when you came and read to them this past winter. Word has it you didn't leave Hancock

County without getting a book into the hands of every child, student and teacher in the Pearlington and Kiln area. I even heard some of the students at the Community College say you'd brought some art books for them. One of the students going into fashion design was telling me about the book she used for a final project. It had come from you."

"I wouldn't go that far," Charlotte blushed, "but we did try to make sure children and students at all levels had books available to them. I can't take credit for all that. The particular art book you're speaking of was a gift from the book's publisher. I merely got to be the person who delivered it. It's the same with most of those books. They came from students and churches all over the country. Some even came from Hancock County, Ohio, where a few of our volunteers are from. What I think is incredible about that scenario is they suffered their own devastating flood in August of 2007, merely days before the second anniversary of Katrina. Yet, the year before, the library there hosted a huge event, one of the first we did, and we collected over 200 new books for these Gulf children. Then, when the Ohio's Blanchard River flooded, they lost thousands of books. This is the beauty of what I do, and the beauty of what I'm seeing here. People reaching out and helping others. We all need help from time to time, including those who've given help at other times. God made us to serve, each in our own capacity."

She gave an appreciative smile. "You daughter's talent did that for us today. She unknowingly, but certainly willingly, served us, the helpers by leaving us with a gift money could never buy. It does go to show that what goes around comes around."

Suddenly, the extent of what all the volunteers were doing struck Charlotte. Yet, at the same time, it made her also realize enough wasn't being done. She felt so insignificant in the scheme of things, a hungering desire to do even more going off within her.

"I'm surprised there weren't more fatalities and casualties than there were," she stated, still caught up in the dismal details of the storm.

"What's more of a surprise is before the storm, we weren't even on the map. They didn't know we were here. If it hadn't been for the rescue helicopters finding a man floating in the water and pulling him out, more people would have drowned and they'd have never found a lot of them. When the helicopter pilot asked the man to point out his home on the map, there wasn't even a dot where we were. The rescued man literally had to ***show*** them where Pearlington was, and with everything completely under water, that was difficult."

A slight smile flashed across Jeremiah's face. "We're on the map now, by golly."

Charlotte laughed for a moment, but then her face fell back to the horror of his words which had come earlier. "It's hard for us, who've never encountered anything like that, to even think about any of this, much less fathom it. We hurt with you, but it's impossible to feel your pain, as hard as we may try. I think the real crux, the real benefit we volunteers glean are the stories of hope and inspiration you give to the rest of the world. I've never, in all my life and in all my travels, heard anything as incredulous, nor incredible, as some of the things you've shared."

"And the stories go on and on," replied Jeremiah. "Everyone, although sharing the same basic story, has a different story, all his own. And the bad thing is, every single one of them is unbelievable, even to us who lived through the storm." For the first time since he'd begun talking, he gave a solemn sigh. "But what you said about helping others, I don't know of a person in this whole area of Mississippi who isn't reaching out to help their neighbor. Those who have houses are anxious to make sure others are in that same boat, and those who don't have houses are helping, knowing their chance to be in that same boat will eventually happen."

Charlotte drew a visual image from his words, an image which spoke volumes to her. During the first year after the hurricane, she had witnessed the expressions and emotions of survivors filled with hope, appreciative of all the volunteers and helpers, and the countless contributions from around the world. When she returned near the time of the second anniversary of the storm, it seemed many had lost hope, seeing they were no farther ahead than they'd been the year before. Their expressions, and their outlooks, were subdued and void of energy. But it seemed that now, with the approaching opening of the new South Hancock Elementary School, the community's spirits had soared. She saw where houses had sprung up, and repairs were finally significant enough to be noticed, as several communities in the Bay St. Louis area were beginning to resemble regular communities again, only they looked cleaner, refreshed, filled with new breath and new life. Mentally and emotionally, they had gone from fighting the riptide to stay alive, to becoming so tireless they saw no way to the rainbow, and then, with a few upward surges, they gained new hope, new energy and swam for the shore, realizing the race they had finished. And for many, they were at least able to now paddle along until they could finally, once again, step out of the boat and onto dry land. ***Ah, what a legacy, what a history, these children have.***

She looked at Jeremiah, seeing him with different eyes, as she fully understood the lesson and reality check he'd just given her. These weren't "the poor little children." They were "the precious little children," in His sight, and in the sight of anyone who'd been blessed enough to come in contact with them. They were richer in spirit and more sharing of their gifts and talents than many people in their big, fine mansions. Suddenly, she saw the inhabitants of Katrina's path in a different light. ***His light***, she realized, offering an appreciative prayer of thanks for the opening of her eyes.

"I know you said the children told you I was an artist," said Jeremiah, a subdued tone in his voice as he interrupted Charlotte's time of reflection. "Do you have one more minute? I can actually show you firsthand the kind of miracles we saw down here."

"I'd love that," answered Charlotte. After the account she'd just heard, she was ready for something to take the edge off the chill running up her spine. It was so haunting she wasn't quite sure how to grasp it all.

"I have something," he told her as he walked to the back of his SUV, "it's actually a sketch I did before the storm. There were two of them, both of which were in the back of my Jeep when Katrina came. I've told you about the water and how forceful and how high it was in our area right next to the river."

He walked back with a rolled up piece of paper, unrolled it and handed it to the observant author. "I think you can fully appreciate this."

She felt the blood rush within her, sensing an omnipotent source of Power had also touched this sketch, as her hands detected its startlingly thin, crinkly paper. There was no denying what she held had gotten wet, making it feel like aged parchment against her fingertips.

Charlotte observed every minute detail of the sketch, the skilled shading that breathed life into the trees of the forest which were unmistakably in the Alps, obvious from the height and shape of the snow-tipped mountains. The scene looked much like one of the many she had visited on one of her trips to Europe when she'd done a graduate project on the churches, and their historic place in their communities, there. To add to that similarity was the church, its architecture of stucco, standing out proudly as the sketch's focal point against the stark contrast of the mountainside behind it.

She noted every tiny facet birthed by this artist's skill, from the distinct shape of the window, to the turret-shaped tower that housed the bell far above the roofline of the pristinely picturesque sanctuary, until her eyes fell to rest on an angel carving that stood perched, high atop one of the eaves of a wing of the structure, overlooking all that lay beyond.

What lay beyond, Charlotte saw, looking deeper into the lines and shading, was a river with a tiny dock only steps away from the sanctuary. At the exact juncture of the building was a spot where it appeared that two rivers met, one leading between the mountains as it went one way, and the other going toward the valleys below in the other direction. ***How ironic, seeing how the road where Jeremiah lives is situated where the Gulf meets the Pearl River.***

"When did you do this?" she asked, suspecting she knew the answer.

"About a week before the storm hit. That's why it was still in my Jeep. I hadn't had a chance to take it to the gallery yet."

"Have you done anything since the storm?" Charlotte suspected she also knew the unwelcome answer to this question as well.

"Nah...it seems it's taken all my time getting things back, as much as I could, to the way they were before Katrina." His gaze fell to the sketch in the author's hands. "I don't know...I just haven't been inspired to do anything since the storm. The gallery's gone and everybody's had it so hard."

The artistic side of Charlotte understood that. It wasn't a lack of motivation as much as it was a healing. She also understood that the best method of healing for an artistic person was exactly what had happened with Alexis and the pottery. ***Her ability to create and tell her story, while releasing her pain and hurt, through her art.***

"Jeremiah," she requested, "would you consider doing some sketches for me? I'm truly moved by your work, and I'd love to have a rendering of this area pre-Katrina, during Katrina and after Katrina. Do you think you might have either the time or interest in doing those?"

There was no hesitation in his voice as he replied, "I'd love to do that. I really miss the art, but it's just like I said. I haven't had the inspiration." He looked from the sketch back to Charlotte's face. "Maybe that's what I need to get the inspiration back," he shared.

The author didn't bother to tell him that was her exact thought, and her reason for making the request.

"It might take me a few days. I need to research what I want to do and make sure I have all the details right. I have to feel it, you know...,"

"Yes, I do know," she nodded, comprehending fully the need for the divine in her creative inspiration, a factor she'd already discovered was present in this, her brother artist.

Her keen eyes examined the sketch a final time before she turned it over, hoping for a better view of the crinkles that lined the paper, void of the pencil markings. What she viewed, however, suddenly took on the role as the most dominantly striking feature of the artwork, for there was no damage -***none***- on the sketch. The back of the paper was covered with several water spots and splotches of discoloration, but not one of them had bled through to the front.

But drops of grief can ne'er repay the debt of love I owe, Here, Lord, I give myself away, 'tis all that I can do. Charlotte trembled as words to a hymn she'd played hundreds of times became as much a part of her as if they had literally been flowing through her veins.

She now understood the reason for the sudden rush of blood when her fingers first met this masterpiece. There were numerous miracles associated with this drawing, not simply the one she was still waiting to hear which was surely connected to Katrina. ***The first miracle***, she surmised, ***is the ability of Jeremiah to touch others through his gifted hands. The second miracle is the creation of the landscape depicted in the sketch, through the hands of the master Artist. The third miracle was that this sketch was still intact, with no blemish or flaw, after its encounter with the hurricane. And the fourth miracle***, she anticipated, is yet to be shared by this artist. ***But the last, and most life-changing miracle,*** she reasoned, ***is that drops of Jesus' blood, drops from that spotless Lamb of God, made the lives of all who accepted him as free of spots and blemishes as this sketch that rests in my hands.***

The rush of blood from earlier, she noticed, had turned to a placid trickling of internal peace and tranquility, the same calming qualities of peace and tranquility she could imagine being reverberated by anyone who laid eyes on the soothing scene before her, drawn with a simple pencil.

"Jeremiah, I know there's more involved with the story behind this sketch," Charlotte stated.

"Yeah, there is...," he hesitated, "but I wanted you to sense the wonder of it yourself first. I could tell it would strike you the way it did me. Like I told you, I had just completed two sketches. I had them in the back of the Jeep on a flat surface, as I had planned to take them by the art gallery. However, when the reports of Katrina threatened the Gulf, our attentions turned to securing our homes. My mind was no longer on the art gallery, much less the sketches.

"It's important here that you understand the sketches

were side by side in the back of the Jeep. When the area was flooded, the Jeep was under water for who knows how many hours. The other sketch was completely destroyed, but this one was just as you see it now."

"Did the other sketch have a church on it?" Charlotte didn't know why she even bothered to ask.

"No," Jeremiah answered, his eyes meeting hers. "No church and no angel overlooking the spot where the two rivers came together." He stood silent for a moment. "You know, this paper with pencil markings has become more than just a sketch to me. To me, it proves that God was right there with all of us during that storm. As bad as it was, He was still in the midst of it. There are so many stories of destruction and devastation which came out of Katrina, but you know, sometimes I think there are more stories of miracles. I wish the world could hear all of those, too.

"That's why I keep this drawing in my vehicle," he admitted. "It has the ability to speak to people in a way I never could."

"You're definitely right about that," agreed Charlotte. "They say a picture's worth a thousand words. I believe this picture is worth a million." She offered him a warm smile which said she was of the same heart and the same spirit of a shared artistic mind. "Do you mind if I keep this tonight and use it for our bedtime devotional with my volunteers? I'd really like for them to experience what I did with it."

"That'll be alright. I wouldn't let anyone else keep it, but I can tell you'll take good care of it." With that, Jeremiah walked back to the door and motioned for Alexis, who came running along with her two brothers.

Charlotte watched the father talking with his children about the events of the day as they left the building. She often wondered whether parents realized what rare treasures their children were. This man obviously did. It was evident in the way he spoke about them and the activities in which he participated with them, including being a coach for their athletic teams. She looked back to see Levi and the boy under the tent, whose sister was now there with him. *Too bad there aren't more parents like him.*

She looked down at the paper still resting in her hands. *And too bad there aren't more artists who not only accept, but also decipher, the gift of the Master's hands through theirs.*

17

"Who wants pizza?" inquired James when everyone was on the bus. "I'm buying."

"Only if we can invite Lena's dad," joked Brice.

"I do want to see the Yankee Stadium, though," Ebony yelled above the din of laughter, "since we're taking requests."

"I happen to know where it is," replied James. "When I was here once before with a building team, we ate our lunch there each day. There's a great Vietnamese bakery near there. One of our workers would stop and pick up pastries for us every morning. They're closed now or we could get some for breakfast tomorrow."

"Speaking of breakfast tomorrow," said Paula, "I understand you can make some mean pancakes, James."

"You wouldn't want to try out your recipe tomorrow morning, would you?" asked Brice's father.

"I suspect we could work that out," James consented.

"Now about supper, my ***real*** vote is for ice cream instead of pizza."

"Your dinner tonight is being supplied by the church where we are staying," Charlotte informed them. "They asked if we might do a Wednesday night program for them and I agreed. I felt it was the least we could do for their gracious hospitality. They've welcomed many groups from many places into their facility, and it's largely due to them, and other churches like them, that you see the recovery that you see. What impresses me most down here is it doesn't matter whether they were directly affected by Katrina or not, they are ***all***, every single one of them, appreciative and eager to show their thanks in any way they can. Therefore, tonight we're showing our thanks back to them.

"So," she concluded, "I'd like for each of you to think of the one thing which has impacted you most thus far this week and speak on it for a couple of minutes. ***Then*** we're hitting the Dairy Queen for ice cream."

"Are you sure they can stand us two nights in a row?" asked Tiffany. "We closed the place down last night."

"All this talk about ice cream is making me miss Dietsch's," said Mary Magdalena.

"What's Dietsch's?" asked Paula.

"Dietsch's is to Findlay, and everyone who's been there, what sweet tea is to the south. That was one of the first places I heard about when I arrived there and it has become a regular stop ever since. It's owned by a German family who has been making chocolates there since the 1930s. I'm not sure when they began making ice cream, but it's second to none."

"They have every flavor you can imagine and it's all made right in their facility," added Ebony, also a regular patron of the establishment. "All those chocolate pretzels, snowballs and Buckeyes you've been enjoying these past three days came from there. They were our contribution to the trip.

"And it's ***how long*** of a drive back to Findlay?" asked James.

"While you're checking the map for Ohio," interrupted Pamela, "I have a question. Did any of you notice how those kids just came in today, went straight to their group's line on the floor and listened to everything we told them, waiting from one project to the next for instructions? It's like the difference between night and day in only three days."

"I don't think we're the only ones who noticed," said Paula, nodding affirmatively with the others.

"I wish I had a dollar for every parent who came inside this afternoon and expressed their appreciation for us being here," stated Dottie.

"We've done nothing, really, but they went on and on about how their children are behaving better at home," added Marjorie.

"One mother told me her son has come home and told her every single detail of everything we've done for the past two days. She said she's never seen him go on about anything like this, even before Katrina," recalled Tiffany.

"They basically all commented on how they've not seen this side of their children since they returned here after the storm," said James.

"I even had a father tell me that his son's attitude is having an effect on the attitude of everyone in their entire family," said Brice's father. "Maybe Brice will go home with that same attitude!"

Random responses continued to trickle from the volunteers as they shared the numerous comments they'd received from the parents, all of them showering words of gratitude on the work of the volunteers.

"And my mom tricked you into thinking you were only

coming down here to make a difference in the lives of the children," said Jack. His face then spoke what was really going through his mind. "Frankly, I wish we'd see anyone from Levi's family. He's on that bus that comes in from the Boys and Girls Club and I wonder if they ever see anyone in his family either."

Following dinner, which included sundaes for dessert, Charlotte asked everyone to join her for a quick meeting. She shared her entire encounter with Jeremiah, including how much she loved his accent.

"No wonder he didn't laugh at my dress," interjected Jack when she had concluded her comments. "A basketball coach in a pink nightgown doesn't have a lot of room to talk." His statement, spoken in true sincerity, covered the extremeness and rationale brought about by Katrina, and spoke of the range of emotions tearing through the rest of the group. They were so horrified by what his mother had told them they were afraid to move, afraid to look at the PVC-pipe crosses, afraid of how they would have felt had they lived through such a holistic disaster.

"You're right," agreed his mother, seeing the need he'd fulfilled for everyone. "Before we go to bed, Jack, why don't you bring out your video of the clown making the balloon animals? You'll need a couple of volunteers to help you do that Friday.

This would be a good time for them to get some practice."

Jack headed for the supply room and the DVD, fully aware of why his mother had made this request. They all spent the next two hours in front of the television, in the same room where they'd all just shared the same heartache, laughing hysterically at the comical antics of the clown as he demonstrated the techniques of making balloon sculptures. They even watched some of the segments three and four times, laughing more raucously with each showing. All of them except Dottie's daughter, that is, who had long ago sworn off clowns.

Charlotte watched this company of "angels" from different places with great appreciation. She wasn't sure whether the video was that funny, or they were in that great a need of God's best medicine – laughter – after the clay sculptures and Jeremiah's story. The speculative author then realized that on August 29, 2005, there were a great multitude of angels who needed a good dose of laughter after the ordeals they encountered in their work for that day. ***That's why Jeremiah found it easy to laugh at the nightgown incident today.*** She sat and laughed as she "rang in" the next morning alongside the rest of her "angels."

18

"You were all so wonderfully behaved yesterday, except for that one incident, we have a special surprise for you today," Charlotte said with even more vigor than usual.

"I thought the special surprise was tomorrow," replied Lena, her shy voice vanished as she proudly boomed over the other children.

"There is a ***very*** special surprise tomorrow, but since you were so good, you get ***two*** special surprises. One today and one tomorrow."

"What's the one for today?" several of the children asked at the same time.

"Well," Charlotte spoke, now lackadaisically as she watched their energy mounting, "these past three days, you've all displayed a great love and appreciation for music. And since Mississippi's favorite son happened to be a musician...,"

"Who is Mississippi's favorite son?" interrupted the

little boy under the tent in his most innocent voice.

"Elvis," the other children screamed in unison.

"I thought it might be nice," continued Charlotte, "if we had a jukebox for you to play each time you did something considerate for one of your fellow or sister campers. But then, since I couldn't find a real jukebox down here, I figured we just have to do the best we could with what we have. So, voile," she declared as she pointed toward Jack.

"Try him out," she instructed one of the girls. "Say the name of your favorite Elvis song and poke his arm."

"Let me!"

"I want to!"

"Can I be next?"

The children raced to line up behind Jack.

"Whoa!" yelled Charlotte. "Right now, we're only demonstrating how he works. You'll get to take a turn when your group leader notices you doing something extraordinarily nice to someone else. Then you'll get a token you can take to Jack and redeem to hear your favorite song."

"Does he know any songs besides Elvis?"

"I suspect he knows most any song you want to hear. Maybe we should see if you could stump him instead."

Jack glared at his mother. "Don't push your luck," he warned, still not keen on the idea of being a human jukebox.

Charlotte was grateful when Pamela chose that particular moment to announce the quilt was completed. All eyes turned in the direction of the far right corner, where she had set up her sewing shop, to see her daughters helping her hold the finished product for all to see.

For the second time this week, the room filled with "oohs" and "aahs" as the children rushed to see their combined efforts of a ghastly story turned into a painfully beautiful work of art. Most of the volunteers wiped at their eyes as they viewed the various squares, representing a part of the story from each one of the campers. Charlotte noticed Levi's square bore only his name, but it was enough to make her realize that it spoke volumes of his loneliness, of feeling entirely alone in the world.

It* is *him and the world he lives in, she noted of his square as she watched him, robed in his black fabric Ninja garment, also staring at the brightly-colored fabric creation. The stark contrast of the gloom of his piece of fabric against the backdrop of the lively squares on the quilt gave a much larger picture than the one which most of the other eyes saw. ***Most eyes other than those of Mary Magdalena***, she observed, catching a glimpse of the heartache spilling over onto the young woman's face.

Word of something going on with the children must have spread outside the boundaries of Bay St. Louis and the nearby areas. As the children left the quilt to play the instruments, an activity which had become one of their favorites, Charlotte received a phone call from WLOX, Biloxi's television station, requesting an interview. "We'll have someone there at 11," came the confirmation from the caller.

Within minutes, Charlotte's phone was ringing continuously. Persons from newspapers, magazines and television stations were calling in hopes of an interview and a glimpse of the children. "Welcome to my world," she said apologetically, sorry for bringing all this unwarranted attention on them. Several adult volunteers went to work returning calls from media sources as Charlotte passed off her cell phone and went back to working with the children. Out-of-town stations, including the one from Charlotte's hometown in North Carolina, were hoping to use footage from their sister network's segments shot live in Bay St. Louis.

The author, who was used to interviews and reporters, was surprised when the reporter arrived from WLOX. Rather than the usual sound check and positioning of the minute microphone, he was completely motionless as his eyes moved from one group of children to the other. His moment of silence was short-lived, for the instant the children realized who he was, they all ran over to claim their "fifteen seconds of fame" in the limelight.

He took clips of the children playing the instruments, of their pottery and puppets and of the quilt. He recorded segments of answers from the campers as he gave them specific questions. His few minutes turned into nearly thirty minutes of material, which Charlotte knew would be cut into two minutes, if they were fortunate.

When he finally took the camera from his shoulder, he turned to Charlotte. "Thank you for coming. This is the first time I've seen or heard a group of children running and playing, laughing, having a good time. There are no playgrounds left, at least none in a condition where children can play on them. You don't realize how the gift you're giving them is also a gift to us adults. I can't wait for their parents to see this clip on the news. It's a side of our Gulf children that's been absent for so long we'd all forgotten it."

He then shook Charlotte's hand profusely before packing up all his equipment. "I'm sure this segment will run several times. It's something our citizens of Harrison and Hancock counties need to see."

The reporter had no longer had time to return to the station than Charlotte had a call to be at the station at 4:00 that afternoon. "The evening anchor wants to interview you live on the set as a prequel to the clip with the children."

"I have an idea," Charlotte shared immediately after lunch as she jumped on the stage. "This seems the perfect afternoon for a scavenger hunt along the beach. We're going to see what kinds of treasures we can find to put in your backpacks before you go home today."

The children and youth all broke into a huge round of thunderous applause while some of the adults glared at the author as if she'd completely lost her mind during the hustle-bustle of the morning. She didn't admit the reporter's words served as a messenger, telling her these children needed time to be outside, to run foot-loose and fancy-free on the beach. ***Well, maybe not foot-loose***, she decided, remembering the condition of the sand and the beach. "Keep your shoes on while we search for treasures," she added.

"We got ***four*** special surprises!" exclaimed Lena. "The live jukebox, the TV station, the scavenger hunt on the beach, and we still have our biggest surprise tomorrow."

"Make that five surprises," Pamela loudly pronounced.

"A reporter for a state magazine just called to say she's coming to interview you tomorrow morning and take a picture of the children."

Charlotte put her hand to her forehead and wiped her hair back from her face.

"Does this mean we're famous?" asked Lena, cocking her head to one side and shrugging her shoulders, the last remaining remnant of her shy little manner.

The naïve question made Charlotte laugh. "You're not only famous. You're ***very*** famous. There are people all over the world who know about you children and your story." ***No,*** not ***their stories***, she corrected herself. ***I've never heard anything like their stories.***

There was a unison whoop and holler as the children went wild with excitement. Charlotte thought of the television reporter's comment about this being the first time he'd seen Mississippi's Gulf children running and playing since Katrina. ***Thank you, God, for loud children who climb the walls, and for the opportunity which caused them to run and play and go wild.*** She listened to the children yelling for a moment and then added, ***And thank you, God, for the media. I had a little help down here with all this loud frivolity and laughter!***

Charlotte walked out of the station, Jack following closely behind her with Mary Magdalena and Ebony on his heels. "That's that," she said, starting the van's engine. "I'm glad those children got the attention they deserve, but we've got work waiting for us. With tomorrow being the last day we have with this group, we need to have everything organized."

"Does that mean no dinner?" asked Jack, puffing out his bottom lip.

"Doesn't she ever let up?" taunted Ebony.

Mary Magdalena gazed at the author, as if sizing her up for the first time. "Does it ever stop?"

"Does what stop?" asked Charlotte, keeping her eyes on the traffic.

"God's work?"

Charlotte never even blinked as she answered, "God never sleeps." As she stopped for a red light, she turned to the young woman in genuine earnestness. "But that doesn't mean He expects the same of us. He gave us a need to sleep, eat and take time for ourselves to rest and rejuvenate. Why do you think Jesus went to the hillside or the lake so often?

"It just so happens I find laughter and rejuvenation in the faces of these children, in the appreciative comments of their parents, in the fascination of the news reporter...," She paused as she glanced in her rear-view mirror at Jack. "And mostly in a son who refuses to let me grow up!" With that, she let out a roar of laughter.

"Mary Magdalena," she said, again serious. "God's work never stops, but we don't have to wear ourselves out trying to do all of it. Besides, if we do that, we're robbing someone else of the same type of blessing we're receiving. I know that while I'm here, I give all I have. But then when I leave here, I take time for myself, even if that time is nothing more than the twelve-hour ride home. A good night's sleep can work wonders. And then I'm ready to go again."

"Don't let her fool you, Mary Magdalena," Jack warned. "She finds time for a release from all the work wherever she goes. It's just her release is typically in the enjoyment she finds from meeting people and discovering new tidbits for her next book. Mom really gets off on that."

"He's right," Charlotte replied. "We're not all made from the same ilk, so each individual has to find his or her own way to chill. But for me, it seems God is continually throwing so many wonderful opportunities at me while I'm chilling that I merely defrost and start all over again!

"There is not a test on how much and how often you do the Lord's work. You'll learn to identify your own strengths and weaknesses and pace your own schedule. That should be true whether it involves the Lord's work, your job or your home life. It's a good rule to follow."

"But take it from me, Mom always breaks the rule. That's just her." Jack gave his mom a loving pat on the shoulder.

"It's simply my joy of life and joy of people. When I crash, I crash hard. When I play, I play hard. And when I work...,"

Her words were cut short as the other three yelled, "you work hard!" in unison.

"It's the only way I know," she admitted, not boastful, nor regretful, simply matter-of-factly. "It's who I am. God would not expect someone else to live by my pattern, and I certainly wouldn't recommend my lifestyle for anyone else."

"Any more questions?" asked Ebony. "If not, this conversation is cutting into my 'chill' time."

Charlotte used the rest of the ride from the station back to Main Street UMC to rest and rejuvenate as Mary Magdalena pondered the author's words. Jack and Ebony rested their heads on the back of the seat and closed their eyes, relaxing in their own ways.

After the hectic events of the day and all the media interviews, a relaxing walk along the sandy shore with the children, as they hunted for "treasures," had seemed a perfect ending. So perfect, in fact, it doubled as the perfect beginning for a renewal of the volunteers' baptisms at the Gulf – even though they did use water from one of the bottles they'd brought for their drinking supply. As soon as the last camper had been picked up by a parent or guardian, Charlotte led the group of volunteers back to the water's edge. There was no doubt they all felt consumed by the many various ways the Spirit had blessed the day.

"The same water, the same sand...the same love," she began. "You are ***all*** His children, in whom He is well pleased." There was not a sound as Charlotte moved from person to person, forming a cross from the water on each person's forehead and then pouring a handful of water in each one's clasped palms, which could either be used to pour over their heads, splash their faces or do whatever reminded them of their own baptism and relationship with the Holy Spirit. Not a sound, at least, until she came to Jack. She didn't fight the quiet tears of pride at her own beloved, or the beauty of the moment she had experienced at his childhood baptism, nor the shared love between a mother and child, both of whom had grown up in "the temple," as he had once called it.

When she had formed the shape of a cross on his forehead and poured the cleansing water into his palms, Charlotte then handed Jack the bottle. He repeated the process with his mother in such a poignant and touching manner that heads bowed in reverence to the same God they all worshipped, no matter their hometown, their home congregation or their denomination. The same God that had allowed all of them this same destination.

Charlotte walked down the beach, gazing across the water as it gently rolled up and sprayed the worn sand, while she uttered silent prayers. Others of the group did the same, going in the direction that each felt led as the solitude and the holiness of the moment totally consumed their individual bodies and spirits.

"Did you notice not one of us was on a time clock back there?" asked Ebony, whispering to her dearest friend so as not to break the silence that had followed them on the bus.

"I didn't, but you're right," noticed Mary Magdalena. "It was like time stood still for however long we needed in order to allow us a spirit-filled interval of renewal and reflection."

"I keep wondering if anything more awe-inspiring or humbling can happen down here," Ebony admitted, "and then it does."

It wasn't long before the bus was back in Diamondhead. Instead of their usual showers, everyone opted to hold onto the sensation of being re-baptized as long as possible, voting to take showers after dinner.

"While we're voting," said Jack, "maybe we could take a count about dinner. I know we'd planned to go to some nice place in Biloxi, but Pamela and I found a place that might be more meaningful, especially in light of what happened on the beach this afternoon."

"There's a restaurant next to the Diamondhead exit," Pamela continued. "Jack and I went there last night to catch up on old times and get away for a while."

"I'd had about all I could handle of being a constant keeper," admitted Jack. "My mom and I are not exactly made of the same ilk...at least in some departments."

"While there, we met a guy whom Jack and I think you might all like to meet."

"Actually, I think he needs to meet all of you, too," Jack said. He began to share how the man had "adopted" a boy whose mother had "jumped ship" when the going got tough following Katrina.

"He didn't even live here," explained Pamela. "He had lost his home in a tornado in Texas, and had come here to do some repair work on a house that belonged to a friend. In return, the friend gave him a place to live and food to eat until the work was finished and he could find a job."

"Shortly after he got here, though," finished Jack, "Katrina hit and...well, you can figure out the rest for yourselves. We talked to him for hours last night and told him about what we were doing here. He keeps this job as a bartender at the restaurant because it allows him to get the child off to school and be there when the child gets home every afternoon. An elderly lady comes over after the boy's asleep each night and stays until this guy can get home every morning after the bar closes."

"Do they live in a FEMA trailer?" asked Harry.

"Where else would they have to live down here?" Ebony asked as she leaned in toward Mary Magdalena.

"They weren't eligible for a FEMA trailer," explained Jack. "You had to be a tax-paying citizen to be able to get a trailer, and since he'd just moved here, he had no way to get one."

"So what ***is*** he living in?" asked Brice's father.

"A tent," answered Pamela slowly.

Jack looked earnestly at the faces of the persons who'd come to be his spiritual family. "I think he needs us as much as these children do."

The expressions on the faces of the volunteers showed the Bread of Life they were about to share was more important than any meal of which they could partake as they all packed in the bus and headed out to spend the evening with a man in need, a bartender.

Charlotte was right, mused Mary Magdalena, regretfully thinking of how many nights she'd worked in a place that had a bartender. ***Even with what I did for four years, nothing prepares you for this.*** She noticed, however, she felt no anxiousness as she stepped on the bus with others of whom she knew nothing of their backgrounds, and who also showed no fear of treading new territory.

They must have all heard the same call...

19

As many times as Charlotte had gone over the "Don't let them see you cry" speech on the bus ride to the camp on the last morning, it was her who had to first fight the urge when one of the troublemakers of the week walked in and handed her a plastic sandwich bag that contained one of the catfish bones that resembled Christ on the cross.

"I found it yesterday during our scavenger hunt," he admitted, his face beaming. "I made sure you didn't see it, and I took it home and bleached it so it would be beautiful for a long time. I wanted you to remember me."

She prayed he didn't see her straining not to choke as she tried to swallow the giant orb suddenly lodged in her throat. Fighting it back with each word, she assured him, "I don't think there's any way I could not remember you. I'm going to put this up on the wall in my office, that is, after I show it to all my friends and family when I get back home."

As she stood at the door and personally thanked each parent for the privilege of working with their child during the week, she was laden with cards and gifts, ranging from baskets of brownies for the group's ride home, to offers for dinner on their next visit to the Gulf when the parent's house would be finished.

"Isn't it strange?" asked Brice. "We came here to give them something and we're the ones going home with all the loot."

"I think that's the point of the lesson Lady Charlotte," which Tiffany was fond of calling their leader, "was hoping to teach us," she answered.

"If you think this is something," added James, who had been in Pearlington with the author previously, "wait until Friday of next week. She warned you that you wouldn't want to leave, and you will definitely be begging to come back."

"Looks like our 'strayer' is back," Ebony informed Mary Magdalena.

"What do you mean?" her friend asked, looking up from helping one of the children finish a project from the day before. "What's he doing?" she asked as she spotted Levi back in his corner, behaving exactly as he had on that first morning. "He seemed to be doing so well."

Then it struck her, the barely-noticeable twinge she'd felt each time Levi had been called "the strayer." ***He's no different from anyone else,*** she assessed, solving her quest for the reason of the twinge. ***"All we like sheep have strayed"...All that Levi needs is a shepherd, in the absence of his mother. He's a lost sheep; we've got to make sure he finds something concrete to hold onto after we're gone. We've got to find a way to make sure he knows he's in the arms of the shepherd before we leave today.*** Her thoughts all turned to a silent prayer for him and for his welfare.

"What's going on?" asked Jack as he appeared from taking a piece of fabric to the costume box, holding the hand of the small boy who'd decided he no longer needed a tent under which to hide. "What happened to my buddy?"

"You're not my friend!" Levi yelled.

"One moves forward and one moves backward," noted Paula, feeling sudden sorrow for both Levi and Jack, as she spoke of the progress of Jack's two "projects."

"Of course I'm your friend. You and I have been best buddies all week."

"If you were really my friend, you wouldn't be leaving me today. You'll go away and I'll never see you again."

Jack's heart sank as he stood there at a total loss of what to say or do next. He understood the depth of this boy's words, words he'd shared with no one besides his mother and their two dear friends. ***What would Mom do?*** Immediately he uttered a quick prayer, knowing exactly what his mother would do. ***She would ask what Jesus would do. She would try to imagine what Jesus would do in this predicament.***

As he tried to comfort Levi, other children and volunteers rallied around the pair in support. Even the little boy holding Jack's hand let go and went over to sit beside Levi, adding his newly-found confidence to the situation by placing a hand on his "buddy's" knee.

Charlotte, who had been preparing for the day's story and drama, was oblivious to the commotion until then. As she walked toward the crowd, Jack gave her an acknowledging nod. "I've got this one, Mom."

He turned to the group. "How many of you knew Jesus was with you during Katrina?"

Hands shot up throughout the children.

"How many of you were like Lena and knew that Jesus was with you when you came back after Katrina?"

Again, all the hands of the children shot into the air.

"And how many of you know Jesus is here with you now?"

Charlotte watched in awe, seeing a similar pattern to how she'd gotten out of a difficult corner on Wednesday. ***He knows what he's doing***, she observed, realizing, though, her astute son was getting Levi out of "the corner" instead of himself and the rest of the group.

"Do you think Jesus will be with you after we leave?" Jack asked, a coy smile taking the place of the serious look of the past three inquiries.

"Yes," yelled all the children in a high-spirited chorus.

"How do you know that?"

Charlotte uttered her own prayer that God had so wonderfully and poignantly rescued not only her son, but a hurting lad, from this seemingly alarming dilemma.

Answers abounded as the children each began to offer their thoughts.

"Now," said Jack, "I have one last question. Do you think we're going to be here with you, even after we leave, through the things we've done together and the many words and songs we've shared this week?"

The air was silent and faces were blank for a moment as the children began to mentally list all the ways their friendships would last after the volunteers were gone. Then, one by one until their voices again echoed off the cement-block walls, they expressed how they would remember the bond made during the past week.

Charlotte's face lit up as one African-American girl, whose vivacious enthusiasm for whatever was going on during the last four days had been an example for campers and volunteers alike, ran to stand beside Jack. It seemed that in their shared love for peanut butter, to which thankfully none of the children had been allergic, she and Jack had held a contest each day to see who could eat the weirdest thing with peanut butter. Neither of them had succumbed to a challenge, eating everything from pizza to pineapple to spaghetti with peanut butter. "I'll never eat peanut butter again without thinking of you," she declared.

That's a good thing, thought Charlotte, aware Jack had bought his culinary opponent a 4-pound container of peanut butter the evening before.

"Nor will I forget you each time I eat peanut butter," replied Jack. "And when you get that restaurant you want, I'm going to be looking for you on Oprah's show and I want to be your first customer. By the way, you'd better have peanut butter pie for me on the menu!"

The story, drama and music got waylaid in the midst of the wave of spontaneous relationships being built, all because of Levi's fear. ***A positive wave that will live on in the memories of these children***, recognized Charlotte, ***as vividly as that deadly devastating wave of Katrina.***

Her story, which would be shortened greatly and would have no drama, would be the perfect ending to the "almost storm" caused by Levi, as well as to the culmination of everything they'd accomplished during the course of the week. She went over the story in her mind, making sure she'd included every detail she wanted to mention as she left them with the message that "out of all bad things, no matter how bad they are or seem, God can make good things happen."

I Know Who Holds Tomorrow

"I've prayed about a lot of things in my lifetime, but I don't believe a carnival was one of them," Charlotte shared with the volunteers who were busily setting up for the afternoon's festivities.

"I don't think you need to pray about this one," stated Dottie. "I feel certain this will be the biggest event these children have had in quite some time."

"It's not just a good time I want them to have. I want these children to go home better than they were when they arrived here this past Monday."

"I don't think you need to worry about that either," noted Beverly, who'd just arrived and joined the group to offer her assistance. "A part of my job has been to work as a case manager for some of these children and their families. You have made a greater difference than you'll ever know. Not only in the children, but in their families, too. I dare say that sometime down the road, something you've done during the course of this week will trigger their memory and help them along the way."

Charlotte said nothing, but prayed Beverly was right.

"Looks like we're all ready," called Brice's father, whose job for the carnival was to judge the juggling contest. He'd spent the better part of the week teaching the children how to toss the three balls in the air and keep them going.

Jack had the balloons and air pumps in place for the children to make poodles, giraffes, apples, tulips and bumblebees. For those who wanted to spend tickets for a special balloon sculpture, he was ready with an assortment of designs as the "Master Balloon Sculptor."

Paula and Dottie made sure the food stations were filled with cookies, popcorn, Cheerwine and Sun-Drop while Pamela and Marjorie helped James and Brice set up the games and lay out the prizes. What the children didn't know was, in addition to the Cracker Jack prizes they could win, the volunteers had gone shopping and bought a specially-selected gift for each child to take home in his or her backpack. There was everything from Levi's basketball to Lena's "Princess" comb and brush set.

"I want every child to leave here feeling like a winner," Charlotte instructed her trusty team. "This is a no-competition event, even though there are a couple of extra contests." She called them into a huddle, where they joined hands and threw them up in the air, giving a big cheer.

"Let the carnival begin!" heralded Jack as he blew a loud whistle. No one said a word as the children ran wild, climbed the walls and yelled to the top of their lungs.

20

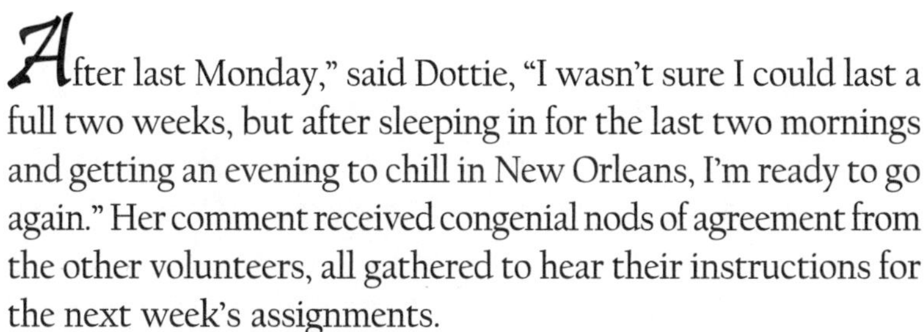

After last Monday," said Dottie, "I wasn't sure I could last a full two weeks, but after sleeping in for the last two mornings and getting an evening to chill in New Orleans, I'm ready to go again." Her comment received congenial nods of agreement from the other volunteers, all gathered to hear their instructions for the next week's assignments.

"Don't forget the trip to Orange Beach in Florida yesterday," yelled Tiffany.

"Or the meal at Lambert's Café in Foley, Alabama, on the way there," reminded Pamela.

"Hey, I liked them throwing the rolls at us," stated Brice. "Do you think we'd get in trouble if we did that at school?" he asked Paula, who happened to be ***his*** math teacher. Her sideways glance obviously gave him all the answer he needed as he added, "Nah, I guess we'd better not."

"This week's going to be a breeze," noted Marjorie. "All

we have to do is repeat everything we did last week and we're home free."

"Minus the Ninja," begged Jack, pretending to fall on his knees at Marjorie's feet, his hands in a praying position.

"I hate to burst your bubbles," Charlotte spoke as she walked into the room. "We may be doing the same activities, but the children of Mississippi are exactly like the state flower."

"Huh?" asked Brice, fearing his forthcoming words were going to take more brain power than he was willing to give at the moment. "I know Mississippi is called 'the Magnolia State.' What do the children have to do with a flower?"

"Good point!" acknowledged Charlotte. "I was hoping one of you would catch that. Magnolias are like snowflakes. No two are alike. What I've learned about all the children I've come in contact with down here is exactly that - no two are alike. Even though they all endured Katrina, every story is different. Every loss is different. The only thing the same is they all lost something.

"Think about the magnolia. It's an evergreen, full of life year round. Children are full of life. Through the turmoil the adults are trying to cope with, it's the children who are their bright spots, who give them the inspiration, the desire to keep going. Think about the magnolia's leaves. They're tough and leathery. These children are extremely resilient. They've proven that they can sustain a lot and keep on ticking, although for many of them, their tickers are somewhat disturbed at the moment. But they'll get back to where they were, even though the scenery around them and the material things won't. Lastly, think of the majestic petals. Most of the magnolias we see have nine petals, in three layers, but there can be as many as fourteen petals. I think of those various petals as the talents and characteristics of each child. Those petals, together forming such a beautiful creation, can go from a startlingly beautiful magnolia blossom to having lost its vigor in only one day, depending on the temperature...the weather. But then another season comes and the glorious beauty returns."

Understanding eyes and nods of heads showed her listeners had comprehended her analogy.

"How did she come up with that?" Ebony asked, turning to Jack.

"Don't look at me. She's always coming up with examples like that. It's like she draws them out of a hat for whatever circumstance she's in."

"But she's exactly right," noted Marjorie.

"There's definitely a method in her madness," agreed Dottie.

Charlotte smiled at all the comments. "Now that I've gotten your attention, I'd like to tell you something about Pearlington."

"Here we go," joked Ebony, "another briefing session. I think she's taking this recruitment business a little too far. I feel like I belong to the Marines instead of a mission team."

"Stop it!" scolded Mary Magdalena. "You're going to make her mad, or at best hurt her feelings."

"Not Mom," Jack stated. "When it comes to children, she lets nothing stand in her way as long as she gets what she wants. And what she wants here is for us to give the children the best experiences we can. She'll accept no less. I've seen her in action before."

The group listened with increasing sorrow to the accounts Charlotte shared of the devastation in the area of Pearlington, the area where they would be working for the next week. "The location is at one of the old schools. What you'll see is the only building left from the entire school. You'll also see 'Pearlmart,' the building that had been a part of the middle school, which became the local distribution center for their necessities since even the nearest convenience store was twelve miles away.

"I don't think I'll ever laugh at getting underwear for Christmas again," said Brice. "I never realized what a commodity that and toothpaste were." His effort to be funny turned into a powerfully prophetic statement.

"If Pearlington was so far off the coast, why did they suffer so much damage?" asked Pamela.

Charlotte went on to explain how the surge of the Gulf literally swallowed the Pearl River, and everything in its path.

"This topic started out so beautifully, with the subject of beautiful magnolia petals, and went downhill from there. Just when I said it couldn't get any worse," said Mary Magdalena, "it did."

"I think we'd all better turn in," stated Ebony, speaking for the rest of the group. "Monday may not be so easy after all."

The group joined hands and said a sentence prayer, just like they'd all done as young children. Each volunteer lifted up a special need or desire for the upcoming week before James ended with asking God to grant them the same blessings with the children of Pearlington that they'd experienced with the children of Bay St. Louis.

21

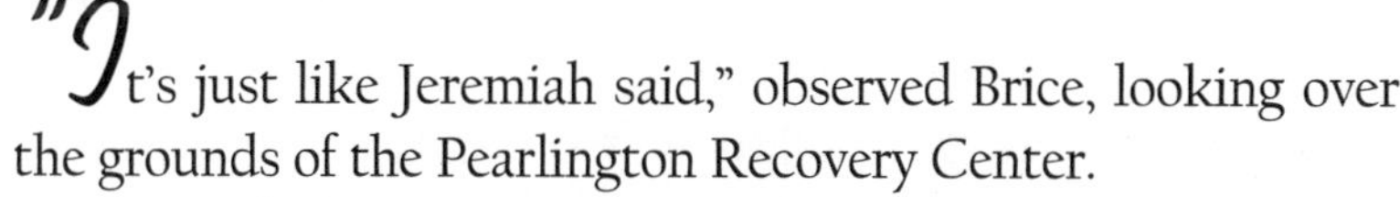

"It's just like Jeremiah said," observed Brice, looking over the grounds of the Pearlington Recovery Center.

"What was it someone said about when you thought it couldn't get any worse, it did?" asked Dottie.

"This breaks my heart," Paula uttered in a non-descript voice. "To think there was a whole school here where children once ran and played."

"Think of it in a positive light," Charlotte said with her usual ray of encouragement. "It could be lots worse. This facility has been remodeled and is in good shape. You'll be amazed when you see all that's been done to make this a viable safe haven for children once you go inside. This is where we worked this past January as the clearinghouse for our books. James and his wife spent many hours here, as did Brice's mom. There have been many changes here just since then." She didn't bother to tell them how grateful she was they didn't see it as she'd first seen it.

Tiffany turned her focus from the yard, which was barren except for the huge tents and "Pearlmart," to the wall which welcomed them. "Look at that!"

Everyone's eyes moved to the brightly-colored sign that covered the front of the one remaining building. At the top of the sign was a huge red border with large white letters spelling the word "Pearlington," and on the bottom was the same border with blue letters spelling "Mississippi," both borders also bearing big white hearts. Between the borders was a picture that resembled something a kindergartener might draw, complete with a light-blue sky, green grass, a bright-blue river, a tree with lots of green leaves and a stocky brown trunk, white clouds and a bright yellow sun. The only thing out of the ordinary from what any child in America might have drawn was the tall rocket ship over to the right of the picture, symbolizing the fact that NASA owned the land west of Pearlington all the way to the Louisiana border, in its entirety.

As the volunteers unloaded the bus to get a better view of the sign, they noticed it was covered in names of other volunteers who had come here from around the world as a part of the recovery effort.

"Look!" exclaimed Tiffany's sister. "The largest name on the sign is from North Carolina."

"Can we sign it?" asked Brice's sister.

"You bet we can!" answered Charlotte. "We want the world to know God left His mark here through us, and it's a much larger mark than the one left by Katrina."

"I wonder how many names are on here," Dottie's daughter pondered aloud.

"A bunch," replied Paula, with no need of her math skills.

Marjorie pulled a Sharpie pen from her purse and passed it around, making sure everyone who wanted to leave their mark got the opportunity.

"It makes you see just how small you are in comparison to the rest of the world, doesn't it?" asked Brice's father.

"Yes, but at the same time, it allows you to realize you *are* a part of the grand scheme of things," answered Charlotte.

"It really is all connectional, isn't it?" queried Mary Magdalena. Her question left the rest of the volunteers' comments hanging, unspoken, in the air.

"Good morning!" Jeanne Brooks greeted Charlotte with her usual glowing face, twinkling eyes and friendly hug. "The children and I have all been so excited about your arrival we could hardly stand it."

Jeanne - who once served as the librarian at the school which had stood here, and who had been the contact for Charlotte's work in the Pearlington area - then turned to Mary Magdalena and also gave her a cordial hug. "It's nice to see you again."

Mary Magdalena stared, her mouth gaping open, at the woman who'd been seated beside her on the return flight home from Mississippi at spring break. ***The woman who shared the hymn title and the words* I Know Who Holds Tomorrow *with me!***

"I'm glad to see the rest of the books all arrived safely," stated Charlotte, "and are still here," she added with a quiet chuckle. She walked toward three pallets of books and began ripping into the boxes. Getting a head start on their duties for the upcoming week, she began to sort the books for Jeanne and the new soon-to-open South Hancock Elementary School.

"Yes, after that last fiasco, when the delivery driver couldn't find the school...,"

"...because it was no longer here...," Charlotte hastily interjected.

"...I made sure someone here was on the lookout for him this time." Jeanne turned to Mary Magdalena and explained how a shipment of several pallets of books had arrived from the author back in January. "The only problem was the driver, from Louisiana, had no clue this building is still known to everyone around here as the old Charles B. Murphy School. Since he drove the books here and saw no school, the pallets were all carried back to New Orleans. There was a huge mess in trying to get them delivered back to the right place, but they finally got here."

"Only after Jeanne's relentless badgering and refusal to allow someone else to be the recipients of books we'd worked to collect for her school for two years," Charlotte added with a slight snicker.

"Even if that had meant driving to Louisiana and bringing them back here, a few boxes at a time."

"If there's anyone in the world who will go to any extreme to make life and education better for her students, it's Jeanne Brooks. I've never met anyone who loved her job and her students any more than this woman. Not only that, she'll fight anyone who gets in her way if she sees a person standing in the way of her students' learning opportunities. And that 'anyone' has occasionally been a 'thing.'"

"Are you sure you two aren't sisters?" Mary Magdalena inquired, noting the likenesses in the dispositions of the women before her.

The author and librarian exchanged humored glances.

"I'll leave you here to sort books," Jeanne said to Charlotte. "If there's anyone I know who's as picky about books as I am, it's you. Keep the helpers you want and I'll take the rest to organize your workspace for the camp this week. The children will be arriving in approximately one hour."

Mary Magdalena and Ebony stayed back with Charlotte as Jeanne left with the rest of the volunteers.

"Did you know all along?" Mary Magdalena asked.

"Know what?" Charlotte responded.

"That your Jeanne was the same librarian I met on the airplane back from Mississippi this past Easter?"

"I had a strong suspicion."

"Why didn't you say something?"

"It wasn't God's time. He wasn't through planting the seed in you."

Mary Magdalena waited for more of an explanation, but seeing there was none, ventured, "What seed?" She sensed the answer would be similar to the author's illustration of the magnolia, the snowflakes and the children from the evening before.

Charlotte, continuing to take books from the boxes and sort them by reading levels, responded, "Do you remember the morning you got behind the dump trucks filled with sand on your way to Florida?"

"Yes, I remember it well, but what does that have to do with this truckload of books?"

"Nothing...at least that I know of, but what it does 'have to do with' was you finding that 'perfect man' – the same 'perfect man' you told me you'd gone to find the Easter when you decided to say 'Good riddance' to Northern Exposure. Those dump trucks didn't just magically appear one Monday morning. And all the delays you encountered the evening before, when it became impossible for you to reach your destination, were not solely for your benefit. However, they ***did*** allow you to be where you needed to be when you needed to be there."

"Okay, I'm a little bit confused now," stated Ebony, her comment totally ignored by the other two women.

"And then, do you think it was by accident that you found your way to Miller's and met Joni?" continued Charlotte. "Who, I might add, is still a dear friend and sounding board for you? It's her who's pulling your load so you can be here these two weeks."

"What about me?" asked Ebony, still going unnoticed. "She's pulling my load, too."

"***And*** if you'll recall," Charlotte went on, "I prayed for us to touch the life of someone in a moving way at Court Street."

"I should just be moving out of the way of you two," said Ebony.

"Followed with a prayer that at least one of us would receive an extra blessing through their congregation," Mary Magdalena offered slowly, finally working her way through the maze of questions which the author had been leading her. "Then, in speaking to that one lady, their choir director, I learned she, too, had a connection with Italian missionaries and our families knew each other."

"I'm glad someone in this crowd has a connection that matters," declared Ebony, shaking her head.

Charlotte nodded. "A seed was planted. A seed that was planted many years ago, back when your grandparents began their work, and that seed continued to grow and bloom and blossom into another branch, you. That seed also drops seeds along the way which sprout into plants bearing other seeds."

"Excuse me, all this talk about seeds is making me hungry," voiced Ebony. "Tomatoes, anyone?"

The choir director at Court Street also bloomed and blossomed into a flowering branch, whose voice is more grand

and glorious than the birds that fly among the branches. Look how many people she touches in her capacity at that multi-cultural church in the Hattiesburg area and at the William Carey University where she teaches, where she plants other seeds. Your meeting her was no coincidence."

Mary Magdalena smiled. "Nor was I in that seat on the airplane, next to Jeanne, by accident."

"Speaking of seats, I think I'll have one," said Ebony, sitting on one of the nearby boxes of books.

"You get an A+!" Charlotte exclaimed in her best congratulatory tone. "You will run into others during this trip who will impact your life greatly. You may see them again many times, or you may not see them at all, but it's like Jack explained to the children. It only takes a moment to plant a seed that can grow and grow and grow for many generations."

"I'm growing tired from all this talk," Ebony stated with a yawn.

For the first time, Charlotte looked up from the boxes of books. "***Why*** do you think the Bible goes through all that 'begat' stuff? It's important for people to not only see, but understand, the significance of the root of the tree, and the importance of the branches." She gave a somber smile. "It's also important that we understand we are all 'begat' – that we are all a part of that rich heritage, and that we are all descendants of that root. We are all seeds."

"Well, I'm glad we got all of that straight," mumbled Ebony, talking only to herself and the concrete wall of the room.

"Wow!" Mary Magdalena was so overjoyed her face shone like a child who'd just received the greatest birthday present of her life.

Which, Charlotte mused, ***was the greatest "birth" day present of her life.*** For even though it wasn't the anniversary of Mary Magdalena's birth, the astute author was certain it was an invaluable comprehension on the part of this young woman of her role in society, her place in all the "begats" and a deeper appreciation of the fact she had been born of such a rich heritage – ***a deeply planted seed***.

Charlotte had long before determined God was only beginning with this young woman who would plant many seeds in her lifetime. She looked at the other young woman, now sleeping on the boxes, and thought of the disciples who had also fallen asleep while their beloved friend was in the garden.

22

The first three days of the second week sped by pretty much on automatic pilot for the volunteers, at least as far as the activities went. But certainly not in the emotional department as they wound their way to the quiet and secluded location of the Pearlington Recovery Center each day.

Although there were less than fifteen miles distance between the locale of last week's camp and this week's camp, it could very easily have been a few hundred. The topography was totally different. Where one lay within view of the beach and was covered in sand, the other lay five miles off the coast's beaten path and was covered in dirt. The open sky that surrounded the Gulf's water was replaced by branches of hanging trees that created a natural sanctuary. Rows of casinos, exploding with bright lights and bursting forth with lavishness as they sought to rebuild their once-overflowing clientele, were a far cry from the vast stretches of stripped and beaten land with only a lone tent, FEMA trailer or house covered in tarp or battered boards.

Although rows of bright pastel FEMA cottages were popping up in one area like budding spring flowers, the other was still struggling with simply affording demolition crews just to clear a spot which they could once again call their "own."

The one connecting factor between these two seemingly opposite poles was a living hell on earth. A storm that blew in with a rush of the demons, but was no match for God's lasting and redeeming love. Sure, neither of the places would ever look the same again. Decades of time would cover the nakedness of the ground and forests, as grass, shrubs and trees would again take root. And experiences and life in general would mute the physical anguish over years. But nothing would lessen the harshness of what these survivors had been dealt, sealed by the scars that would forever remain etched on the minds, on the analogs of memories, of all who had endured a fast, but forcefully furious, Hurricane Katrina.

Especially the children, mused Mary Magdalena as she watched the youngsters move from table to table, setting about the tasks - or in this case, art projects - that had been laid before them. She glanced in the direction of Alexis, who with her two brothers, were here for the week. Alexis looked up in time to catch her stare and held up the picture she was drawing, which was of the boat. A young girl, approximately of the same age, also held up her drawing. It was of a Virgin Mary statue which greatly resembled an angel on the paper and was the same thing she'd drawn each day of this week.

As despicable as the occurrence which had led to this day, she glimpsed a thread of strength interwoven in the makings of these children. It was there, as visible as a thread hanging from a garment, not in sync with the rest of the garment, but nevertheless there, for all the world to see. It was evident in their faces and in their body language. ***And, yes, it is evident in their voices, too,*** she determined, listening to them sing as they worked.

"Are you okay?" asked Ebony.

"Yes...no...I don't know...,"

"Well, you can't get any clearer than that." Ebony's sarcastic comment brought the hint of a familiar smile to the face of her best friend. "Maggie, ol' girl," she said, reminiscing back to their "Exposure" days, "there's something going on inside of you. It's as plain to me as it was when you were toying with the idea of putting Ypsilanti, Michigan and that horrid lifestyle behind you."

"Maybe I'm pregnant," teased Mary Magdalena.

"C'mon, now, girl. You can't fool Bubbling Brown Sugar. I know better than that."

"Okay," Mary Magdalena chuckled. "But what if I were great...with a brainchild...one of putting something into the lives of these children rather than putting something behind me."

"Don't be goin' there. I'm not ready to be a godmother yet!"

"C'mon, now, girl," mimicked Mary Magdalena. "You know we're like peas in a pod. Who else to help with whatever is going on with me?"

"I only have one thing further to say on the matter at the moment. You just make sure it stays a 'brainchild' and not some 'hair-brained' idea."

Charlotte called the activity to an end as the children made a huge semi-circle, anxious to get their hands on the drums and the instruments. The size of the room had caused changes in the layout of the activities, but this one Mary Magdalena loved. She could now watch the faces of all the children at the same time as they played and sang.

It had become evident on the first day at Pearlington

that one of the older guys was a natural-born percussionist. Charlotte had made him the leader with the drums, allowing him the chance to hone his God-given talent. She also quickly discovered that these children were adept at playing the small colored-plastic handbells she'd brought. It was only halfway into the week and these campers were already "rocking and rolling" the building with strains of ***Amen*** and ***This Little Light of Mine***, both songs of the campers' choosing.

Even their choice of songs shows their strong spiritual backgrounds, surmised Mary Magdalena, noticing that every one of the children knew all the words to the songs. She turned to Ebony. "Isn't it funny that Katrina rocked and rolled their houses, and tore the roofs off most of them, yet here they are, young children, 'raising the roof' with songs of praises in their love and devotion to God?"

"What isn't funny is over half these children still go home to FEMA trailers and tents when they leave here every afternoon."

Mary Magdalena's looked around the room at the children singing and making music, all of them participating and having great fun, as the merriment written on their faces expressed. "Ebony, have you noticed that not one child, ***not one***, has uttered a single complaint? Not last week, nor this week?"

"You're right. They've learned the lesson that it isn't about ***what*** you have, but ***Who*** you have that holds the key to happiness. They've learned at an early age what the ***real*** priorities in life are. I hope it's a lesson which remains with them throughout their lifetimes. It was a lesson that kept my grandmother happy with what she had."

"I almost feel the unfortunate ones are the ones who will never learn that lesson, who will never know the joy we're seeing on the faces of all these children right now." Mary Magdalena felt the swell within her own soul as she recognized the lesson she had learned through these children. No longer did she feel driven by owning "things." What mattered to her most at this very moment was realizing she'd had a part in helping put the vibrant glows on the faces in front of her. She had shown them love, and they had in return given her a love she'd never forget.

23

"Of course the phone decides to ring now," Charlotte said, sardonically, as she led the convoy of vehicles and volunteers from the two-lane road onto the ramp that led to the four-lane highway that would take them to Hattiesburg and Court Street United Methodist Church.

"Do you mind playing secretary?" she directed toward Mary Magdalena. "It's probably Jack with a question, but if it's anything important, could you take a message and tell them I'll get back to them? I really need to watch the road. I get turned around every time I get into the historic section of Hattiesburg and that's where the church is." She watched her directions and navigated while Mary Magdalena answered the phone. "Hello...no, I'm sorry, this is her secretary. Could I take a message? I'm afraid she's in the middle of something at the moment." There was a moment of silence before she said, "No, she hasn't heard from them."

Charlotte glanced in "her secretary's" direction, wondering from whom she had not heard.

"Yes, I'm positive. She'd have mentioned that if they'd called." There was a long hesitation. "I see... I'll give her the message."

Mary Magdalena hung up the phone and looked down at her lap. "Uh, Charlotte," she stammered, "uh... that was the secretary at the Pearlington Recovery Center."

"What did she want?"

"Uh..., uh..., she uh...,"

Charlotte looked with expectant eyes at the young woman who'd taken over playing secretary for her, and then quickly shifted her focus back to the road.

"She uh...wanted to let you know that...that...," Mary Magdalena took a deep breath and spit out the rest, hoping that would ease the blow. "The television station is sending a reporter and cameraman to go with us on the alligator cruise tomorrow."

"They're doing ***what?***" Charlotte bolted, her head spinning sharply toward her messenger.

"Uh...,"

"Don't tell me there's more," the author said disparagingly, sensing more words on the way.

"The newspaper is sending a reporter, too," added Mary Magdalena, rushing to get out the words.

Charlotte gave a long, deep breath which was followed by a slow sigh, her eyes glued to the road in front of her as if she were in a trance. "Well," she finally managed, "I guess we might as well get it all over and out of the way at one time." Her voice was tinged with anguish. "All I can say is that they'd better not get in the way of our good time."

She said nothing for a few minutes and then looked at Mary Magdalena. "I guess it's okay. Those children will feel like a big star if they get to be on TV." A slight smile appeared on her face. "And they are stars, you know...every single one of them."

Mary Magdalena smiled, glad no storm was ensuing from the news of yet another round of reporters. "Yes, I do know."

"I heard that!" exclaimed Ebony, throwing out the three words that had been her trademark with the girls at Northern Exposure.

Isn't it funny? Mary Magdalena thought to herself. ***I haven't heard those words come out of her mouth in three years, but they sound like salve to the soul.*** She realized that the past was not forgotten, it hadn't completely faded away, yet reminders of those days she'd spent denying her upbringing and her heritage no longer hurt.

"That's tomorrow," Charlotte commented after a while, having mulled over the situation. "I refuse to worry about it today." She gave a satisfied chuckle. "Besides, if God is okay with our time with the children being made public, so be it!" she declared decisively. "It might be the icing on the cake."

"I thought you told us we already had an iced cake for the party after the cruise," replied Ebony.

Mary Magdalena and Charlotte glanced at each other before turning their heads to look at Ebony in the back seat, both saying loudly, "I heard that!" With that statement, they turned into the parking lot of Court Street United Methodist Church.

When everyone was off the bus, Charlotte had them to join hands. "This is a new and different experience for most of you, and especially you teens. Court Street had done what all churches are called to do, and that is minister to everyone. This is going to be quite different from what you see when you walk into your middle-class, all-white church on Sunday morning.

Yet, what you feel should be exactly the same thing you feel every Sunday morning. If it isn't, then you need to pack yourselves a bag of whatever they serve here this evening and take it home to your own churches."

"I just got a whiff of the chicken tetrazzini they're serving for dinner and I'm taking a big bagful home," stated Ebony, as she returned from carrying a box of supplies into the church. "You talk about home cooking, ummm, ummm. From the looks and smells of things I passed on my way through that building, it looks like my grandmother could have risen from the grave and spent all afternoon here in their kitchen."

Her comment received lots of anxious stares, their owners all ready for a scrumptious home-cooked meal.

"I heard that!" yelled everyone at the same time.

"It would appear that God has already taken care of things, at least the important things, before our arrival. Let's go in and serve the Lord together. Amen!"

The teenagers rushed to the door while the adults stood for a moment in the parking lot, basking in the moment of silence, aware that within the next two hours, their entire beings would be fed.

24

The giggles of delighted enthusiasm and the twinkles in the children's eyes were enough to make Charlotte forget the television reporter who was already at the Pearlington camp when she arrived on Thursday morning. He was so unobtrusive in his actions that the author determined he would be a terrific "behind the scenes" reporter. ***Which is a good thing***, she decided, positive a boatload of children in an alligator swamp needed no extra attention.

Volunteers and campers alike piled into the big yellow school bus that carried them to Slidell, Louisiana, the location of Cajun Encounters Swamp Tour. Bug spray, ball caps and sunscreen abounded as the children prepared to board one of the four boats that would carry them through the swamps in search of "Big Al." It was a successful day, as many of the children saw the famed gator open his mouth wide to chomp down on the marshmallows thrown at him by the boat's driver and guide.

It was a day filled with perfect weather for the perfect outing, complete with a gargantuan-sized cake in the shape of an alligator, made by a baker famous for his King cakes in the Picayune area. He had decorated it to look exactly like Big Al. Children called out which piece of the gator they wanted as two adult volunteers cut the cake and Tiffany and her sister served it. Brice and his dad took care of serving the Cherry-Lemon Sun-Drop to cap off the perfect day. ***A far stretch from the day that brought us all together***, Charlotte observed, watching the gleeful faces of each child. ***And of each volunteer***, she added, peering at the faces of the youth and adults who'd come to offer a blessing, but rather, had been blessed.

"It ***is*** a perfect day!" she heralded, more to herself than anyone else.

"Hey, Ms. Charlotte, I'm glad I caught you. I was afraid ya'll would be gone for the day, and I knew I wouldn't get here tomorrow before you left for North Carolina, or wherever it is you're going from here. One thing my children have learned during the past two weeks is that you get around."

Charlotte instantly recognized the welcome voice and turned to see Jeremiah. "You could say that, but this time, I ***am*** going back to North Carolina. I'm looking forward to a couple of weeks in my own home." Immediately she wished she could retract the words as she faced this man who'd lost two homes and was still working on one.

"It's alright," Jeremiah assured her, seeing the regret plastered all over her face.

In her effort to backtrack and start anew, she added, "I'm glad for this chance to tell you how wonderful it has been to spend another week with three of your children. They are all so different, yet each has an enchanting characteristic. I can't believe all this artistic talent landed in one family."

"That's why I'm here," he said quietly, causing Charlotte to immediately appreciate his modest demeanor. "I have something for you."

Charlotte stood silent as he pulled two sketches from a thick, oversized cardboard envelope.

"If you don't like them, or you've seen something else you'd rather have, please let me know," he told her.

She felt the emotion of the drawings seep through the paper and into her fingers as she stared at the sharp, clear details of Jeremiah's work, every bit as astonishing as the sketch of the church he'd earlier shown her. The first one was of the boat that had landed on the car.

"I knew you said you'd seen that scene. I thought it might be nice if I did something you could relate to." He waited as she lifted that one to get a view of the other one. "I did a lot of research, but I kept coming back to this one. It's the scene I think is the most recognized picture of the destruction in Pearlington."

"I've seen this one, too," she observed. "It tore at me the very first time I came here after Katrina, and it is still just as gut-wrenching every time I go past it," she said of the sketch depicting the place where the Catholic Church once stood.

Mary Magdalena neared the couple. "I hate to interrupt, Charlotte, but you have a phone call. Shall I take a message?"

"Yes, please." As the young woman turned back toward

the building, Charlotte called her back. "Take a look at this, Mary Magdalena. You will especially appreciate it given your Catholic background."

Mary Magdalena's mouth fell open as she stared at the drawing, the same image which the child inside had repeatedly done so primitively. Every detail in this man's artwork was so crystal clear she felt she could reach out and touch it, yet there was such an unspoken mystique about it she shuddered where she stood.

"This statue of the Virgin Mary was all that was left of one of the nearby churches," shared Jeremiah, "except for the front two steps where you see her now standing. Someone picked her up and placed her on the front step, since that's all that was left of the church," he explained. "Her head was messed up, but I didn't want it that way for you. She looks the way she did before the storm because that's the way I still see her...just as she was when I grew up here."

Charlotte carefully scanned the sketch, observing and appreciating each minute detail. What spoke to her most about it was the way the Virgin Mary's arms were outstretched, not bothered whatsoever by the effects of the storm, as she still welcomed passersby to "the church" - a holy place of worship. She'd always known a church was not the building, but rather the people inside. In her hands lay living proof.

Jeremiah noticed her eyes frozen on the one odd feature of the drawing. "I did put the baby doll at her feet on the front step, though," he added, "just as she appears now. Someone, probably some child, found that doll lying nearby following Katrina and placed it at her feet." He waited. "Like I said, if they're not what you want, I'll be glad to do something else."

"They're perfect, Jeremiah," she assured him, still staring at the pencil lines that spoke so strongly of a once-before community and the memories of a man who had lived there, and of a ruinous storm that robbed him of that rural, scenic beauty. His sketch said to her that he would rebuild and be stronger than ever, just as this place would once again be a restful solace to the inhabitants who withstood the adversity of a nightmarish monster called Katrina. "They're exactly what I want."

Charlotte looked down at the sketch still in her hand, mesmerized that her life had been forever touched by two artful masters in two different Hancock Counties, yet whose hands were led by the same Master. ***And that both of their meaningful works of art came about due to strange occurrences of nature - one who didn't receive the usual mass of snow, and the other who received more of a storm than anyone should ever have to endure.*** "I wanted to take something home to remind me of this place and of the people. Your work has provided exactly that, Jeremiah. There's no way I can ever forget Hancock County or all these precious children. Especially when I look at these."

She extended her hand. "Thank you." The author then whispered something in Mary Magdalena's ear, causing her to rush back inside the building. In a matter of seconds, she was back with Charlotte's purse. Reaching into it, the author asked, "How much?"

"I didn't do these for the money. I wanted to do them for you. I think I needed this to prompt me into getting back into my art and I was grateful for the opportunity."

Charlotte wrote a check and handed it to him. "Put this on something for your house that will be a reminder for you to continue with your art. I'll accept your art as a gift, but in turn, I want you to accept that gift from me."

Jeremiah smiled and gave an understanding nod.

The author watched admiringly as he went as quietly as he came. ***Such an unassuming person***, she observed as he drove away with his three children whom he'd shared with her during the past two weeks. ***The world needs more like him.***

She turned to eye the children who were still left. The one family of eight children who had lost everything, and still had no home, yet whose mother not only had cooked a delicious Cajun meal for all the volunteers for one day's lunch, but also brought it and served it to them under the big outdoor tent. ***The same tent where hundreds of people were fed daily following the storm. The same tent where, no doubt, these same eight children had partaken of many meals following the devastation. The same family who realized the value of their closeness and their role of support in the community***, as Jeanne had shared of the parents of these eight children who stayed actively involved in whatever was going on in the lives of their children. ***Which shows,*** Charlotte noted, witnessing how well groomed and dressed the children were – clean clothes, no wrinkles, pride in themselves – even without the luxury of material "things." ***They will make it – all of them!*** she deduced, appreciating their respect of others and others' property. ***The world needs more like them.***

The boy who had smiled as largely as if all had been right with the world from the moment she'd first laid eyes on him, and was still smiling as he wore the big crocodile hat she'd brought for the "Citizen of the Day" to wear. ***The world needs more like him***.

The girl who sat alone at a table and drew angel after angel on sheets of drawing paper, giving one to each volunteer. ***A girl who's obviously seen plenty of angels unaware in her short lifetime... and recognizes them.*** Charlotte smiled. ***The world needs more like her***.

The list went on and on as the author made mental notes of the unique traits and abilities of each child, storing them for a lasting treasure in the caverns of her mind. ***The world needs***

more like them.

"Look what I have," stated Mary Magdalena. "It's just like yours, minus a few years of skilled experience and strokes of practice."

Charlotte looked down to see the paper that had just been handed to Mary Magdalena by the young girl drawing all the angels. Suddenly she realized the image on the paper was not an angel at all, but rather an amateur attempt at the same image of the Virgin Mary in her sketch by Jeremiah. "But where's the doll?" she asked, noting its absence in the girl's impression of the statue.

"I don't know. Maybe she hasn't seen it lately, or at least since the doll was placed there. Why don't we take Jeremiah's rendition over and show her? Since she's seemingly so captivated by the statue, perhaps she'd like to add the doll to her drawings."

"Good idea!"

"Angelina?" Mary Magdalena called, interrupting the girl's next drawing of the statue.

Angelina? Charlotte repeated to herself. ***Talk about an appropriate name!***

"I have something I'd like to show you," said Mary Magdalena as Charlotte held Jeremiah's sketch at eye-level for her to see. "Do you see anything different in this drawing from yours?"

"Uh-huh," answered Angelina nonchalantly in her soft, sweet voice, unmoved as her hand continued to draw while she snatched a quick glance at the professional sketch. "My doll."

"Your doll?" inquired Charlotte.

"Uh-huh," replied Angelina, this time without even bothering to look up from her work.

"The doll in the sketch is your doll?" questioned Mary Magdalena, beginning to feel like a detective.

"Uh-huh," came the same answer for a third time, this time expected by the two interrogators.

Mary Magdalena and Charlotte glared at each other, both impatiently awaiting the truth of how the doll landed at the foot of the statue, an answer obviously long in coming.

"Your doll was found at the foot of the statue?" Mary Magdalena finally ventured.

"No, it was found by some nice lady nearly a half-mile from my house after the hurricane."

"And she put it at the foot of the statue?" Charlotte asked.

"No. She asked around until she found out it was my doll. She told my daddy she suspected it was the only thing I would ever see of my toys again and she was determined to get it back to me." Still her eyes remained glued on the paper with her drawing.

"So your father put it on the statue?" Mary Magdalena felt like she was pulling a never-ending rope.

"No." Angelina finished her drawing, handed it to a volunteer along with a hug and immediately reached for a new piece of paper.

"How exactly did the doll wind up with the statue?" Charlotte inquired, surmising this was more difficult than digging up answers to any research she'd ever done with her books.

"I put it there. When my father took me to get the doll and we were walking back to my house, I saw the statue on the steps. She looked so sad without her baby Jesus. I asked my daddy if it would be okay if I gave her mine 'cause I figured she needed it worse than I did. She looked very lonely without her baby. At least I still had my mommy and daddy and my baby sister to keep me company. Mary didn't have a house or a baby left."

Angelina stopped moving her crayon and looked up for

the first time since the questioning had begun. "That's why there's no doll in my pictures. I gave it to Mary." Her face was expressionless as she presented her listeners with the well-sought answer that left them with a "Well, Duh!" punch.

Both Mary Magdalena and Charlotte stood speechless as they watched the young girl go back to drawing with her crayon. Their glares at each other moved to her paper as they watched her finish another picture.

"Here," Angelina announced, handing her work of art to Charlotte after she had signed it with an assortment of upper and lowercase letters spelling out her name. "I saved yours 'til last." She gave the author a long, hard hug with the tightest squeeze she could muster. "I want to write children's books just like you, except I want to draw the pictures in mine."

The lump in Charlotte's throat would not be ignored. She prayed Angelina could not feel the tears falling onto her light blonde tresses as the child's arms remained firmly locked in a bear hug.

Content she had accomplished her mission of leaving a gift with all the volunteers, Angelina ran to another table to make a craft of her own to take home.

It was then Charlotte realized she was humming the notes of an old hymn a great-uncle had loved to sing during her childhood visits to his home on Sunday afternoons. She kept humming, trying to recall the words until they came... ***When the storms of life are raging, stand by me.***

She glanced over the room filled with children, paying particular attention to the parents arriving to take them home. ***There's not one of them who hasn't stood by Him in the raging storms.*** Charlotte peered at the two sketches still in her hand. ***Or didn't recognize He was standing by them, too, in the rage of Katrina.***

The words of the hymn formed into song as the author

began to sing, suddenly aware that every "storm" she had faced in life had made her a stronger person. ***And shaped my life so that one day I would come to Mississippi to show love to these children.***

That's what prepared me, Charlotte concluded, looking into the face of the young woman standing beside her. She shared her finding with Mary Magdalena – glad she could provide the answer to her young friend's question before her return to Hancock County, Ohio – even if it had taken over five decades to discover.

Five decades? Charlotte laughed to herself. ***When you think of it that way, Angelina didn't take so long to answer our question after all!***

PART THREE

Mary Magdalena stood in Riverside Park, on the bank of the Blanchard River, overlooking the spot where Sabrina's lifeless body had been found. She hadn't forgotten Sabrina, or that horrible episode, yet she had finally stopped blaming herself for the chain of events which led to her dear friend's murder. When those times of guilt reappeared, she tried to remind herself of all she had done to bring her co-worker from Northern Exposure to know the Christ who was sculpted in the sand, the Christ who shared his final meal with his brothers – his disciples – and the Christ who had risen from the dead.

"A Christ whom Sabrina did know in her final days," she said, speaking only to the gentle wind, as she sat on one of the nearby benches where she could continue to view the spot.

"So you've gone to talking to yourself, have you?" asked Joni, the life of any party, as she also took a seat on the bench.

"You're just the person I need to see," Mary Magdalena

replied, ignoring Joni's question as she immediately spouted off the story of Levi, her heart aching more with each word. "Charlotte warned me when I first told her I'd like to go work with the Katrina children that I would come back a changed person, and that my life would never be the same again."

"You know, Mary Magdalena, we all have to face change in our lives. Some people bring it on themselves, but it isn't always self-induced. There are many reasons for change, and oftentimes those reasons are out of our hands. God gets us where we need to be, even through our own self-inflicted mistakes along the way."

Thinking of how she'd gotten to this point, going where she felt God had led her, Mary Magdalena thought how appropriate this fall day was with its dull, dismal gray sky, barren trees and wind whose chill nipped at her flesh. She gazed across the park at the tree whose two low, far-extending branches swept toward her, reminding her of Christ with his arms outstretched for all who would accept him.

"It's just like that tree," continued Joni, recalling the past significance of this particular tree to her friend. "You noticed it in a time of darkness in your life and allowed it to speak to you in a special way. You found a source of strength in it and through that, you changed to not only dodge the obstacles in your path, but face them head-on. People can accept the challenge and go on with their lives, or they can sit in total darkness, longing for the way things were."

Mary Magdalena sat silent for a bit, deep in thought as she stared at the tree. "And had it not been for a bleak time in the season of this tree's life, I'd have never seen those two branches reaching toward me. It was the same when I first saw it, getting ready to burst forth with life in a new spring. It was only in the dark period of its life that its true message showed."

"Exactly."

"Can you wait here a moment, Joni?" Mary Magdalena asked, a irrefutable urgency in her voice. "I have something I want to show you."

Receiving the nod she hoped for, she rushed across the street to her house and was back momentarily with a photo of a boy draped in a black piece of fabric. "There's this boy in Mississippi named Levi and I've not felt comfortable sharing his story with anyone, but you're the very first person I met when I originally came to Findlay. You saw through me from the beginning and became God's messenger to me. There have been several occasions since I've known you that you were there for me, even at times when I would have wanted no one near me, like that time in the hospital when you brought the pies. Through your face and your actions, I have felt the touch of God many times, sometimes so strongly that I even felt I could see His face if I looked hard enough." Her voice stopped as she stared hard at the photo. "That's exactly what I wish I could be for Levi. The touch and the face of God."

Mary Magdalena took a deep breath as she looked back at the tree where she'd seen "the arms of Christ" and felt the smile of his face. "There is a tree exactly like this one in Mississippi. It's in Bay St. Louis, in an area I suppose is considered the Old Town. To me, it was a part of town that was so picturesque and quaint it was much like I imagined it had been for generations. That is, except for the fact that most of the trees were new, replacing the massive ones that had stood there before Hurricane Katrina. But there was this one tree, the focal point of the whole area, which looked exactly like this tree.

"You said God puts us where we need to be. That's exactly how I felt the day I saw the tree in Bay St. Louis. I'd have never noticed it had it not been for a series of events that led me to it. It all began when Charlotte wanted to go and get an oyster po' boy from some landmark restaurant, pretty much like Miller's was here. You know how she is, always hunting down the establishments the locals frequent."

Joni gave an understanding nod.

"She'd uncovered this place on her first visit down there after Katrina," Mary Magdalena continued, "Frankly, I didn't mind as I was starving at the time. Besides, after she explained it had been owned by the same family for about as long as Miller's, I thought it might be fun to give it a try.

"We took a break from sorting through all the books, and carnival games and prizes, long enough to go there. It was only fifteen minutes from Diamondhead, where we were "camping out" in the Methodist church's sanctuary. When we got there, the place was closed. Not to be outdone, Charlotte spotted a newer restaurant next door. There was a menu on the window and when she saw they served po' boys, she was content so we went in and took a seat.

"It's funny now," Mary Magdalena said with a soft laugh, "I don't even remember why, but we decided to change places the minute they took our order. We moved to a table right in front of the window, with Charlotte's back to the window. From my vantage point, I could see this tree straight out in front of me. It looked for the world like this tree.

"I was about to point it out when I saw something shiny dangling from high up in its branches. The rays of the sun were hitting the object just right so that it shimmered, reflecting the sun's rays straight in my eyes. I guess I was staring at it pretty intently, for Charlotte turned around. 'It looks exactly like your tree in Riverside Park,' she observed."

Mary Magdalena scrunched up her mouth. "I guess I have a reputation with that tree, huh?" she asked, looking squarely at Joni. "Seems everyone knows the story behind it."

"Not everyone," Joni teased, "only the significant people. That would include Charlotte and myself." Her comment caused a smile to flash across Mary Magdalena's face, the reaction she'd hoped to receive.

"Anyway, our food came then, and I forgot about the shiny object. I'm sure it was nothing, but for whatever reason, I felt it speaking to me, just as the two out-stretched branches of this tree here in Riverside Park. Every time I look in this park, I see Christ. I see him on the cross, I see him at the Last Supper and I see him beside the empty tomb."

"That's because Christ is where we can turn as a source of solace in those times of change. You see," explained Joni, "our Lord, even though he was the son of the Most High, also had to endure many changes."

The pair sat there for nearly two hours, chatting about the changes that had come to Findlay just in the short time Mary Magdalena had been there, the changes that had overwhelmed the Gulf coast, and the changes that would continue to come to people all over the world.

"I'd worked at Miller's ever since I was a teenager," shared Joni. "It's hard to believe that it's not still sitting on Main Street. But after a while, when I saw it could not re-open following our flood, I had to get another job. I love my new job, for it allows me to see so many of the high school and college students. Not only do they get food at McDonald's, but I make sure they get at least one friendly face, and a hearty laugh to go with their meal before they get out of that place. It's an opportunity I'd have never gotten had long-standing circumstances not changed."

"I see your point," Mary Magdalena replied, pulling back her jacket to reveal her 'I Survived the Flood of 2007' T-shirt. "In the midst of what little I've seen and experienced in the Gulf, there has been an abundance, a literal outpouring of goodness from all over the world, and from the locals who themselves are hurting and in need."

"Change is hard," noted Joni, more serious than Mary Magdalena had ever seen her to be, "but it is only through change that we can grow."

"I've heard that saying! It was on the wall in the dorm's study area. I'd never thought about its meaning, though, in all the times I've stared at this tree with its falling, yet vibrantly colorful, leaves. I guess a tree can hold a lot of messages, huh?"

Joni nodded.

"There's one thing I'm learning will never change," admitted Mary Magdalena, a light, but definite resoluteness in her voice. "I love working with children and youth, and I'm determined to one day have a place where I can make a difference in the lives of hurting children. Sometimes, the more I'm around Charlotte, the more I see how much we think and feel alike on that subject."

She smiled at Joni. "There was never a doubt God placed you in my life, and there's never a doubt He placed Charlotte in my life."

"It's called 'planting seeds.'"

26

Charlotte stood silently peering out the large front window of the sanctuary of Diamondhead United Methodist Church, making sure not to awaken Mary Magdalena. In many ways, this was the morning she had been working toward over the course of the past two-and-a-half years, although at the time she was unaware of that. It was a morning which marked - not only for Hancock County, Mississippi, but for the world – a new beginning for the demolished Gulf. ***And how fitting it is the Katrina children get to give that message***, she thought, seeing their precious faces in her mind, as she said a prayer of thanks for the new school's opening.

The morning of October 31st, which was the day chosen for her to host a fall carnival in celebration of the event, was still hidden behind a shroud of blackness, as wisps of willowy clouds fought to be seen in the tiny patches of gray where the light was trying to peek through. The angel hanging in front of the window provided one of those picture-perfect moments as it radiated a ray of hope against a world of darkness. ***How strange***, she observed, noticing the shapes of the clouds in the background seemed to be aligning themselves to match the shape of the angel in the window, its back arched with a flowing gown billowing in the back. ***Like the shape of all the shells you brought from North Carolina's coast for these children.***

Her sudden realization sent tingles down her spine as she recalled walking the beach for an entire week, with the help of a friend, as the friend introduced a craft she had done with children using the interestingly-shaped shells. The pair then set out, like two women on a mission, searching for enough shells to give one to each student at the new school. With every step, it seemed they found an "angel."

"A sign we're doing exactly what we're supposed to be doing," Charlotte had commented to the friend during that week. By the time their week was over, they had enough "angels" to fill up three banker boxes, certainly enough to share with each of the students.

The thought of that week encouraged her as she replayed the conversation with Mary Magdalena from the evening before when the group of volunteers, slated to help them with today's Fall Festival, called to say they would be unable to join them. "What are we going to do?" her young friend had asked. Charlotte, feeling like the disciples when they saw the multitude and had no food except for what was held by one child, had no answer. "All I can tell you," she had answered, "is if they fed that many people with the help of one child, we're in for a big blessing considering the number of children we'll have at that school tomorrow." With those prophetic words, she had gone to bed, praying for a goodly helping of "loaves and fishes" – in the form of volunteers – come morning.

The author now stared at the morning's picturesque

arrival, combined with the thought of the shell "angels" she had brought, and watched as an azure blue sky crept upward on the horizon, gently nudging the black away as the sky began to fill with color. Suddenly, the gathering clouds turned into a host of angels as their defined shapes glowed with mixed shades of neon oranges and pinks, resembling an array of billowing gowns against the golden-colored angel in the window.

Charlotte inhaled slowly and deeply, trying to fill her entire being with the miracle of the dawn, as her soul sent messages of praise and adoration to the Maker of the scene before her. She watched in awe, thoughts scrambling through her mind as visions of the torrents that ravaged this same area three years earlier faded into an image of rare beauty, reminding her of the kind of illustrious beauty which illuminated through people when they allowed the Light to shine through them.

Within a matter of a few minutes, the color had transformed into a brilliantly-blinding iridescent glow behind masses of white clouds, still resembling a multitude of angels as the sun's giant orb filled the sky, removing all remaining traces of darkness.

"Who turned on the lights?" asked Mary Magdalena, sitting up and stretching.

"God," Charlotte answered simply, still focused on the Masterful painting in front of her.

The young woman discerned there was more than one meaning in the author's comment, but chose not to delve any deeper into that issue at the moment. "Any earth-shattering solutions to the problem of no volunteers for today yet?"

The ringing of Charlotte's cell phone interrupted her answer. "Yes," was all she said. She answered the phone and listened intently to the words coming through the small gadget, with Mary Magdalena watching closely for any reaction as she decided the call must be from the same One who turned on the lights.

"Okay, Miss Queen of One-Word Answers, what is going on and what did I miss? Undoubtedly I slept through something."

The author laughed. "In 'a word,' yes, you did."

"I should know better than to play word games with you," teased Mary Magdalena.

"Hurry and get ready. I'll tell you over breakfast. My treat! We're going to need a lot of nourishment to make it through this day."

"The call was from a man in my church," shared Charlotte.

"In Concord?" asked Mary Magdalena.

"Yes, only he isn't in Concord, he is in Biloxi."

"I'm liking this story already," Magdalena replied, a huge grin reiterating her comment, "but please don't tell me he came down here just to help us, and that he drove all night to get here."

"No," Charlotte answered with her own huge grin. "He and four other men from my church are down here this week on a building team. They were planning to work until noon today and go home, but...,"

"Don't tell me," interrupted Mary Magdalena. "The voice of God told them we desperately needed their help today so they're going to meet us at the school."

"In 'a word,' yes." The author gave a loud guffaw.

"Okay, Charlotte, that's enough with the word games. You're already so far ahead I'll never catch up." Mary Magdalena wolfed down the rest of her waffle and guzzled her milk as the author shared the details of the morning's sunrise and the tale of the angel shells.

"When I saw that first angel take shape in the clouds, I knew we were going to have all the angels we needed before the day was done," admitted Charlotte. "I've been a strong believer all my life, but all the goodness I've seen in my lifetime pales in comparison with what I've seen this morning."

"I hope I have a few angels of my own today. I have this weird feeling, something I can't explain or put my finger on."

"From what I witnessed this morning, there will be plenty to go around for everybody."

When they pulled in the parking lot at the school, there was a sensation in the air that matched the brilliance of the sky Charlotte had witnessed. It showed on the faces of the parents dropping off children and on the faces of all the dignitaries who'd shown up to see "the beginning of a new era" for the education of southwestern Mississippi. It showed in the twinkles of the eyes of students and in the sparkling smiles on the faces of teachers for whom classrooms of the past three years had consisted of few, if any, desks and textbooks inside barren, dull walls covered by whatever posters they could find in the "care packages" sent from other schools and school supply houses.

People were lining the sidewalks, trying not to disrupt the day, but anxious to get a quick glimpse of this project which had taken over three years to complete.

"Can't you just feel the excitement in the air?" shot a familiar voice, causing the two women to turn in its direction. Mike Wolf was getting out of his car and swiftly moving toward them. "What can I do to help?" he asked in his usual energetic manner.

"Don't tell me you got a call from God, too?" asked Mary Magdalena, not sure whether she was joking or not.

"In a word, yes, I guess you could say I did," replied Mike.

"That's it, I give up!" exclaimed the young woman.

"We'll explain later," offered Charlotte. "What does bring you here this morning?"

"I was already up and dressed for work when I got a call telling me there was some problem with the offshore rig and not to bother to come in today. I knew this was your big day with the kids so I decided to come lend a helping hand."

"You're right," acknowledged Mary Magdalena in amazement. "It was a call from God."

They headed toward the main entrance of the school just in time to see the bus with the bright orange and blue letters approaching. "Wow, there's a sight for sore eyes!" proclaimed Mike.

"You're telling us," agreed Mary Magdalena.

"I didn't know they were going to be here."

"Neither did we," replied Charlotte.

"They got a call from God, too," said Mary Magdalena.

The bus door opened as James shouted, "Hello, all! How are you today?"

A calming peace radiated within Charlotte as she answered, "All is well," knowing her words were powerfully true.

Mike showed James where to park the bus while Charlotte and Mary Magdalena went inside to check in all the volunteers. The halls were bursting with life, as wide-eyed students and teachers alike found their ways to their classrooms. In no time, Jeanne Brooks was in the front office to lead the procession – which had grown from two to eight in the course of the morning – to the gym where the Fall Festival was to be held.

"You don't even have to flush the toilet," was the first remark Charlotte heard when she entered the hallway. "It does it all by itself." She smiled profusely at the words of the young boy whose face and small body were completely mesmerized.

"I think that one comment says it all," Jeanne said. "We're all in a dream, not knowing what to look at or do first. Can you believe this is the first ***real*** school that over half of our students have ever seen?"

Charlotte quickly calculated the time lapse since Hurricane Katrina.

"It hit right at the beginning of the school year in 2005, so students from second grade down have never been inside a real school of their own," Jeanne continued.

The blank stare of Charlotte's matched the one on Mary Magdalena's face. "You know," noted the author, "I've been down here at least seven times now, and that reality never crossed my mind." She peered up and down the hallways at the dazed glares on the faces of the children. "No wonder they look like they're off in another world. They are."

"The sad thing," added Jeanne, "is that when they leave this, forty percent of them still have no real home of their own." A glimmer of a smile lit up her face. "But compared to where we were at this time three years ago, this is heaven."

The heaven of all the angels I saw this morning, observed Charlotte, grabbing a quick glance over her shoulder at the six men who were following Mary Magdalena and her down the hall. ***And the heaven of all the angels I see now***, she concluded as the words of ***Wind Beneath My Wings*** played through her mind, followed by a vision of all her 'heroes' who had made it possible for her to be walking down this hallway at this instant.

Heroes in all the tiny hands who had touched the books that were now in the hands of children, students, teachers and parents of Hancock County, Mississippi; heroes in the hands of her mother, a former librarian, who had catalogued and processed, ***with the help of my father***, the thousands of book donations from all over the country; heroes who had contributed games and prizes, and baked cookies, for all the students of the school. ***And heroes who were angels unaware***, she noted, with one final glance over her shoulder as they reached the gym. She looked at Mary Magdalena. ***And a hero who, I have a feeling, is going to touch many more lives in her lifetime.***

A floodgate of tears ripped at the back of her eyes, a floodgate which she pushed back with all the force she could muster, along with the promise of a healing unleashing following the end of the day's carnival. Tiny kindnesses from thousands of people were culminated in the boxes of prizes, and cookies and coolers of drinks, now housed in the kitchen of the concession area. Combined with the willingness of eight individuals now facing her and awaiting instructions for their mission of the day – a mission which had taken two and a half years of preparation – she prayed she'd be worthy to lead it.

Mary Magdalena recruited Mike to help her place tables in front of the concession stand window, which faced the hallway at the gym's entrance. "We put Cherry-Lemon Sun-Drop and Cheerwine sodas in the coolers yesterday afternoon," she told him. "All we need to do at the moment is set out enough cups for the first group. I'll take care of filling them later as the groups file in. Then we'll place a cookie on a napkin and lay them on the tables for the children. The ladies in Charlotte's church provided fresh-baked cookies for all the children. There are four kinds, so we'll put a few of each variety out and let the children take the kind they want."

"Mmmm," mumbled Mike, sampling one of the chocolate-chip cookies that had broken in transit. "I like this job."

"Don't get too comfortable with it," warned Charlotte, entering the kitchen of the concession area. "Your services will be needed to man one of the game stations once we get them all set up. Mary Magdalena will handle the KP duty once we get started."

"It's okay, Mike," Mary Magdalena assured him. "I'll make sure to save all the broken cookies for us volunteers. If there aren't enough, I'm sure I can drop a few while placing them on napkins." Her comment received an appreciative wink.

Charlotte quickly gave instructions for each station. "We'd have never accomplished all this set-up in time had we not been able to get in here yesterday with all the games and prizes," she said to Mary Magdalena, glancing at the clock on the wall of the gym. However, instead of the clock, her eyes spotted something else that demanded her attention. "Looks like Jeanne dug up another volunteer," said Charlotte, nodding toward the door.

"'Dug up' is right!" remarked Mary Magdalena loudly enough to cause everyone in the room to glare toward the gym door. "I think she went to the grave to get this one. He looks more like Elvis than Elvis!"

"I'd like you to meet our art and music teacher," introduced Jeanne. "Can you guess why the students adore him so much?"

"I figured if the students could dress for career day," he admitted, "I could dress as a character I'd like to be when I grow up."

Charlotte eyed the man she'd heard so much about from Jeanne in past conversations. "I have a feeling you're not going to grow up any more than I am," she said, already sensing the bond of their creative kindred spirits.

"He's going to float, in other words, come in and help at times between classes," Jeanne informed the group.

"Elvis floating in on Halloween in Mississippi...wait until I use that line back home," said one of the men from Charlotte's church.

"Your friends will never believe you were helping with an innocent, little children's carnival!" stated Mike.

"That's right! They'll probably think you were in the next state over on Bourbon Street!" seconded another man.

"How about that for a comeback the next time someone tells me 'The King is not dead!'?" sneered Mary Magdalena.

"I hope your voice matches the outfit," observed James, directing his comment at the music teacher.

"Don't worry," replied Jeanne, "it does! And his gift of art is just as great as his voice." She grinned at "Elvis." "He's a real asset to our school."

Five minutes before the scheduled arrival of the first group of children, Jeanne returned, followed by her student helper from the nearby high school. "I brought you another volunteer. I thought you might need her worse than me today."

Charlotte beamed as she looked around at her assembled crew. "Well," she proclaimed proudly and thankfully, "it appears we have just enough volunteers to man each one of our stations. And," she swiftly added, "enough time to say a prayer." She uttered words of thankfulness, a plea for guidance and a request for bursts of energy to match those of the children. "And most of all, make us shining examples to these precious children who have come dressed for the hopes and dreams of their futures in these costumes. We give you utmost thanks for allowing us not only to see those hopes and dreams, but to be a part of them. Amen."

Rounds of "Amens" echoed hers as she gave a robust wipe at her eyes and opened them just in time to see the first group of students at the door. "Places everyone!" she announced, giving one more brisk wipe of her eyes.

"Charlotte," said Jeanne, waving to get her attention from the gym door. "There are a couple of people at the office to see you. Should I send them back here?"

"Yes, that's fine. I can't leave the children right now," the author answered, pointing to the hundred-plus small bodies rushing from one station to the next to fill their plastic bags with prizes.

"It's probably two more angels," said Mary Magdalena, who overheard Jeanne's question.

In a matter of minutes, a man and a woman entered the gym, following Jeanne. From the expression on Charlotte's face, Mary Magdalena decided she'd been right in her assessment. She saw Charlotte greet the couple with hugs and then saw them deeply engaged in conversation as the author's face lit up and she gave them another hug. Jeanne then exited the gym, the pair again following her.

"What was that all about?" Mary Magdalena asked James.

"That was Larry and Carol, a couple from our church. They've been down here for every one of the mission trips with Charlotte. They're the ones who brought all the supplies down for the camp we held this summer. They drove all the way back down here to take all the equipment and drums back after the camp was over. We couldn't have done the work last year or this year without them. Chances are they've brought something else she has planned for the school."

As one group of students exited and another entered for their thirty minutes of games and prizes, Charlotte called a quick meeting of her helpers. "The best is yet to come," she shared.

"Are the rockers here?" asked one of the men from St. John's.

"They are!" she blurted, looking as if she could explode

from the excitement. "Along with the benches and also a special surprise I haven't even told you about."

"Is she always this way?" Mary Magdalena asked tauntingly, enjoying Charlotte's impish enthusiasm.

"You heard Jack this summer," answered James. "He said it didn't take much. She loves surprises, especially when she's the one giving them."

"We have lunch after this group," Charlotte said, interrupting them. "If we eat in a hurry, we can go to the library to see the rockers. They're putting them together now."

"What rockers?" asked Mary Magdalena as Charlotte and she went to the kitchen to prepare another batch of drinks and cookies.

"Contributors purchased rockers for each classroom, from kindergarten through second grade. When I was asking Jeanne for a wish list in one of our phone calls in the wee hours of one of our conversations, she said how wonderful it would be if each of those early grade teachers had a rocker in which to read to their students. Having read in so many classrooms all over the country, I'd seen lots of rockers in classrooms, many painted with themes. I simply took Jeanne's wish one step farther and had these rockers all painted with a Dolphin theme."

"Wait!" interrupted Mary Magdalena. "That's what you were talking about with the youth director at St. Andrews the week after Easter when you were in Findlay."

"That's right! Their youth raised enough money the very next Sunday to purchase six rockers. Several came from St. John's and three more came from friends of Marjorie, one of the volunteers you met this past summer. We've had them painted by artists from all over the country, including two young blind artists. Can you believe that? That's what I find most amazing. The woman who just arrived painted one of them and another lady in our church painted one. One of the rockers donated by

St. Andrews was also painted by an artist in their congregation. Two were painted by blind students at the Helen Keller Institute in New York."

"Totally blind?" Mary Magdalena's pitch rose with each letter of the words as did her astonished disbelief.

"Yes," Charlotte confirmed. "It was amazing the talent that came forth and offered to share their artistic abilities to create a positive learning environment for these students."

Mary Magdalena's expression hinted that she was deep in thought. "So, Charlotte, how many hundreds of people have helped you with what is going on here today?"

Charlotte smiled, a radiant glow on her face. "My child, there are thousands of people who have made what we've done here during the past three years possible. But the important thing you must realize is that they weren't helping ***me***, they were answering a call to help others. That call didn't come from me. I happened to be the open vessel who heard it first." She paused. "Let me rephrase that. I'm sure many people heard it before me, but they perhaps had neither the means, nor the time, to pilot the ship. When you have a son like Jack, who looks at you and pleads, 'Mom, you've gotta do something to help these children,' there's no way you can ignore the issue. I had the support of my entire family and all my friends, and God provided the means of brainpower to pull it off.

"All it took was me saying, 'Yes,' to the call and I was equipped with what I needed at the times I needed it." She gave a brief chuckle and added, "And not one minute before!" The radiant glow turned to an appreciative sigh. "A project like this naturally attracts people who are willing to help. How can you look at the faces of these precious children and not want to reach out and do something for them?"

Mary Magdalena turned toward Charlotte. "The faces of these precious children," she repeated slowly, recalling a childhood song. "That's what God sees when he looks at every one of us, isn't it?" Her question required no answer as she continued to think aloud. "Red and yellow, black and white, they are precious in His sight."

"Yes." The author said no more, aware that a Greater Power was speaking to her friend, and amazed once again at the many various ways in which God spoke to each person who reached out to help others. She could tell whatever was going on inside Mary Magdalena's head was going to last long past this morning.

"That's enough until the groups after lunch," stated Mike, turning his counting skills to the number of cookies Mary Magdalena had placed on napkins rather than the number of people who had made this day possible.

"Good!" proclaimed Charlotte. "Mary Magdalena, I want you to come out and see the children playing the games. I've never seen such appreciative children. You'd think we had given them the Hope Diamond instead of all these tiny inexpensive trinkets, from the overjoyed elation on their faces.

"Can you believe most of these children have never been to a carnival other than the ones we held at the summer arts camps? One child asked the man at the 'Go Fishing' booth if we made up that game. Why, that game was around when I was in first grade. It was always my favorite at the school carnivals." Charlotte walked from station to station, speaking to the children and interacting with them. "Have you ever seen anything like this? I don't know whether to laugh or to cry. All I can say is I've never been more moved in all my life.

"I was brokenhearted the first time I came here. It was unbelievable to think that something so horrible, that such a poverty level, was so close to my home. This is only a day's drive away. And to look at them now, and see how far they've come. It boggles my mind to think how many volunteers from this country have come here and given a day, a week, some since the storm, to make a difference in the lives of these people. And the greatest thing is these people are so anxious to reach out and help us with what little some of them still have. That truly *is* love in action." Charlotte gave another hard swallow, still refusing to let the tears escape until the end of the day.

She has enough adrenaline left to make sure that doesn't happen, Mary Magdalena observed.

"Okay, team, let's go," called Charlotte after swallowing her lunch nearly whole.

"That woman's a slave driver," joked one of the men.

"You should see her in choir," laughed James.

"That woman's on a mission," teased one of the other men.

"You got that right!" Charlotte called over her shoulder. "I'm ***always*** on a mission."

She led the group to the library and began to pull books from shelves.

"What's she doing?" asked one of the men.

"This is what I'm doing." Charlotte opened the books to reveal the special stickers that had been placed, mostly by the hands of her parents, in all the books given by thousands of contributors. "And there are thousands more where these came from, spread all over the coast of the Gulf." Her enthusiasm turned to a somber stare. "I wanted you to see what your time and money have accomplished. You're some of the lucky few, for many people who've given and done haven't reaped that reward. I sincerely admire them, and their gifts of selfless love," she said, taking time to look at each face in front of her. "Now you see why I do what I do and why this means so much to me. Thank you for allowing this to happen."

The author placed the books back on their appropriate shelves and peered around the large room. "Ah, there they are," she announced, spying three of the rockers already assembled and in the back area of the library. "As soon as they all arrive, there will be sixteen of them. Our next project will be to get director's chairs for the teachers of the older grades."

Jeanne came from her office in the back of the room when she saw the visitors. "We found a great home out in our courtyard for the two benches. They're more beautiful than I could have ever imagined. They look just like the ones I wanted from Wales."

"A woodworker in our congregation made these," James explained to Mary Magdalena as they moved to the courtyard. He pointed to two magnificent wooden benches, each adorned with a large dolphin across the back of the seat. "When we recently added a new building, the cedar fence which had been there for years had to be taken down. He was able to use some of the cedar for the benches, so that a part of our history and heritage could be preserved for these children. Carol, the woman you saw earlier and who painted one of the rockers, drew the dolphins that are on them."

Another of the men went on to tell Mary Magdalena and Jeanne about the church's rich German heritage, which began when Bach was still alive. "The church actually sits on 131 acres of land that was granted to the congregation by the King of England. Seventeen Lutheran congregations have stemmed from the seeds planted there."

"Planted seeds, huh?" Mary Magdalena asked, looking in the direction of Charlotte, who was now at the front of the school standing beside a large dolphin carved from wood.

"Ladies and gentlemen," the author announced, making a big production of her introduction. "I'd like you to meet Miss Caroline Doshe."

"Caroline I can understand," replied one of the men, "seeing as how this specimen of chainsaw art obviously came from North Carolina. But Doshe?"

"I had to speak at a convention for the North and South Carolina state and county fair association," explained Charlotte. "A wood carver had done this at last year's fair in Wilson, North Carolina." She turned to Mary Magdalena and Mike. "That's a good bit east of Charlotte and Concord. Anyway, there was a drawing for it at the fair. The couple who won it didn't have room to give it the home they felt it deserved, so they donated it to the auction for scholarships given by the fair association. When I saw it at the Banquet Auction, I knew it had my name on it...or rather South Hancock Elementary's name on it.

"I won the bid, but had it gone for ten dollars more, it would have capped my limit and gone to another bidder. I was so excited the auctioneer announced that he thought I was going to get up and dance on the banquet table.

"The next morning during my keynote speech, I explained why I had so desperately wanted the dolphin. I also told the audience I was holding a contest for them to name it, complete with a prize. There were so many good entries that I had a tough time choosing a name. But Caroline won, since both the Carolinas were represented at the event. I wanted the students here to always remember they are loved by the Carolinians. And Doshe, well, one of the vets for the state of North Carolina came up with 'Dolphin of South Hancock Elementary...D-O-S-H-E.' I loved it because it had a nice Cajun ring to it. Doo-shay," she said, pronouncing it the proper way. "Caroline Doshe."

Charlotte eyed her watch while everyone around her eyed the craftsmanship of the dolphin. "I hate to break up this lovely party, but we have approximately two hundred more children waiting for their turns at the fun and prizes."

"And cookies," added Mike. "Those are great cookies! I'd hate to have to eat all of them."

"I'll be sure to tell the ladies at the church you approve," Charlotte said with a grin.

"No need. Diann and I have decided to come up and tell them ourselves in November on our way back to Ohio."

The author turned to Mary Magdalena. "Planting...,"

"I know...seeds," interjected the young woman. "I'm beginning to see your point now." She smiled. "Or rather, your stem peeking up from the ground."

By the time the last group of classes had come through the gym, the volunteers had gone through over thirty boxes of candy and prizes, not to mention over six hundred cookies and many gallons of sodas, and several hundred angel-shaped shells. There were enough buckeyes, symbols of good luck brought by Mary Magdalena from Hancock County, Ohio, to give one to each of the "angels." There were even enough of the collectible Boyd

Bears, given by one generous donor, for each kindergartner and first grader, and one left over for the teacher who collected them. The few leftover cookies were distributed between each vehicle for the long ride home, and the bottles of soda were left for the next day's Opening Ceremony and Ribbon Cutting.

The men, who had so graciously shown up that morning, helped crush the boxes, carry out tables, and load all the re-usable games into the cargo van in which the couple had brought the rockers, benches and Caroline Doshe. In less than thirty minutes, the team of now ten persons stood on the sidewalk posing for a couple of photos together. No one moved for a moment as they all stood silent, staring at the old dilapidated ruins of a school several hundred yards in front of them, the reality of what they had just done sinking in.

"Mission accomplished," Charlotte said simply, not bothering to brush away the tears this time.

The crew, which had all heard the same call, said their final farewells as Mike headed north and the church bus headed east. Larry and Carol had decided to stay overnight to attend the opening ceremony and see the sand sculpture, and Mary Magdalena was anxiously awaiting the arrival of the contingency – including her husband – from Hancock County, Ohio, who were coming in the next morning to do a sand sculpture as a part of the school's opening celebration.

"How does dinner in New Orleans sound?" Charlotte asked the remaining three helpers. "I've never been there for Halloween. It's my treat, no tricks."

27

"I can hardly wait to see Nick," Mary Magdalena shared over breakfast. "I'm not sure whether I'm excited about telling him all about yesterday, or whether I'm more excited that he'll finally get a chance to see what I've been doing down here and meet the children."

"You'll love seeing Joshua's sculpture unfold before your very eyes," Charlotte informed Larry and Carol. "I'm thrilled you stayed over last night."

"It was our pleasure," replied Carol.

"I'm like the guys from the church," said Larry. "Yesterday was the greatest treat I think I've ever given anyone. It was worth the drive down here and back just to see the smiles on the faces of the children."

"Can you believe our carnival fell on Halloween?" Charlotte asked. "It was perfect timing. And no one mentioned Halloween or 'trick or treat', we simply spread lots of love."

"I think it's great the way the children were allowed to dress for career day," noted Carol.

"Me, too," agreed Charlotte. "It encourages them to keep their hopes and dreams. I hope they aspire to be great people and do great things. You know, my highest goal with our efforts here is to let the children know any one of them can work with their gifts and talents and reach any goal they set. I'm all for reaching up, not being content with less than we can do. They may never be 'the absolute best' in their field, but they can surely reach the top and touch the lives of others while doing it. The lesson here is they can be stars and achieve goals, right here from Hancock County, Mississippi, or from Hancock County, Ohio. And they can help others, right from their own back yards...even if they're not sure where their own back yards are," she added somberly. "The stories of these children and these residents of Hancock County, Mississippi, have touched people all over the world."

With her positive outlook back in her voice, Charlotte concluded, "How fitting it is that today is November 1st, All Saints' Day. And I don't mean as in the New Orleans' football team," she quickly added. "But in my eyes, these children and all these who have suffered so greatly, yet carry on with such a sense of pride and stamina and resilience...now ***there's*** an example of a saint. I've not seen one person here, no matter how downtrodden, who wasn't anxious to reach out and lend a helping hand to their neighbor, or another person also in need. I think the perfect ending to this day is going to be when the children get a chance to go to the beach after the school's Ribbon Cutting Ceremony and all get their hands in the sand alongside Joshua. I don't know of a child anywhere who doesn't like to play in the sand."

"Speaking of helping hands," Mary Magdalena interrupted, "we'd better get going. Nick just called to tell me that

Joshua and he, along with Harry and two other workers have just gotten off I-59 and are taking the Pearlington exit off I-10 right now. If we leave this minute, we should all reach the beach about the same time."

"You don't think she's a little anxious to see her husband, do you?" Charlotte replied with a wink. "Larry, if Carol and you will take Mary Magdalena to the beach where the guys are doing the sculpture, which is about five miles from Pearlington, I'll pick Ebony and Jack up at the airport and meet you there."

"They're coming, too?" shrieked a very surprised Mary Magdalena.

"You don't think Ebony is going to let you be one up on her, do you? Jack knew Joshua could use his help, so he suggested Ebony catch a connecting flight in Charlotte and they come down together. Then he'll ride home with me so I won't be alone, and Ebony can go back to Ohio with you and the Findlay crew."

"Charlotte Crenshaw, you don't miss a trick, do you?" Mary Magdalena teased.

"Not at Halloween, I don't!' Charlotte playfully shot back at her young friend, aware many more "treats" were in store for her before this trip ended.

The opening ceremony for the school was a huge success. Being the first public building to have been built from the ground up in Mississippi since Katrina, it marked a huge step forward, for FEMA, MEMA, and the community. It risked becoming a media spectacle, but the school's administration kept it as low key as possible, wanting to focus on the students and their accomplishments, and their "new home" – at least their new "home" for several hours a day.

Standing back and getting a chance to see the entire facility, filled with supportive students and parents, Charlotte was even more moved than the day before.

"It's something else, isn't it?" The familiar voice, from the day before, once again caught Charlotte unexpectedly. "I had to bring Diann," continued Mike. "Seeing as how she's a teacher, she couldn't wait to see this." The couple then ventured on through the hallways to make sure they didn't miss anything.

Larry, Carol and Charlotte walked through the facility, gleaning all they could to take back in the form of stories for their own congregation, as Mary Magdalena headed in another direction to hurriedly give the "grand tour" to the rest of her Findlay friends and Jack so they could get back to their project in the sand. They were all greeted – with hugs from small hands to shakes from big hands – as students, parents and school personnel alike extended a farewell word of grateful thanks and appreciation.

With each accolade, Charlotte uttered a simple "Thank you," but recalled Jeremiah's words. "I didn't do it for the money," – ***which in my case was the thanks***, Charlotte noted – "I wanted to do it for you." ***You felt the need to give him a check; these people feel a need to express their appreciation. Say "Thank you" and graciously accept what they're capable of offering you – their words. Otherwise you're robbing them of a blessing.***

"Thank you for allowing us to be a part of this," offered

Carol as Larry and she prepared to leave. "Seeing Joshua's work in the sand was incredible, but being in this school amidst all these children, I'm not sure I'll ever do anything to top that."

Charlotte nodded her agreement, finding it hard to speak as she waved good-bye to students and parents leaving the school with cups of Cheerwine punch. She hugged Larry and Carol and managed to mutter, "Thank *you*! Safe travels and I'll see you back in Concord on Monday."

She watched the couple drive away, thinking how life goes on, as she shed the leftover tears which hadn't managed to escape the afternoon before. As she walked to her van, she looked up at the sky. Unlike the hosts of angels in the clouds that she had witnessed the day before, it was now a vibrant blue, void of any clouds, as the sun rained down on this new facility, and the Son reigned down on God's children. That realization was enough to erase the tears as she headed for the beach, anxious to see Noah's ark, the animals and the dolphin taking shape.

There was a note of melancholy in her voice as she passed the field where the school had once stood. She dared not look back.

"Remember when you told us about Levi and I asked if you'd been watching too many FBI shows?" Ebony asked when Charlotte finally arrived back at the sand sculpture.

The author nodded, smiling at the number of children

and families who had come to see and experience Joshua's work in the sand.

"Now I feel I'm caught up in one of those shows myself. You know at the end of each episode when they've solved a case, or caught the criminal, and the team walks toward the jet together. That's exactly how I feel right now."

"Except our jet is a convoy of two trucks," corrected Mary Magdalena.

"And Mom's van," Jack added.

"You know what I mean," said Mary Magdalena. "All of us are getting in our separate vehicles and leaving this place, a place where our combined efforts have hopefully left it a better place than we found it."

"I don't know about better," noted Charlotte, "but certainly with a bigger sugar rush. Between all those cookies, Cherry-Lemon Sun-Drop and Cheerwine punch those kids have consumed in these past two days, they will still be climbing the walls when they go back to school on Monday."

"And the parents will be climbing the walls, counting down the hours, until they go back to school," Jack commented. "Especially after they see and hear all the loot in their bags from yesterday's carnival. Some of those things are so noisy, they're obnoxious." He became suddenly quiet.

The others understood, for his comment struck a chord within each of them, too. They were all drawn to the memory of their first mission trip here together, when the children carried all of their 'loot' in their backpacks. They also recalled all the crafts the children had made and carted home in a huge bag on the last day of camp. Crafts which they all kept beside where they slept at night, a touching fact of the stories they'd shared these past two days.

"Sorry, I didn't mean to end things on a bad note," Jack apologized.

"It isn't bad," replied Mary Magdalena. "Bittersweet."

"I wonder if this is how Dolly Parton felt when she penned the words of the second verse of *I Will Always Love You*," Jack reflected, singing the words about bittersweet memories.

"I don't want to leave," said Mary Magdalena.

"Didn't I warn you about that?" Charlotte reminded her. "That day we were alone in the hallway at St. Andrews in Findlay, I told you it would be this way."

"It gets harder to leave every time I come. Those children have a way of endearing themselves to you."

Charlotte noticed the pain in Jack's eyes. She could tell his thoughts were on Levi, and wishing he could locate the boy. Were he able to find him, she suspected he'd try to take him back to North Carolina, a solution that would solve nothing. A glance in Mary Magdalena's direction found another face with the same expression, but this one weary about Levi's mother.

"We'd better get going before Pearlington has another flood," said Ebony.

"Right!" agreed Jack, instantly changing the subject. "I guess the next time we'll see you two is in Findlay for the 10th anniversary of the sand sculpture. Mom and I will get to be there this year."

"Tenth anniversary?" asked Ebony. "You mean it's been going on that long?"

"We're not getting any younger," was Mary Magdalena's answer, picking up on the conversation's change of course.

"I didn't hear ***that***!" she blared, causing uproarious laughter within the group.

Jack reached inside Charlotte's van and retrieved a set of juggling balls which he handed to Ebony, along with a bag of balloons and an air pump which he handed to Mary Magdalena. "Start practicing and we should be able to have fun with ***your*** Hancock County children next April when we get there."

"I wish you could juggle my schedule as well as you can juggle those balls," Charlotte blared at Jack, causing a loud chuckle from the group.

"I just hope these children can use the juggling and balloon sculpting, as well as all the other crafts and art mediums we taught them," replied Jack, "to relieve the stresses of their lives as they continue to rebuild."

"Maybe we should have also taught their parents to juggle and make balloon animals," suggested Ebony.

"Maybe you should go get us something to eat," shouted Nick across the beach.

"That's a great idea!" exclaimed Charlotte. "Hop in," she politely ordered, motioning for Ebony and Mary Magdalena to join Jack and her in the van. "I can take you to that place we missed the last trip," she said, looking over her shoulder at Mary Magdalena.

"Benigno's?" asked Jack, receiving an affirmative nod. "That place has the best po'boy sandwiches. I can't believe Mom hasn't already taken you there."

"She did," replied Mary Magdalena, "before the rest of you arrived this past summer, but it was closed that day. We never got a chance to go back. You know how busy we were."

"You're right. I do remember. Mom and I ate there the first time Larry and Carol came to bring supplies. They loved it, too. They're going to hate they missed it when I get back and tell them we went without them."

"I would have invited them, but I knew they were anxious to get in five hours of good driving before stopping for the evening. Besides, we're not going to stay long enough to read all the memorabilia and see all the photos on the wall. We're simply going to eat and get a carry-out order for the guys back at the sculpture." Her words stopped as she suddenly slammed on brakes.

"Don't tell me there's another alligator crossing the road?" asked Ebony cynically before computing the significant reverence of this stop.

"Would you look at that?" Charlotte asked, pulling the car over to the side of the road as she reached for her camera. It was the sign she'd seen on her first trip to the Gulf following Katrina, the one that stopped her dead in her tracks then, too. It was still having the same effect on her.

"It would appear that Hurricane Ike also had a shot at this sign," noted Mary Magdalena, noting the top half of the sign had been torn away so that now it only read "BUT GOD IS BIGGER." This was the third time she had ridden past the sign, each of them with Charlotte, and each time something had gone off inside her, something akin to a mental alarm trying to alert her. It even happened when she viewed the picture she'd taken of it, or even thought about it. But now, she sensed whatever it was struggling to come out, longing to be recognized, to be known, to breathe. Mary Magdalena felt her body grow limp as all of her energy seemed to fulfill a mission of its own.

"Are you okay?" asked Ebony, seeing her friend suddenly wobble.

"Yes," she managed. "I ***am*** okay, and I have this strange feeling that everything is going to be wonderful, but I don't know why yet."

"O...kay...," Ebony replied skeptically. "And you're sure you haven't been in the communion wine?"

Mary Magdalena's eyes told her this was no laughing matter.

"Alright, Maggie, my girl," Ebony said, cognitively, as she used her friend's nickname from the past when their sisterly bond had so strongly begun. A past in a time when they'd both strayed from the paths of their childhoods, but from which both allowed the spiritual influence of their grandmothers to lead them back to a path of righteousness, to bring them back "into the fold." "I heard that look, clearer than any words. I'm here for you."

Mary Magdalena, holding onto Ebony's arm, crossed the highway and walked out to the water's edge, staring into the horizon. ***What is it, God? What is my mind and body trying to tell me?*** she pleaded. ***I know that whatever it is, it's deeply instilled inside me. It's something I can't change; I can sense that. But I have no idea what You want or what is happening.***

She closed her eyes and began to pray, using the words she'd heard on so many occasions in her grandmother's prayers, reciting the words she had learned as a young child and recited through her early and mid-teenage years. Feeling the strength of this friend holding her up in a time of need, she continued to pray, clearing her mind of all else as she focused on herself being in the path of Christ. The Christ she'd found when she'd gone on her first mission, a mission in search of that "perfect man," the day she dared to drive out of the parking lot of Northern Exposure.

Slowly, breathing in the salt-water air, and feeling the sand between her toes, she tried to envision the presence of Christ in this place, as he had been by so many lakeshores in his lifetime. ***As he was...***, she said, yearning to find the message hidden inside. Her thoughts stopped as she yielded herself fully to her inner self, her body completely at peace and perfectly still and quiet.

Ebony silently watched the transformation happening before her, all the while praying for her friend, sensing, and recognizing herself, the reality of the spiritual force at work in Mary Magdalena. She wasn't sure how long it had been when her friend's eyes opened and she stood, strong and sure, again looking out over the water as she whispered, "As he was."

Mary Magdalena, a vision of divine calm and serenity, looked at Ebony. "Would you go and get Charlotte and Jack?" she asked.

"Shall I call Nick on your cell phone?" her friend asked, also aware of the veil of calm and serenity encompassing her.

"No, I'll explain this to him later. Right now, I need to speak with the three of you for a moment."

Ebony was back in no time as the three stared in baited anticipation at Mary Magdalena.

"We've all seen this sign," she began, as she walked them to a spot where they stood squarely in front of the battered board, "and it's spoken to every one of us. Probably to everyone who has seen it, or has seen a photo of it. It has become a well-known icon to the world in the wake of Katrina." She paused just long enough to re-read it. "But there was something besides these words that lunged at me each time I saw it, and today, I knew there was something from it, combined with something inside of me, demanding to be heard." She took a deep breath. "It wasn't until I stopped and put everything else aside, praying as I learned in the Catholic tradition and from my grandmother, that I figured it out. Look at the water," she invited, holding her hand out in its direction. "As it was in the beginning, is now and ever shall be."

"Glory be to the father," said Charlotte, reciting the words to the response she'd played every Sunday for thirty-seven years.

"And to the Son, and to the Holy Ghost," continued Jack, singing the words that followed.

The four joined in chorus as they sang the words they had all learned as a part of their communicative faith. "As it was in the beginning, is now and ever shall be. World without end, Amen, Amen."

"This sign says more than most people realize," Mary

Magdalena shared. "See where it's sitting? It's on the site where the Catholic Church once stood. Where countless numbers of God's children came regularly, and recited prayers, and sang and gave praise to the Father, Son and Holy Ghost."

She pulled a picture from her purse, where she'd stuffed it securely inside a compartment of her wallet. "Look at this," she instructed as she held it out for them to see. "It's a picture of the Catholic Church in Pearlington after the storm."

Charlotte stared in disbelief as she noticed the photo was the same as the sketch Jeremiah had done for her, a photo this young woman obviously kept with her at all times, a photo of a place she had visited many times during her work here. ***And a photo of the same image as Angelina's drawing.***

"There is no church," said Jack.

"My point exactly. But what do you see?"

"I see the pillars that once supported the building," he answered.

"And the front steps," offered Ebony.

"And the Virgin Mary standing on the top step," noted Charlotte, slowing adding, "with a baby doll laid at her feet." ***Just like in the sketch...Angelina's doll.***

"Look at the Virgin Mary's head," Mary Magdalena instructed. "I heard Alexis' dad tell Charlotte that the top of her head was broken off from the storm, but she was the only thing left standing on the grounds of the church after Katrina. Her," she paused, "and the pillars, the foundation of the church. Christ was, and is, and will always be the foundation of the church. The building may be gone, but God is still here. The Father, the Son and the Holy Spirit are still right here and all around us. I wonder if whoever wrote these words on this piece of plywood had any idea as to the depth of their meaning."

Ebony looked in awe at her friend. "That was very profound. Girl, no wonder you needed all your power. That was about the most powerful statement I've ever heard."

"Then just wait," warned Mary Magdalena. "The good part is yet to come."

"Do I need to get Mom tissues?" asked Jack, punching his mother with his elbow.

"Possibly, and you'd better bring some for yourself."

"Then I know I need some," chimed Ebony.

"Jack, when Levi was with you, moaning in the corner, did you catch anything he said?"

"No, he sounded more like a wounded animal to me." He thought long and hard. "It was more like the moans and groans I'd think of coming from the ghost of Jacob Marley when he visits his partner, Ebenezer Scrooge."

"And then when your mother began questioning the children about praying during Katrina, and after Katrina, and since Katrina...do you remember how he reacted?"

"That really seemed to trouble him," said Ebony. "I remember because he got louder and louder, as if someone were sticking something in him, prodding deeper and deeper with each question."

"I remember that well," noted Charlotte. "He got up and ran out, and I was begging God to give me something to lure the children's focus back on sculpting something from the clay. That was after a young boy asked if that's how God made us?"

"Yes," acknowledged Mary Magdalena. "Jack, can you remember anything...anything at all or anything unusual that Levi either said or did then?"

"No...," he replied, his interest piqued as his mind replayed that day. "All I remember is how I prayed God would give me something, a key to open that boy's shell, to stir inside him, to get him in touch with his feelings and his soul."

"I think you probably did have something," she speculated, "when you allowed him to be the Ninja. You let him know it was not only okay, but special to be different."

Mary Magdalena's eyes moved to Charlotte. "And then when your mother began to ask the questions the next day, she gave him something which spoke to his soul. Something which spoke to his soul as his mother had once done."

"But I couldn't make out any words from what he said," Jack mournfully admitted. "It all sounded like gibberish."

Mary Magdalena took her rosary beads, the black onyx ones her grandmother had left her, and held them in her hands. She held them as if they were the greatest treasure on earth, lovingly feeling the individual beads and softly chanting the prayers of each one. "Did his gibberish sound anything like that?" she asked after a couple of minutes.

Jack stood spellbound. "It could have. I just don't know. I can't tell."

"I believe what God was saying to me through this sign is that Levi's mother was indeed holding her rosary beads in her hand, and they weren't gnarled and tangled, she was simply praying so fervently in her hour of need that it appeared that way to Levi.

"You see," she went on to explain, "in the Catholic faith, we have different prayers and different Mysteries. As we pray, we are instructed to literally place ourselves in Jesus' path, allowing us to feel his pain and suffering so that we may become closer to God. I believe his mother was praying the prayers she'd been taught to say. She was not oblivious to the storm, or ignoring her family, she was reciting the words that she'd been instructed for God to watch over her family, in life or in death."

No one spoke a word as Mary Magdalena's suspicion filtrated through their minds, allowing them to paint their own image of Levi's mother in the chair, praying with the beads.

"And that's why the empty bag meant so much. When I caught him that day when his backpack got hung on the nail of that board in the church's attic, he was indeed muttering. I saw it as the whimper of a scared puppy, but you're saying he could have been praying," Jack surmised.

"That's exactly what I'm saying, and what I believe with all my heart. And, because there was a nail holding his bag, it could have caused him to think of the crucified Christ, the nails in his hand, that would have been a part of those prayers his mother was reciting."

Charlotte reached out and took the hands of Ebony and Mary Magdalena, who in turn reached out and took the hands of Jack as they formed a small circle. The author began to pray, thanking God for placing the four of them into each others' paths, asking Him to watch over and protect Levi, and beseeching Him to be with Levi's mother, wherever she was.

"Do you think she's still alive?" asked Ebony.

"I don't know," answered Mary Magdalena. "But I do know I surely wish I could learn something about her. I'd love to be able to give that boy some closure in his life."

"If Levi's mother taught him all the prayers," Jack speculated, "he certainly has plenty of time to say them all in that closet while he's locked up." With that, he shared the whole story of what he'd learned about "the strayer" to Ebony and Mary Magdalena as they listened in horror and shock.

"That makes me angry," voiced Ebony.

"Me, too," agreed Jack, but if we help him, it must be done in peace and in love. Not out of anger."

"You're right," Ebony conceded as she looked toward Charlotte. "What can we do to help him?"

"Let me think on that," said the author. "For the moment, I think we all need to pray about this, as fervently as Levi's mother was obviously praying. God will lead us to an answer. I have no doubt." The author squeezed Mary Magdalena's hand. "He's led us this far through you, my dear child."

Mary Magdalena stared at the photo one last time before putting it away, fingered the beads as her grandmother had done so many times before her, and took a final look at the sign. "Katrina was big," she said. "The longer I'm down here and the more places I go, the bigger I see that it was." Her grip tightened on the beads. "But with each thing I see, I also see that God ***is*** bigger." She focused on the sign. "I wish I could meet the person who wrote the words on that sign."

"The important thing is not the person," offered Charlotte. "Just as we are not the important things in the scheme of things in Hancock County. In this case, the words were the important things which were left behind. In our case, the love and support are the important things that were left behind. Not only ***our*** love and support, but the love and support of each contributor, wrapped inside the pages of each of those thousands of books which are now in the hands of children."

"Amen!" shouted Ebony. "I don't know about you three, but I'm ready for some dinner. If I have any more spiritual food right now, I think I'm gonna explode!"

"Progress always means road construction," said Charlotte, taking detours down lots of side streets off Highway 90. "I'm not complaining, though. You can actually drive your car down the roads here now without knocking it out of line from all the potholes."

"Or dodging houses and boats in the middle of the road," noted Jack, recollecting his first unbelievable jaunt down this path following the hurricane. "Remember that one house the water picked up and literally sat down right on Highway 90. The poor man who had lived in that house said it didn't even get water up past the bed, but then the water picked it up and took it back out toward the Gulf. A front-end loader came down the street and literally demolished it right in front of the poor man's eyes. He was devastated, for he'd been sure he could have it moved back to his lot and set back on the foundation. Imagine...knowing your home had at least stayed in one piece, at least from the floor up, and then to see it shattered to pieces and thrown over into a pile of rubbish with countless other homes ravaged by the storm."

"This is surely a different picture from three years ago," Charlotte said, admiring the view as she drove down the scenic coastline. "You can again recognize all the natural beauty that made this such a popular place to live. The only things missing are the massive limbs of the trees which once shaded all the yards. I can actually see the resemblance to when Jack and I first came through Biloxi after my seminary years."

"Look at the rows of houses," Ebony added. "They're picture perfect, like a brand new community. Everything is freshly painted, and it looks like most of the houses have new windows. I can't believe the change just since the summer. Things are really clicking along for some of the residents now."

"They look like rows of dollhouses," Charlotte said, navigating slowly enough to appreciate each one.

"It's certainly a welcome change from the houses we saw on our first trip here," surmised Jack. "There were so few houses anywhere down here, and some of them weren't even on the right streets any longer. I'll never forget the horror I felt each time I saw an 'X' on one of the houses with a repulsive number that denoted the number of people found dead in each one. That was spine-chilling.

"On our first visit here, I think the most dreadful story I heard was of a girl in her late teens. She'd run away from home, but in hearing of the storm, came back to check on her family. When she arrived, there was an 'X' on the house. Not knowing what it meant, she went inside to find both her parents and two brothers dead. There is no word to describe the repulsiveness of that kind of situation, not to mention the disgusting and sickening stench. She'll never be able to erase that from her memory."

Jack paused to let the wave of nausea which had settled in his stomach pass. "I can still see those houses in my mind and remember right where they were on these streets, so I can't imagine what these children must relive day in and day out. My heart aches uncontrollably at times, but then I think of Lena and that story about how good it was they found their steps. Every person in America needs a video of that sweet child to watch every time they think they're having a bad day."

He continued to stare out the windows, thrilled to see that welcome signs or decorative plaques, many hinting of the loves of hobbies of the residents of each particular home, had replaced the terrifying 'X' marks.

Home, observed Mary Magdalena as she carefully took note of each residence, as their trip to get sandwiches turned into a long, purposeful tour through the streets of Waveland and Bay St. Louis. ***That's the difference. When I saw this area the first time, there was nothing but masses of shells of what was left of houses. Now you can actually feel the love and the pride, as real and tangible as any wood, brick or siding.***

"I've said it many times," said Charlotte, sounding overwhelmed. "Many people never see the growth from the seeds they've sown. They come, they plant and nurture, and all they can do is pray that some of the seeds, like in Jesus' parable, land in good soil and not only grow and flourish, but spread to others. The love multiplies.

"I'm one of the lucky ones. Through what we've done in the past two days, I've reaped the harvest, not only of our work, but of the many volunteers who've come from all over the world in an effort to show these people love."

"When I came here the first time," Mary Magdalena shared, "what I felt was deep pity for these children and their families. I felt sorry for them. You know, 'that poor person' syndrome."

Charlotte gave an understanding nod as she listened for the words she knew were coming.

"But when I left after that first time down here, I realized I had gained more than anything we'd left with these children. They weren't poor at all. We were the ones who were lacking in the faith exhibited by most of them."

The last few minutes of the ride passed in silence as each of the four tried to digest the scenes and memories they'd just shared before trying to digest their meal. Blaize Street was a welcome sight after the lengthy stint of reminiscing.

"I can taste the oysters from here," Jack said, opening the doors of Benigno's for Ebony and Mary Magdalena.

"Charlotte's right!" exclaimed Ebony. "This feels like walking in Miller's, before the flood, except with a Gulf coast atmosphere." She stared at all the old photographs and newspaper clippings hanging on the walls.

"I wonder if they have an equivalent of Joni," teased Mary Magdalena.

"Well, if they do," Jack replied, "she'll drop a witch earring in your coffee instead of an Easter bunny."

The quartet laughed heartily at the now infamous tale of Mary Magdalena's first encounter with Joni and Miller's when the waitress dropped an earring in Joshua's coffee and kept pouring.

"I can see this is a fun group," welcomed the waitress.

"Always!" Ebony responded, not taking into account what would transpire in the next few minutes.

"Look at this," Jack said, pointing to the back of the menu. "It even sounds like Miller's." With that, he read the note about the restaurant aloud, "Our family and small quaint atmosphere will make your feel right at home!"

Equivalent of Joni...children...faith...family...home..., Suddenly Mary Magdalena felt as if she were putting together the pieces of a puzzle instead of ordering a sandwich from a menu.

"Are you okay?" asked Jack. "You look as if you've just seen a ghost."

"I'm fine," Mary Magdalena answered. "There's just this eerie feeling about this place, and I don't know why. I love its charm, the menu selections are great and the prices are right, yet I have this strange feeling, almost like the walls are talking to me."

"It's just all the memorabilia on the walls," he replied, lightly excusing her wave of emotion. "It reminds you of that family atmosphere you used to feel in Miller's in Findlay. You're simply having flashbacks since we all miss going there."

"I don't know...," ***Miller's...Joni...home...*** Pieces of the puzzle kept leaping from her subconscious.

"Maybe it's a lack of ***real*** food combined with the sun shining directly in your eyes," suggested Ebony. "You're not used to the sun being this bright at home."

"Perhaps it's a touch of car sickness, too," Charlotte added.

"Here," offered Jack, "switch places with me so you're not staring straight into the sunlight."

Sunlight...talking with Joni...switching places...feel

right at home...sunlight...switching places..., Mary Magdalena jumped from her chair and rushed to the sidewalk, her body pivoting from one side to the other until she caught a slight glimpse of it. She tore off across the street and into the park-like setting diagonally across from the restaurant to get a good look at the shiny object, reflecting in the sunlight.

"We'll be right back," Charlotte yelled to the waitress. "I promise."

"It's part of our fun together," Ebony added, trying to politely defend her friend's behavior.

Jack simply shrugged and headed out the door behind the others.

"There is something there," she shouted to her comrades. "I see it...up in the tree."

The four cast their eyes upward until they all saw what had been gnawing at her.

"They're beads," said Ebony.

"They look like Mardi Gras beads," spoke Jack.

"They looks like what were once silver Mardi Gras beads," noted Charlotte.

Mary Magdalena grabbed at the tree's strong trunk as she tried to climb up the branches.

"The sign says, 'Please do not climb the tree,'" Ebony told her.

"This may be a matter of life or death," replied Mary Magdalena. "The worst thing they can do is charge me a fine."

"The worst thing they can do is arrest you," shuddered Charlotte.

"Good! Then I'd have time to stay down here and find the owner of these beads."

"Well, she's right about one thing," observed Jack. "There's no way those beads could have been thrown that far. That's at least two stories high."

"I can't reach them." Mary Magdalena's frustrated voice rang through the branches.

"There's got to be a way to get to them," Jack said. He spotted his mother combing the area and didn't ask, but knew she had a plan. ***If anyone's more on a mission than Mary Magdalena at this moment, it's my mother.***

"Come back down, Mary Magdalena," instructed the scheming author as she held a thin broken branch, approximately the length of a yardstick, in her hand. "I have an idea that I think just might work."

"I think she's read far too many novels," offered Ebony.

"I think she's ***written*** far too many novels," retaliated Jack, "but if she wants something badly enough, she'll work until she gets it. She's determined to see that Mary Magdalena gets those beads. I can see it in her eyes."

"And you want her to have them just as badly," noted Ebony. "I can see it in your eyes."

"I wonder how many people are watching out of the nearby businesses and houses to see what we're doing," Jack commented, snatching a quick glance around the perimeter.

"Oh, relax," Ebony told him. "It's Halloween weekend. I'm sure they're used to seeing all kinds of antics down here. They'll merely think we partied a little too hearty last night."

"Okay, you two," warned Charlotte. "Enough with the fun and games. Ebony, you pull down on this branch," she instructed, pointing with the stick in her hand. "That will allow Jack to be able to grab the great big limb. Jack, yank it down with all your might. Mary Magdalena, when he gets it down far enough for you to reach the bough above it, you grab it and pull down as hard as you can. I'll use this long stick to jerk the beads loose from the branch holding them."

The team went into action, Ebony pulling her designated branch, Jack grabbing the huge limb and Mary Magdalena taking hold of the bough just below the upper branch which held the beads.

"Try to move the limb up and down, Jack!" Charlotte yelled, stretching as high as she could, but still unable to ring the stick through the beads.

The limb rocked enough that she was finally able to get the stick centered through the beads, but they were hung.

"Here, Mom," suggested Jack. "I've got this limb down. Come here and try to hang onto it while I've got it in this position. I'll try to knock the beads up and over the top of the branch that's keeping them in place."

Charlotte fought the limb, unwavering in her attempt to rescue the beads.

"Got 'em!" shouted Jack, his words causing the other three to let go with such spontaneity that the tree literally jerked back and forth.

"I'll bet that's the hardest anyone's ever worked for a string of Mardi Gras beads," Ebony declared, panting in her half-serious wit.

"Any ***one***?" repeated Jack. "There were four of us working for the same string of beads and they still nearly whipped us!"

The four laughed, relishing in their successful teamwork, as Jack handed the beads, tarnished nearly to the point of being black, to Mary Magdalena.

"Do you think these have been here since Katrina?" she asked.

"They must have," answered Jack. "Look at the finish on them."

Charlotte examined them closely. "I'm fairly certain they were silver-colored. Even from the wear and tear of the weather, that's distinguishable."

"Look at how they're all tangled in the top section. Do

you think they've been that way since they landed in the tree?" Mary Magdalena questioned, running her fingers gently around the knotted round balls that made up the beads, so stiff they looked as if they'd been forever molded in that shape.

All comments stopped as the four looked back and forth from each other. The shared expression masked on their faces proved the same question was running through each of their minds.

"Do you think...?" Ebony finally ventured.

"What I think," stated Jack, "is we'd better get back in there and order our food or that waitress is going to call the 'looney farm' after all of us."

"Can you believe I saw these glimmering from the tree months ago and did nothing about them?" Mary Magdalena asked, securely holding the treasure they'd pulled from the tree.

"And you'd have done what with them then?" ventured Jack. "Throw them away? You'd have had no reason to even contemplate on them at that point in time. God didn't want you to discover them then."

"Then do you think...?" Ebony ventured again.

"I think we need to sit and eat while we rationalize our thoughts on these beads," suggested Charlotte. "There are any number of ways they could have washed here, and more numbers of people they could have belonged to. If God led us to them, then He'll lead us further with them."

"But one thing's for sure," Mary Magdalena firmly stated, "they're not going out of my sight. At least not until I can track down Levi and see if he recognizes them."

They ordered their food and then projected how they could feasibly contact Levi, and whether they would even be allowed to see him, should they find the location of his family. "Do you think we should quit playing detective and call the local authorities?" asked Mary Magdalena, thinking aloud.

"I'll tell you what I think. I think this po'boy is even better than Jack said it would be," said Ebony, sneaking a bite from the sandwich as the waitress set their orders on the table.

"Told you," bragged Jack. "This is my favorite eating establishment we've found down here. Actually, when we first came down here, it was the ***only*** eating establishment open. We just happened to stumble across it."

The foursome stared at the beads which now lay in the middle of their table.

"I don't think we stumbled across it, Jack," admitted Charlotte.

He glared at his mother. "I guess you're right. No more than you brought Mary Magdalena here on a day it was closed and had to go next door. She'd have never seen the beads from the front window had you been here. The sunlight had to be just right for her to catch a glimpse of them."

"And no more than we wound up here today with all four of us to retrieve the beads," concluded Ebony.

"So, maybe they ***were*** rosary beads, at least to Levi's mother, and she was praying with each bead," suggested Mary Magdalena. "I've watched my grandmother on many occasions like that. She'd prayed so hard and rubbed those beads so zealously that she had them all twisted and gnarled by the time she finished."

"That looks exactly like what might have happened to these," agreed Jack. "I just wish I could have made out any words Levi was saying back in the summer. That might be a clue."

"Where do we go from here?" asked Mary Magdalena.

"We go back to the sculpture," said Charlotte. "I have a feeling if these beads have anything to do with Levi's mother, more clues will come. What I think we ***don't*** do is make the beads public just yet. We might become the laughing stock of Hancock County, Mississippi." Her eyes moved to each of the other three, one at a time. "For now, I think Mary Magdalena should hold onto them. We'll all pray about whether there is any merit to this finding. If there is, we must also pray God will lead our steps from this point forward, and then truly believe that He will."

"I have a feeling there's more to these beads than what would appear," Mary Magdalena added, for the first time relaxing against the back of her chair.

"Is that what you got from the tree?" asked the waitress. "We were watching to see what you'd found." She leaned her head down and took a closer look at the beads. "Those things must have been there ever since Katrina. Isn't that odd? I've been here all this time since we were finally able to re-open and I've never noticed them up there."

Ebony scowled at Mary Magdalena, carefully watching to see if her friend caught that comment.

"I guess they had your name on them," the waitress concluded, offering a pleasant smile as she laid their ticket on the table and walked away.

"Well, Mary Magdalena," stated Jack. "Even she says they have your name on them. Since God seems to be using you as the connection with these beads, I'm thinking that He'll continue that pattern."

"I agree," added Charlotte. "We'll all be aware and open to the situation, taking careful note should we come up with any good solutions."

"Why do I feel I'm in the middle of one of Charlotte's novels?" Mary Magdalena inquired.

"Because this is the kind of real stuff that good novels are made of," Charlotte answered. "I do suggest that for now, we don't share our thoughts on the subject with anyone. Not until we're a good bit more certain these aren't simply some trashed beads nor they didn't just happen to be here. For now," she added, leaving money for the food and tip where the beads had laid, "I think we'd better get back. There are five hungry men playing in the sand back toward Pearlington."

28

It was a perfect Sabbath morning as Jack packed the van for their return to North Carolina while his mother deflated their air mattresses and tidied up the facility of Diamondhead United Methodist Church, making sure it was ready for the services that would commence in less than two hours. The sky was slightly overcast, but with no hint of any downpours.

Perfect weather for Joshua's sculpture, Charlotte noted. ***No wind to dry out the sand and just enough clouds to keep the sun from scorching it.*** She'd been around enough of his masterpieces to know even a shower or two couldn't hurt. The valleys he built into the lines of the sculptures served as automatic troughs for the occasional rains and actually kept the sand from drying out.

The mother and son duo arrived at the scene of the sand sculpture to discover hundreds had already gathered to see the Master at work through the master, and to practice their own handiwork in the sand. Children ran to greet them, pushing the imaginary "button" on Jack's arm to see if he was still a human jukebox. Parents rushed to thank her for giving their children a memorable experience at the school's carnival. Teachers swarmed to express their gratitude for the gift of the uniquely-painted rockers. Local residents gathered to show their sincere appreciation for so much morale-building and attentive interest in their community.

Charlotte sensed she had been given the greatest gift in the entire world by receiving, and answering, a call to fill a need. Yet, at the same time, she felt humbled by her own inadequacies, all the while wondering why God had seen fit to choose her for His purpose here.

"Well, Mom," observed Jack, placing an arm around his mother's shoulder, "it's a long way from this Hancock County to Ohio's Hancock County, but it appears you've managed to make quite a few friends in both." He smiled, reaching up to wipe away the tear on her cheek. "I'm proud of you and I love you."

"I love you, too," she replied softly, wishing she could say more, but afraid of turning into a fountain of tears. She secretly wondered whether this would be their last work of mission together, now that he had acquired a full-time job and was starting a life of his own.

"Hey, Joshua," called Harry, "ask and you shall receive."

"What do you mean?" asked the sculptor, his mind totally on his creation which continued to draw a sizable crowd of spectators, as he worked toward his goal of having it completely finished by sundown.

"You know how you and Mary Magdalena have this thing about asking and receiving?"

"Yes." The sculptor threw a quick glance in the direction of his daughter-in-law and gave a knowing wink which she returned along with a gleeful smile.

"Well, about an hour ago, you asked for packers to help you pack the sand, and I have two good arms coming for you."

"Thanks, Harry! That's great, but if you'll recall, I asked for 'a couple' of packers, not just two arms."

"I know, but you'll like these. They are two of the best arms in the business."

Hearing exciting whispers from the bystanders wafting through the air like a spring breeze, Mary Magdalena turned her head slightly. Her jaw dropped as she caught sight of the two approaching men. One face she recognized well, but the other – whom the bystanders recognized extremely well – she had only seen in the newspapers, magazines and on the television. She turned back to see Joshua's reaction only to discover he was so caught up in shaping the sculpture he was oblivious to the noise of the crowd.

"In what business?" he asked, still busily perfecting the details of the section of the ark on which he was working. He paused, barely long enough to look back at Harry, and then suddenly stopped and did a double take. "B...en?" he uttered quietly, noticing the hometown football star of Findlay, Ohio, Ben Roethlisberger, coming toward him. As if that weren't enough of a surprise, Big Ben was walking alongside Brett Favre, the hometown football star of "The Kill," Mississippi.

The look of astonishment on Joshua's face could not have been much more had he seen God in the flesh. However, Mary Magdalena recognized the miraculous arrival of these "two arms" as a sign of God in the flesh. God's timing was perfect as the quarterback of the Pittsburgh Steelers and the recently retired quarterback of sixteen seasons with the Green Bay Packers, and a final season with the New York Jets, strode across the sand as calmly as if they were on the familiar field of green. She smiled as she watched Joshua take a long, slow breath, his head bobbing as he gave a big gulp. It took a few seconds for his mouth to close from the gasp of surprise he'd inhaled moments earlier.

"You know," Ben began as he took one of the wooden packing tools and handed another to Brett, "that Brett is from Hancock County, Mississippi. We have more in common than a strong arm."

"Wow!" was all Joshua could manage as he stood there, still in awe and wonder at the vision before him. "You guys really are an answer to prayer."

Mary Magdalena gave a quiet laugh, sure that wasn't the first time those words had been spoken by fans of these quarterbacks' respective teams. She watched as these two celebrities, each from a Hancock County and each from an area that had been torn apart by devastation – although one much worse than the other – united their strength to make a difference in this healing and rebuilding partnership.

"Okay, coach," said Brett to Joshua, "you call the plays on this one."

Joshua's face flashed a full grin, one common for him when he was ready to begin a new project, as he commenced to show these two super sports heroes how to use the packing tool in order to shape the sand in the right way.

Onlookers stood, flashing pictures and watching with

the same awe that Joshua's face had shown, as they, too, realized this beach truly was "Common Ground," a place where people from all walks of life could come together to both find and offer healing.

This is not about building sand castles, Mary Magdalene mused to herself, remembering the phrase she had used to plead her case to all her helpers from Hancock County, Ohio, ***it's about building relationships***. She proudly watched as she saw parents and students alike, from the prior rival school areas of Mississippi now united in the South Hancock Elementary School as Dolphins, jump in alongside the pair of "arms."

"Ah, my child," she sensed from above. "Precisely my idea."

Mary Magdalena listened intently to the still small voice, the same one she'd heard the day she sat in the pew at St. Andrew's United Methodist Church back in Findlay as she'd stared at the window. The same one which had spoken to her through Charlotte's sermon on United Methodist Women's Sunday in that same sanctuary. And the same one she was sure would lead her from this sand sculpture to the next place she was to go.

The young woman glanced toward Charlotte, whose hope and dreams were that every child, not only in the Hancock Counties of the country, but everywhere in the world, would realize they were beautiful "planted seeds" who could grow into big, tall plants that reached for the stars – ***Like the two stars who've just appeared and proven that point to all these tiny watching eyes*** – and who could always be there to lend a helping hand when needed.

Her eyes fell back to the "helping hands" working alongside Joshua and all his team as she recalled Ben's words at the end of the play-off game that took his Steelers to another Super Bowl win. "The Lord is good!"

Indeed, the Lord is good! Mary Magdalena offered upward in a prayer of gratefulnes as she quietly began to hum. The melody was simple, the words were plain, but together they formed a song which she was sure Mary Magdalene would have sung on the days of her journey following that first Easter morning, that morning after having seen the Risen Lord. "I don't know about tomorrow...,"

She walked to the edge of the water, which was still considered unfit for use, scooped up two handfuls, held it up high and let it run over her head, allowing it to give her a renewed sense of her baptism. Contaminated or not, it was Holy Water in her eyes, created by the ultimate Author and Artist, as far as she was concerned. So caught up was she in her own spiritual moment of discovery, she was unaware of others around her who had also begun to sing until she turned around and heard, "but I know who holds tomorrow, and I know who holds my hand."

I Know Who Holds Tomorrow

I don't know about tomorrow,
I just live from day to day;
I don't borrow from its sunshine,
For its sky may turn to gray;
I don't worry o'er the future
For I know what Jesus said,
And today I'll walk beside Him,
For He knows what is ahead.

Many things about tomorrow
I don't seem to understand;
But I know who holds tomorrow,
And I know who holds my hand.

Every step is getting brighter
As the golden stairs I climb;
Every burden's getting lighter,
Every cloud is silver lined.
There the sun is always shining,
There no tear will dim the eye;
At the ending of the rainbow,
Where the mountains touch the sky.

Many things about tomorrow
I don't seem to understand;
But I know who holds tomorrow,
And I know who holds my hand.

I don't know about tomorrow,
It may bring me poverty;
But the one who feeds the sparrow
Is the one who stands by me;
And the path that be my portion,
May be thru the flame or flood,
But His presence goes before me,
And I'm covered with His blood.

Many things about tomorrow
I don't seem to understand;
But I know who holds tomorrow,
And I know who holds my hand.

Ira F. Stanphill

About the Artist

A very special thanks goes to Jeremiah Ritchie, a native of Pearlington, Mississippi, for drawing the sketches of scenes from the aftermath of Hurricane Katrina for use in this book. Jeremiah is currently rebuilding in Kiln ("the Kill"), also in Mississippi's Hancock County, after losing his home during the storm.

About the Author

Catherine Ritch Guess is the author of twenty books, all of the inspirational genre, which include fiction, non-fiction and children's titles. In addition, she is a published composer and a frequent speaker/musician for a wide range of conferences and events.

In the midst of working on her next titles, much of her time is spent reaching out to people throughout the world, whether that be through reading to children and offering cultural arts camps, running her fingers across the ivories of a keyboard, or holding to the value that "laughter is the best medicine" through the portrayal of her comedy character, Miz Eudora Rumph.

Her most treasured activity is spending time with her family at home on her grandfather's land in Indian Trail, North Carolina.